" Your
be
" This

MW01273137

whenever you turn to the
right or the left"

# OPHIR

Isaiah 30:21

April 25, 2016

For Lucy~

Thank you for helping
me to realize that
the "Magic" I have
always sought really does
exist...inside of me!

You are magical +
I'm so grateful to Know
you.

Pamela

# OPHIR

*A Dime Store Romance
for the Urban Intelligentsia*

PAMELA ATKINSON

Order this book online at www.trafford.com
or email orders@trafford.com

Most Trafford titles are also available at major online book retailers.

Printed in the United States of America.

ISBN: 978-1-4269-7362-8 (sc)
ISBN: 978-1-4269-7438-0 (hc)
ISBN: 978-1-4269-7439-7 (e)

Library of Congress Control Number: 2011910914

Trafford rev. 07/24/2014

 www.trafford.com

North America & International
toll-free: 1 888 232 4444 (USA & Canada)
phone: 250 383 6864 ♦ fax: 812 355 4082

# Special Thanks To:

Ann Harmer, my gracious editor; Peter Robson, veteran editor, whose early review gave me confidence and enthusiasm; Ken and Dave for their wonderful generosity; Trevor P. for his artwork; Nicholas B. for his typographical assistance; Dearest David W; Doctor D. Brown for her rare knowledge and kindness; Lora for The Big Hug; Kathryn and CO. for their longtime love, help and understanding; Stuart for his unconditional love.

# TRIBUTE

Rest well, dearest braveheart.


July 11, 2014


"You are my sheep, the sheep of my pasture, and I am
your God, declares Jehovah."


Ezekiel 34: 31

New International Version of the Holy Bible, and
The New World Translation of the Holy Scriptures

This book is

dedicated with love to

Janet Louise Atkinson

Janet showed me the way with her generosity, and with her
ability to pull all out in the practice of her powerful artistry.

*Listen, O daughter, and see...*

*and forget your people and*

*your father's house. And*

*the King will long for your*

*beauty...the queenly consort*

*her stand at your right hand*

*in gold of Ophir.*

Psalm 48: 9-13
New World Translation of the Holy Scriptures

# Chapter One

Terror is negative panic, come true. It's blanking out, not pulling the cord. It's a shut chute and death in thirty seconds. Thirty seconds during which your sense and senses are planed away by the cliffs of air you shoot past, down. Stoned on fear, your heart has no chance to sink because you are weight. Your life has no chance to flash before your eyes.

John Smilie was lounging on the outdoor deck of the restaurant above the marina, at one of the many tables shaded from July by white umbrellas. The air—soft, pastel—was an enhancer of happiness. The sun was warm on his skin. He sat with a group of friends, and they raised their glasses many times, in celebration of nothing. The drinks drugged his muscles, muffled his thoughts. He was twenty-eight, rich in health, uselessly relaxed.

Her legs, long and white against her black dress, flashed past him. What was left of his alcohol haze tugged at the backs of his eyes and stung his scalp.

The woman in black strode along behind a redhead, curvy in white. As the redhead's heels clocked over the deck toward a table, necks snapped in their wake. Clock, clock, snap, snap—a metronome of lust. John chuckled to himself at the sight. This would be easier than he had anticipated, less of a challenge, disappointingly, because he recognized the redhead. He leaned forward and watched the two women.

Seated for mere moments, Madalyn, in black, began to feel the familiar and existential strain of doing nothing, expecting the albatross to shadow her with its wing. Her nerves were inflamed by the sun, like tender eyes accustomed to the dark, suddenly shocked by light. And her darkest glasses were failing her. Irritability, latent but chronic, niggled as usual at the sight of the perfectly sunburnt men in their ice-cream shirts, and of the women who reminded her of the female joggers she just could not understand, fully made up, lips filled in with a sporty bright pink, sweating into their foundation.

She looked across the table at her friend Tina, whose short, orangy gold curls swayed and settled with the movements of her head. Tina was agreeing with the waiter that a pitcher of margs really would be the way to go. Her small-boned, rounded body was draped upon her chair with light, unthreatening seductiveness. Madalyn perched tensely on the edge of her seat. Keyed up and distracted, she pulled a rim of black straw down over her eyes. A sigh accentuated the ribs on her back.

"This is just what you need, Mad—you never get out in the sun," Tina said.

After the second margarita, Madalyn began to admit to herself, reluctantly, that perhaps she could *try* to like summer. If only it wasn't so sunny. But her hat was off. Boats putted in and out of the marina below them. A breeze from off the water rearranged her dark shawl of hair. A seagull circled above.

Tina and Madalyn both heard the splat. Tina looked up, trying to ID the offending gull. Madalyn looked down and eyed the milky blob inches from her foot.

"What drama." She lit the cigarette waiting between her lips, and as she pulled the chunky glass ashtray closer, it skidded on the tabletop, hitting her drink and slopping it into her lap.

"Shat," whispered Tina, but her laughter emanated from their table with embarrassing range, escalating into the danger zone where mascara is at risk. Madalyn plunked her hat back upon her head and secured her huge black bugs-eye glasses onto her nose with the back of her wrist.

She was mopping at her lap and sucking air through her cigarette to calm herself, when she felt the sun disappear from her face. She looked up at a pale pink shirt—strawberry ripple.

During the introductions had taken off her glasses out of instinctive courtesy, and in his self-created shadow, first looked upon the commonplace handsomeness of John Smilie. Just another good-looking, pink-shirted, irretrievably slack-souled had been her irritating reaction. Somehow, though, his knack for securing the upper hand during eye contact—the way he spoke with Tina while his eyes were focused unflinchingly on Madalyn—and the dilatory quality of his conversational style made something of an impression on her. She had always been jealous of people who waited with confidence for others to fill the vacuum of silence, which always made her feel so nervous. And so obligated.

"Well, I think he was rude. To *you*," Madalyn said after John's brief visit. Tina smiled, her eyes dancing with superfatted self-esteem. "You work with him—what a treat that must be," Madalyn continued. "Let me guess. An ego like a black hole, right? God, I hope so."

Sunday morning dawned well before Madalyn's hangover made itself felt: stomach slightly nauseous, muscles weak, eyes buried in the phantom, painful swelling of her head and the grit of regret dirtying the bright, sunwashed morning like so much sawdust.

I must like it this way, she thought, thanking God for the last coffee filter in the box, the very temporary relief of the alcoholic high thudding back to earth the next day, unfairly weighted with newly burgeoned fear and sadness, not successfully drowned forever, oh, no—rather, stronger and healthier than ever before, bobbing up, breaking the surface of consciousness . . . We're back!

The sun mocked her mood. Her morning cigarette geared up her gastrointestinal system unnaturally, with the instantaneous lurch of nicotine through her blood and bowels. Ah, yes. A sunny Sunday morning. The day of worship. She recalled childhood Sunday mornings in Tina's Baptist church; cool, dim and cavernous, the organ's deep tones further sheltering her sun-shy spirit that blinked and teared up just as did her eyes when she stepped out into the shock of real noon.

Then there were her adult Sunday mornings—frightening, jelly-like slabs of unstructured time, which she had still completely failed to master, unlike those who sprang from bed to beach to barbecue with vigour and without pause.

But today a new drug eased things for her, blurred the hard edges of contrast—her thoughts of John Smilie. She could not shake the murky, slightly sickening feeling of excitement that percolated inside her body.

She called Tina because she had questions, but there was no answer. Yesterday all she had been able to glean was that John had a shiny new MBA and had been hired three months ago by Tina's employer, Jerome Stackhouse of Stackhouse Developments, a real estate development firm with commercial properties all over the city and several substantial projects in California and Arizona. John had been hired, apparently, to concentrate on the American properties and to scout out investment interest. Since Tina's work involved overseeing the local conveyancing, she did not interact much with John.

Tina was fairly certain he was single, but that was about all she knew. Still, Madalyn felt, Tina could try a little harder to provide some needed insight. She wanted to know, especially, for example, if John was just one of those soft, self-absorbed types with nine different hair care products in their bathrooms. She wanted to know if Tina really felt he had been "totally attracted" to her.

Madalyn felt less guilty about her usual sunny-day paralysis and settled in on her couch for most of the afternoon, trying to read. But she could bring very little concentration to bear upon John Updike's breathtakingly microscopic descriptions in which she usually found awe-coated sustenance for her deteriorating brain. But she made the attempt and hid away from the sun, eighteen storeys above the city, in the privacy of her head, wherein grew romantic, cinematic fantasies with engorged her heart, softening the clatter of her various fears and insecurities, which usually created a racket of such magnitude that she could maintain a tenuous lack of awareness of the emptiness inside. These activities took her into late afternoon and the promise of darkness, matching and soothing and shrouding her light-phobic soul.

At seven o'clock she ventured outside, to facilitate the burdensome practicality of feeding herself. Most of the vegetables she bought for her tuna salad would languish for weeks in her fridge, transforming themselves into decay, their nutritional potential forever lost.

At around nine o'clock the wedding in her head was interrupted by the alarming chirp of her telephone, that harbinger of dread, or perhaps bliss.

"Regale me," she said to Tina, who did, with the details of her day. Jack, her youngest brother, mid-thirties and unmarried, and a bunch of his friends had pounced on her, metaphorically and unannounced, in the midst of her Sunday morning sleeping-off sleep, had teased her from outside the bathroom door and had escorted her back to the restaurant above the marina for brunch and Bloody Marys, which had quite nicely muzzled the dog that had bitten her on Saturday. And so, subsequently coerced onto a sailboat and surrounded for the rest of the afternoon by an appreciative gaggle of guys, had she ridden out the rest of *her* hangover.

"I was going to call you, but they came at ten. I didn't know if you'd be up . . . but guess what? Roger Kiersted knows

John, so I asked for, you know, details, but as it turns out, he doesn't really know him. So no real useful information."

Envy of Tina's day and of her proximity to even such a skimpily informed intelligence source welled into Madalyn's heart, the contents of which she edited. For the sake of pride.

"Oh, yeah?" she said. "Well, what's really to know?"

Although they had been best friends for years, there were many things Madalyn and Tina did not share. When Madalyn hang up the phone, for example, she wished profoundly to be in Paris, working on deepening her voice with pack after pack of Gauloises, debating the definitive definition of Art with some tortured, ravishing, world-weary artist, whose despair she would be able to assuage by virtue of their intellectual compatibility, combined with her big R romantic optimism and her long slender legs, the insides of which, enfolded around him, feeling like thinned out velvet, would cause him to find renewed hope as he, childlike, discovered the sweetness of her sexual specialness, which would bring tears to his eyes during their first encounter.

Madalyn's open-ended heart continued to fill with fantasy, a bridge to which she felt wholly unable to construct from upon the stagnant, mushy, mundane shores of her reality.

Madalyn envied Tina's normalness. Unburdened by concerns about meaning and purpose, Tina seemed enviably able to find satisfaction in day-to-day life. Bound together by their history—having grown up together—they were, however, true girlfriends, the crux of their relationship being detailed analyses of the men in their lives.

During the fourth grade, Tina had transferred to Madalyn's school and was assigned to Mrs. Van Alstyne's class, where Madalyn vied with Roddy MacIlwraith for top of the class. Tina, from the first day, vied with no one as the girl to be.

One day in the first week at her new school, Tina caught up with Madalyn on the way home and asked her over. Madalyn said okay, but she would have to call home when she got there.

The girls sat facing each other, camped on the frilly spreads of Tina's two beds.

"Same here," said Madalyn. "I would have been so mad too if my parents hadn't gotten me the blonde one. But, plus, you got Midge and Ken," she noted graciously. And so, from upon the common ground of Barbie, began a summit of nine-year-olds, sounding out the details of families and stuff.

During the course of their conversation, it became increasingly apparent that Tina had plenty of both. They were at siblings, trading envy.

"I'm an only child," Madalyn offered, unsure of the impact this would have. Her deficiency-prone little ego was boosted by Tina's "Lucky you!" This was an exotic state for the Tyhurst baby, hounded since birth by fraternal care.

"I have all brothers. There's four," Tina complained, unaware of the priceless osmotic training her childhood would provide. At this point, Mrs. Tyhurst appeared in the room, her stockings and heels amazing Madalyn, who had assumed the mother would come with slacks and archless feet. Further, this parent did not hover above Madalyn in the air space reserved for adults. Suddenly, Mrs. Tyhurst's lips were shimmering below Madalyn. Her arms were tucked under the edge of the bed, and her lady's body lay long and detached on the floor. Madalyn could smell the perfume of the spray that kept Linda Tyhurst's hair suspended in mink-brown curves around her face.

Mrs. Tyhurst did not stay long. Before she left, she volunteered the assurance that Madalyn Paul was an elegant name and added Madalyn to her wide-ranging list of Sweeties. When she was gone, Madalyn wanted to wallow in Tina's description of everything about her mother. She looked over at a friend too new to ask, but Tina had resumed their talk with a career diplomat's natural omission of awe.

"See this—it's a eyebrow pencil," Tina said, holding up a stub. "We could do beauty marks," she suggested, reaching into the drawer of her bedside table. "My mum has a magazine that says that natural beauty marks have a meaning about your personality. But it depends where they are on you."

This was news to Madalyn, whose mother didn't have that or any other issue of *Cosmopolitan*. Tina adjusted a mirrored compact in front of her face and soon showed Madalyn a quite professional-looking dark dot under the corner of one eye.

"You do one here," Tina pointed and handed over the implements. "I can't remember all the meanings, but I think face ones are that you are good at expressing your personality about being a woman—like that you know *how* to be one. And oh yeah, oh yeah! I remember it said, 'the men stick like glue'!" They shrieked over the idea.

Expressing her womanly personality above her lip, Madalyn started to replace the cap, but her hand slipped and the cap sliced the tip of the pencil in half. She braced herself, but spied only kindness on the other girl's face. Its heart shape was Linda's, as were the eyes, dark green, with the depthless shine of a Christmas tree ball. Tina's eyes were lashed as fully, though less crisply than her mother's, in every waking moment without exception.

"It's okay, I've got lots," Tina said, scrabbling in the drawer for more of Linda's leftovers.

Madalyn could only assume it was Mr. Tyhurst who had given his daughter the red hair, which Tina now pawed at with a brush.

"I can never get it to go straight, like yours," she said, switching beds and brushing out Madalyn's long hair.

"I'd rather have curls," Madalyn declared.

"No way!"

"Yes way. Mine is *hopeless*." Madalyn was finally relaxing into this first meeting, where the pooling of hearts had begun.

Tired of grooming, the girls settled onto the carpet around Tina's portable record player. David Cassidy repeated, over and over, that he thought he loved them. Too, as it turned out. Sharing the record cover, absorbing every eyelash and pore, they pined quite openly for his scratchy affections. Just a funny, occasional feeling, at age nine, this longing that would magnetize and trail the filaments of all their grown-up women's plans.

Other records were eventually consulted, and decisions were made with snap consensus, thanks to a shared taste in music and to the handily abbreviated code of aesthetics to which they both subscribed: good song, forget it, forget it, good song.

That night at dinner, Madalyn's parents asked if she thought she had made a new friend. Madalyn raved, with the confidence of a connoisseur, and Grant and Evelyn Paul were brought up to date on all that was really mint.

Madalyn left out the part about Warren Tyhurst's car. Mrs. Tyhurst had asked her second eldest son to drive Madalyn home, and he had done so, slowly and safely. But Madalyn knew that her parents needed protection from worry over the past potential danger of a convertible.

"Would you women like to sit in the back and be chauffeured?" Warren had asked, bouncing the keys to his blue Cadillac. It had been one of the family cars until the previous year, when Don Tyhurst had given it to his son, because Warren had turned sixteen and because it was time for Don to rotate a new model out of the midtown dealership and into his driveway. Tina ignored her brother's teasing. Madalyn memorized enough of him to reproduce him that night in a dream.

"It's January!" Warren had laughed, but then humoured the sweetness of his sister's set lips and took down the top. The girls sat up straight on the white leather seat like two brave beauty queens, ready to wave despite the cold.

"Okey dokey, you have a good day now, y'hear?" John folded the pink message slip and tucked it into his breast pocket. As he opened Tina's office door to leave, he gave her his signature wink, his whole face participating, his mouth open in a smile not quite calculated enough to rein in his excessive self-confidence. When he left, Tina closed the door and picked up the phone.

Over at the law firm of Birk & Samuels, Madalyn was picking and tapping her way through some revision to an agreement that scrolled by, page after green neon page, on her computer screen.

The offices of Birk & Samuels were three floors of fine dark wood and soft green carpeting, a forest refined into perfection. Somewhat fewer than one hundred lawyers bustled through its thickets, breathing the artificial air. There were only fifteen women among them. The gender balance was evened out by the secretaries, or support staff, as if a p.c. moniker would change their actual status as slaves. Everyone had to be at least tagged with dignity. Work at Birk & Samuels was a relentless, macho grinding out of reams of exquisitely prepared paperwork for spoiled and demanding clients who tossed their ruthlessly protean deadlines at their lawyers with careless disregard. The deadlines were always met.

Perhaps as a reward for such grueling work, there was some play at Birk & Samuels—a great deal of it unofficial, some of it official, like the annual office Christmas party and a mid-summer event, this year a Friday dinner-dance at the aquarium. Two hundred people, more or less, spouseless, dateless, in their primes, were invited to drink Birk & Samuels' liquor, free and lots of it, served with the unspoken expectation that tongues would stay leashed and relationships would stay professional. Confusing for the uninitiated. And target practice for some sticklers for policy, like Renata, Lawrence Pickard's secretary, who enjoyed office parties by targeting new support staff and firing off a round or two. Warning shots.

"This is your first Birk & Samuels function, isn't it, Madalyn?" she asked.

"Ahm . . . yes, it is." Madalyn scanned for someone to rescue her from the dainty little woman plucking at her arm.

"Well," Renata continued, "then you should be enjoying yourself." Always the incongruity of Renata's voice struck the listener. It was huge, inescapable, a fat-handed slap.

"I saw you speaking with Mr. Pickard. Lawrence is really a doll to work with—we really are a team," *really* and *are* rolling into the room around them like smoke. Madalyn's stomach cringed.

". . . and you'll find that Birk & Samuels functions aren't anything like the parties some firms have, you know, the other biggies. I shouldn't mention names, but, well, Greyell Webster, for example. You would not *believe* some of the things that go on over there. Our partners are conservative, and it is made very clear to new associates that the staff are off limits."

Renata held her fire long enough to scrutinize Madalyn, trying to determine her potential for mischief and looking for the signs, which she knew well—an insecurity, perhaps—that she could play upon, to loosen Madalyn up for some collaboration. Taller than Renata, Madalyn coiled a skein of hair that had fallen between her breasts. She tossed it over the angle of her shoulder, where it disappeared into black. Her eyebrows were frozen in truculent flight above eyes too dark for Renata to see.

Renata's own hair, baby blonde, was beginning to stick to her forehead. Her dress grazed her chin, camouflage for the signal lights of breath. But her cheeks were lit, giving her away. Beakish, Madalyn thought of Renata's nose, modeled into a point. Renata had resumed her diatribe. Madalyn, disgusted, cornered, silent, a martyr for now, paid the attention that the voice, like most weapons, commanded.

Renata was well wound up, but choking on the good stuff about Greyell Webster. She was greedy for gobs of gossip, but, selfishly, never gave any away. She was a Professional. She was also an Organizer. Birk & Samuels baby showers and Christmas craft parties had been, for years, delivered assembled by Renata. And she was a committed member of the inevitable office anti-smoking Gestapo. Hoping to convert by rudeness, she would stick her nose into the smokers' lounge and reprimand "all you unhealthy people" on their own turf.

Renata had found more to say on inter-office sex. Madalyn listened, ears glazing. She considered how Renata would react to the fairly common knowledge about that tall guy in Insolvency, what was his name, and the third-floor receptionist. Etc. Hmm. No. But. She reached into her purse for a cigarette, and tiny, healthy Renata was blown away by the first exhalation.

The agreement printed, Madalyn placed it on her boss's desk. Ross White and the rest of Corporate Securities were at lunch. She appeared to be alone in her quarter of the floor. Her phone rang. It was Tina.

"He asked. I gave. Be prepared."

After a brief chat, during which promises were made to discuss the John issue ASAP, Madalyn replaced the receiver. As she did so, one of the new articling students stopped by her work station, and she noticed again his terrible youth. All of his clothes were new, his hair still looked wounded from its cut, straining to adjust to its cemented place on its head. He looked like a teenager dressed up for church.

"Have a good time on Friday?" he asked.

Madalyn felt a sudden stab of despair when she realized that to him, a big law-firm splash like last Friday's was something to get excited about. She was twenty-six, university educated, and had worked as a legal secretary for the past five years, a quote unquote career, as she sarcastically described it, which she had fallen into for lack of a better idea. She was amazed by her lack of imagination. And by her profoundly disturbing inability to get out of the field.

She was regularly and deeply alarmed by what she considered to be her own passivity and cowardice. And it certainly did not help to have her mother's feminist disappointment with her daughter's seeming lack of ambition dredging constantly and painfully through Madalyn's insecurities. It was a form of quiet, ladylike rebellion, she'd often supposed, this inertia of hers that had been nurtured over the years into dauntless health by her own disappointment in herself. Madalyn felt as if she were nailed shut in her past.

"Absolutely," she answered, stamping the student's question with the same response she had been using all morning. The tone of her voice—umpteenth office party, run-of-the-mill good time—ended the subject there.

He slapped the shelf of the half wall of her station. "Well, I'm outta here," he said. And off he went for lunch.

Madalyn watched him walk away. He leaned into his walk, like a paper doll bent forward on the tabs of its feet, bouncing out of each step on the ball of each foot.

On Sunday evening, as Madalyn plotted the possibilities of a future with John Smilie, a somewhat stimulating if less soul-satiating alternative to being in Paris, Tina was occupied with her own inner ordeal. Enfolded in a thick white Ritz Carlton terry robe that her father had picked up on her parents' last American holiday, she channel-flipped with one hand, the other raking her red ringlets. Glutted by attention from men, as usual, and as usual feeling only slight gratitude for the ego maintenance she had grown to expect, boredom screeched through her bloodstream, kicking up sprays of a sort of frustration she could not name. She longed for Monday.

Stackhouse Developments was one of Birk & Samuels' biggest clients. With a degree in urban geography and her real estate license, Tina had gone to work for Jerome Stackhouse a little less than two years ago. In addition to handling the local conveyancing, she was also responsible for most of the liaison work with the architects and lawyers.

And so it was that just before two on Monday afternoon, she was being carried toward her appointment with Lawrence Pickard by the Birk & Samuels elevator and by an anticipation that collapsed her breathing into a quick, shallow, rhythmic pulse at the top of her stomach.

Tina could not pinpoint exactly when she had begun to anticipate her meetings with Lawrence in this way. Nor had she fully realized that their meetings had, over the past several months and at his suggestion, become more frequent and also longer and less substantive. Business was usually taken care of in less than twenty minutes, then they would spend at least as much time chatting: about Jerome, loud-mouthed and soft-hearted, politics—Lawrence had some good inside stories about the indiscretions of several provincial politicians—Tina's love of what she termed "black" music, Lawrence's obsession with film noir, and other safely superficial subjects.

Tina and Lawrence were developing a rapport that was enjoyable not because of the actual content of conversation, but rather because of the rarefied aesthetic of the sounds of each other's voices and the glancing of their eyes, bouncing off each other's with courtesy-controlled lightness, the disguise of civility, glances like benign piranha, gobbling up, here and there, bits of the other's aura.

Lawrence's secretary was in fine hyperactive professional form that day, her pink shirt buttoned right up to the collar, squeezing her neck, her sensible flats marching briskly below her long, taupe pleated skirt. She ground the end of a pen into her palm as she approached Tina, then escorted her from the reception area down the hall to Lawrence's office. Renata, as usual, greatly enjoyed addressing Tina by her first name. Lawrence always referred to Tina as Miss Tyhurst, and Renata was privately incensed by the social separation this form of address implied; she dug away at her resentment with every deliberate enunciation of Tina's name.

"Lawrence is incredibly busy today, *Tina*. We almost had to cancel you. Or at least postpone. There was just a huge fiasco over a really big closing this morning. He was so angry, you have no idea. He has no stomach for incompetence. Just none at all, *Tina*."

Lawrence stood at his office door, looking somewhat distracted, as if he had forgotten whether he meant to come in or go out. As Tina approached, Renata noticed he was fiddling with the cufflink on his left shirtsleeve.

Lawrence was not handsome. He was a small man, fine-boned. His hair was straight and dark. The eye of the hurricane of his personality could be seen in his face: dark, bright, almost lidless eyes, oriental in appearance; straight nose and thin, squarish lips set among the sharp bones of his cheeks and jaw. Among his peers he was known and admired for his competence, his energy and his almost supernatural calm, broken only occasionally by a fierce burst of temper.

He was also known for bearing down on people when he spoke to them, flattening them with an unblinking, durable eye contact, its intensity causing a disturbing sort of discomfort. Because he hardly looked the part, the sexual quality of this look was noticed only by women. The women of Birk & Samuels rarely discussed him amongst themselves and when they did, they spoke in false consternation of his wounding temper, hoping to camouflage with criticism the fantasies so clearly evident in their faces.

At the age of forty-three, Lawrence had accomplished much of what he had promised himself in his youth. During his childhood in the cold, rugged landscape of northern Ontario, he had begun the practice of directing his life, formulating sets and subsets of goals and successfully realizing them all. This skill, as well as his self-discipline and intelligence, were noticed by his teachers and appreciated quietly by his small family. His mother and father gave him praise—but not too much—and affection. His sister, and what would be the beginning of a long parade of girls and women, gave him adoration.

"Y'know, I'm falling behind badly in the client relations department," Lawrence was saying half an hour later. "How 'bout if I call you next week for lunch? We've never actually done lunch without Jere, so it could be something of a treat."

Tina paused before responding. Her answer that yes, lunch sounded like a good idea, was spoken in her soft, fleshy, contained voice that seemed to collapse in on itself, with no force or effort behind her carefully chosen and enunciated words.

"I'd better pen that in right now—you know how it is," Lawrence said, looking around his office and indicating his laden desk. He rummaged under a stack of files for his Daytimer.

"Good at helping me keep track of myself, I'll give her that," he said of Renata, who was out at her desk, willing herself into a psychic sweat.

It was after work on Monday evening. A pincer of irritation cramped Madalyn's breathing for a moment as she lacquered her finger instead of her nail. Manicure finished, she flexed her jaw in an effort to alleviate the tension headache from which she always suffered from while waiting for her nails to dry. She stood by the open sliding glass door of her balcony, admiring her fingernails and their frank red glossiness.

The telephone rang. Three rings should be enough to disguise her eagerness, she thought. Minutes later, she set down the receiver just long enough to disconnect, then punched in

Tina's number with the tip of an index finger smudged and stippled for a very good cause.

Madalyn was having dinner with John on Saturday. Tina had urged her to keep their standing Thursday night date so they might discuss this impending event in detail. Thursdays were usually reserved for each other—they would meet for drinks and dinner after work, sometimes dancing, though less frequently lately, since Madalyn was growing sick of everyone trying so hard to get a date for the weekend, and of the talk, which receded into primitive shorthand in the din-stuffed clubs.

"So, is Rose good? I'll pick you up at work, say five forty-five. Don't let Ross keep you," Tina had instructed.

On the short walk to the bar, they ran into a friend of Madalyn's, someone she had met in one of her art college courses.

Eight years ago, Madalyn had received her bachelor's degree in fine arts—history and studio. Large oils had been her forte: three-by-five canvases on which she had patiently layered her backgrounds that were also her foregrounds, partially obscuring in many of her works the figures she had painted on first. In the years following graduation, she had taken a few courses at the local art college.

One year had tried sculpture, but had been intimidated by the medium and the students; her class had been monopolized by too many alienated feminists for Madalyn's comfort. Politically obedient, they had shorn from their dress and their speech all manifestation of conventional femininity, afraid of being mistaken for their former selves. Madalyn had scrambled for new ways to disguise her bourgeois background and pink-collar day job from these women who pounded their taken-back power into chunks of slimy clay.

"Hi, Nihil." Madalyn stopped to greet a young man hunkered into a black leather jacket as heavy as armour. He braked in the air and spun around.

"Madalyn! Kiss-kiss, sweetheart!" He slipped an arm around her waist, then noticing Tina, patted Madalyn's rear and stuffed what he could of his fingertips back into the front pockets of his jeans.

"Nihil, you know Tina."

"Yeah. What's shakin'?" Expecting the lack of response, he turned back to Madalyn.

Nihil Asso, a.k.a. Ronnie Peden to the Unemployment Insurance Commission, was an actual artist who "assembled" sculpture on the top floor of an abandoned warehouse and who lived a lifestyle dedicated to creating the illusion of substantial unsold substance in his soul, a task he accomplished primarily by deliberately depriving his body of nutrition.

Madalyn had been to his studio several times. On one visit he had been preparing for a showing and read to her the curatorial write-up which was to accompany one of his works.

"'The artist employs a sculptural emotive process, utilizing found objects from the decaying industrial hinterland. He rehabilitates the garbage of the exploitive superstructure and transforms it into symbols of rage, which mock the very bourgeois imperative which produced them.' Fucking good shit, eh?" Nihil added with a wink.

"Where are you showing?" Madalyn asked.

"In a space that's too fucking small. It's the old Heden Gallery. My work demands space—I should have gotten the *new* gallery. Anyway, it's all fucking politics with Neil and Helen," he finished, choosing as usual not to use any of the many other available adjectives.

Madalyn took another look at the sculpture. Over eight feet tall, it consisted of two standing figures of painted copper piping, one blue, the other green flecked with red. The green figure held its "hands"—dull black pieces of tire—behind the blue figure, which it appeared to be embracing. On the hands were two balls of pink insulation foam, teased into fuzz and spray-painted gold.

Madalyn took the title card and read, "Laraby Kissing an Agent of Kaos."

"So where are you ladies headed?" Nihil asked.

"Over to Rose," Madalyn answered.

"Gag me," Nihil said. "I'm heading down to the Tile Room later tonight, about eleven, twelve, so if you feel like it . . ."

"That's a gay club, isn't it?" Tina asked.

"I'm happy and gay, aren't you?" Nihil replied. The Tile Room was, in fact, not exclusively a gay club, just a concrete cell for any and all appropriate prisoners of the night. Strictly alternative. Wednesday was Normal Night.

"Now, children," Madalyn said.

Nihil and Tina's mutual dislike had begun the first time they met, when Tina had come down to the art college one day to meet Madalyn. She had worn a mink jacket, a Christmas gift from her father, which sometimes felt a little creepy, but it had been cold that day and she'd been in the mood. Nihil had been appalled by her fur, a political crime. What a princess. He coddled his resentments toward money as if they were the result of a childhood trauma, which, if glamorized, would explain everything. Tina in turn had been appalled by his emaciated face and his stiff, bleached brush of hair, all colour burned away, matching his complexion, the colour of death. What a fake.

After they "escaped" from Nihil, as Tina put it, they started with drinks at Rose.


Before she made it famous, Joanna Klammer's club was a lonely leftover from the wickered, seventies, muffled in dust. The flies on its walls had been a bored lot. When Joanna bought the four-storey building, her money transformed it for the vitaminized young, whose mating grounds had to be slickly tiled and clean.

She had renovated the top three floors of the building for office space: architects, three-person law firms and the like. Very grey on grey. The ground floor contained shops selling overpriced gourmet food products and fashions. And then there was the bar. Just getting used to its makeover, Rose beamed pinkly in the crush of fickle fans.

Well-paid professional prisoners, free at last, adjusted reclaimed personalities during the trek to Rose. Here they reasserted their aristocratic rights, the rich room a salve to the indignities of the day. Rose marble floors, rose-papered walls, brass lamps hung low, glowing like candles. Two slick bars of black marked the ends of the long room, like goalposts.

The population peaked at about seven. Unless you managed to get away early and claim a table by five, it was a sweaty but nonetheless grateful stand, although a woman over by the piano looked to be having trouble relaxing, and no wonder. Handbag, briefcase, cigarette, cocktail, claustrophobia; the burden appeared to be too great, and she looked faint.

Straightening his crouch with legs well trained for upward mobility, a young man reads aloud, "Greyell Webster, Barristers & Solicitors."

"Or Babblers & Scribblers. I'm a Scribbler—what do you do?" The woman who spilled her purse joked her way through another generic encounter.

Heads turned briefly toward an exclusively feminine group at a table by the window. One of them, a women's magazine moonie, drunk on wine and merciless expectations, listed her good points and whined at the god of statistics who might well deny her the perfect mate she so richly deserved. Manless thirties loom. Rescue me.

Across the room, someone surveyed the women, calibrating the warmth in his eyes by the look of each face. Please me.

Barry Klammer lurked expertly under his jacket at the back bar. These youngsters didn't seem to get the hang of the hunch. To Barry, they all looked like those pompous brats from the old-money neighbourhoods, trying to chortle like oldly at their parents' parties. A waitress reached past his shoulder for a drink and he saw what looked like one of his wife's earrings trembling on the girl's ear.

Joanna Brice Lawson Klammer had taken Barry's name as a sort of favour to him, but she hadn't really needed it. Or his money. She had J. Brice Jewellery. She had regular buyers across the continent, a staff of thirty and conspicuous stature in the fundraising gala set. She even had full-page ads in *Vogue*, showing ears and necks concealed by jewel-less jewellery, copper and brass and silver and gold, soldered and hammered and twisted into Art. "J. Brice. Available at Better Stores."

*Better* stores. Nah. It was too late. But Barry imagined the ad for his cleaned-up act. "Select new issues. Fullest disclosure. Minerals actually mined. Available from Better Promoters."

Barry could be called a venture capitalist or, for greater accuracy, a stock promoter. The city's stock exchange had a notoriety across North America because of operators like Barry. Penny stock in papery, newborn companies, mostly "mineral resources," was flogged to receptive local brokers and over-the-counter traders in the States.

Barry had been the best, King of the Boards, in the haydays when he had half a floor in a pink bank tower and played golf with the mayor. Then gold had plunged and the Securities Commission had started prying and exposed a slime of suspiciously timed press releases and manipulated trades.

As Barry's sloppy fortune dwindled, Joanna's careful fortune rose. Since his third and so-far current wife had diversified into real estate, Barry put in an occasional appearance at Rose. Maybe the newness and youth would rub off, or maybe he was punishing himself; he wondered who knew.

Sometimes he chatted up a few of the regulars who called the place the Klammer Klub, but not to his face, of course. Tonight he sat alone and drank, scheming how to save his ass. Better haul in his guy who made cold calls and see how the latest chunk of moose pasture was taking in Florida. And better get on the horn with the lawyers and see how his defence was coming. Damn hearings. Shafted, that's what he was getting. Barry gestured to be done again.

Behind him the night gathered steam, which condensed above bloodshot eyes. Throughout the room, expensive liquor released libido into the air. Eventually, work-day fatigue would wear away the magic. Weekend wallets would lose their heft. And tomorrow, a careful planner would wake up and realize that this month's RRSP contribution was now sloshing in the early-morning bladders of all those girls from the Exchange, waiting to be pissed away.

Madalyn and Tina spent five minutes standing by the bar near the door, waiting for Madalyn to decide if she could "handle the claustrophobia." She could not, and so they left, walking up Robson Street and finally settling on a second-storey nouvelle Italian restaurant where the scraping of their chairs on the terra cotta floor grated on Madalyn's nerves, making her even more thankful for the bottle of California chardonnay. They postponed ordering dinner and began to discuss.

"I don't want to get too excited," Madalyn said, "but I do have a major case of nerves. I think he's probably way too good-looking. I'm sure he knows it. And I really wonder if I should trust that much charm."

"You think he's charming?" Tina asked, and Madalyn thought she heard a subtle note of superiority, as if Madalyn's own impressions were somehow suspect. She knew Tina did not mean to sound this way, but, nevertheless, it made her feel more insecure than ever. And perhaps a bit superficial.

"Well," she said.

"He doesn't lack for self-confidence, if that's what you mean," Tina said, leaning toward Madalyn on her elbows, smiling and sounding now more fully and cozily in cahoots with her friend. "But he's a little flashier than your usual type, isn't he?"

"I don't know if flashy is the word, but I mean, I don't know the man yet. And what usual type?"

"Intellectual. And John is, well, let's just say he seems to me to be more of a social animal."

They went on in this vein for some time, speculating on the nature and person of John Smilie. Madalyn contributed to the conversation with apparent curiosity, but inside, she did not care about the words. Her craving for excitement, unmet to the point of excruciating ennui, had been fully primed by her images of John, by her fantasies about him, by the magic bullet of sexual and romantic stimulation with which she had been shot so definitively last Saturday. In her mind she held his face and kissed it, ran her hands over his chest and floated on the verge of the fantasy she nurtured when she was alone, of pressing herself up next to his skin and placing her hands on his stomach, down low.

"Maybe I just want sex," Madalyn was whispering loudly to Tina as the waiter approached them yet again to ask if they would care to order. The two women were laughing, and their eyes, plumped by wine into live, glistening jewels of sensual avariciousness, caused the waiter to blush and smile weakly, and to feel slightly but deliciously threatened as he stood on one foot and then the other while Tina and Madalyn, tipsy past the point of real hunger, debated their dinner selections.

"Oh, hi, Mom," Madalyn said. "Yes, actually, I'm just getting ready to go out . . . an actual date . . . I don't know, I just met him . . ." She leaned her head to one side to draw on her cigarette, held safely away from her white skirt. What little there was of it rode up her thighs as she sat down.

"My week was fine, thanks, nothing too exciting. Well, except for this date-to-be. How was yours?" Madalyn asked.

She listened to a description of her parents' preparations for a hiking holiday in the Cascades. Why anyone would backpack and camp overnight when they could take day trips from a luxury lodge with hot running water and all the other amenities, Madalyn could not understand. Madalyn had ceased to join her parents on these wilderness ordeals, which they seemed to love so much, when she was seventeen.

"I should really get going," Madalyn said, bouncing a smoothly shaved calf over one knee. She twisted her ankle to one side to admire the look of her thin, arched foot in its red high-heeled shoe. She was relieved to have a real excuse to get off the phone.

For some time now, she and her mother had shared only such small talk, avoiding a number of basic issues, mostly to do with Madalyn's life, which was stagnant according to her mother, during that argument last January.

Madalyn ran her hand over her cleavage, tugging on the low vee of her thin white cotton top. She had a sudden image of herself hiking alongside her parents, dressed as she was for her date.

After they hung up, Madalyn went to the fridge for a medicating glass of wine as she allowed her excited anticipation to smooth over her irritation. She stroked her collarbone as she sipped, already feeling the dull glow of the first drink of the evening. Her fingers travelled down her chest to her waist and over one hip. "You've got so much potential," her mother had said in January. "Do you want to pound a typewriter for the rest of your life?"

So much potential—that heinous trick mirror of feminist pop psychology. Madalyn's irritation rose like nausea, the muscles of her ribcage clamped tight against her lungs. Standing in her tiny, sunlit kitchen, high above the street, she drained her glass and waited, listening for the buzz of her intercom.

They had gone for dinner at an oyster bar on the south side of False Creek, a finger of water that reached into the city, separating downtown from the west-side residential areas. It was flanked by packed condominium developments on the south side and a rotting world exposition site on the north. After what seemed like a surprisingly quick dinner, mostly liquid, during which they exchanged the usual conversational coupons, John suggested a walk down the seawall to Granville Island, not really an island but a formerly rundown industrial stretch between the two bridges spanning the water. It had recently been redeveloped into a magnet for disposable income: theatres, restaurants, art galleries, a gourmet market and two marinas.

John suggested Delancey's, a dinner-and-dancing mecca in the late seventies, just for a laugh, he said. The walk to the Island eased the fuzz inside Madalyn's head from the three glasses of wine she had absorbed at dinner. It was nine thirty when they began their walk, still light, one of those summer nights that filled her with dread.

"So what do you do, normally, on the weekends?" he asked as they walked.

"You mean in the summer?"

"Sure."

"Well, I don't know if I can even talk about it. Summer makes me so uptight."

"Uptight?" he asked, and the smile on his face, half-turned toward her, dissipated her initial reactive stab of embarrassment at the slightly overbearing incredulity in his voice. She held his eyes for a moment and sensed an attraction on his part that transcended his amused yet critical tone. So she decided against an apologetic stance.

"My apartment becomes hot and claustrophobic. Too much sun makes me anxious. I live for the fall. I love darkness. I like to wear black and skulk around the cappuccino bars, psyching myself into feeling like an artist."

"Ah, a woman of substance."

She glanced over at him, catching his eye again, and again noticed his smile just before he turned to look straight ahead. His lips were twisted slightly and his cheeks looked flushed. Silence fell into step with them as they walked. She editorialized then, her insecurities attempting to alleviate any discomfort she might have inflicted upon her audience.

"I guess I'm not very imaginative," she said. Then she asked John what he liked to do in the summers, her disinclination to suffer inanity fighting against her will to attract. He, however, became enthusiastic and told her about his action-packed weekends, camping and water-skiing, heading out, as he put it, to stay with a couple he knew who had big groups up to the wife's parents' house at the money-jammed, year-round recreational community of Whistler, fast becoming one of the most highly acclaimed ski resorts on the continent. They rode mountain bikes, he told her, played golf (*Golf?* Madalyn almost burst out laughing), windsurfed on the tiny, perfect glacial lake that Madalyn herself had stopped at once with her parents.

He agreed that the city was no place to be in the summer, and he did everything he could to get out of town every weekend. If you had to stay in town, he said, it was crucial to know someone with a pool. Luckily for him, his mother had one. Not only that, Madalyn learned, his mother's second husband was a member of the North Shore Golf & Country Club, where John was often invited to play a round on a Sunday afternoon. Madalyn was glad she had made a point of looking closely at him as he elaborated on his second reference to golf. Seeing that he took it quite seriously, she was relieved that she had not let loose with her opinions on the sport. Well, okay, golf.

Upon their arrival at Delancey's, they found a table in the lounge on an outdoor deck with a roof of foliage, tucked away from the dance floor, where mostly tourists, it appeared, generated an awkward good time to the alcoholic AM love ballads.

John commented on the tackiness of the place. "It's so seventies, it's so out that it's in, it's . . ."

"A cult experience," Madalyn said.

"Exactly," he responded, and said that to do it right, they should order Mai Tais or some other elaborate tropical drink, which they did, fooling around with the little umbrellas and laughing at the gardenia floating in Madalyn's glass.

John exercised his particular brand of charm on the waitress, using her name, which he had read on her name tag, asking Kim if she would recommend the Mai Tais, and when she told him, quite earnestly, that they *were* good, but that the Tropical Storms were really something, he patronized her sincerity with so much warmth that Madalyn felt herself on the verge of embarrassment lest Kim should clue into the joke.

Madalyn drew a cigarette out of her purse and was about to light it when John took the matchbook from her hand.

"Unh-unh, that's my job, remember?" he said, reminding her of the lesson he had taught her at dinner. She felt slightly chagrined as the flame flared at the tip of her cigarette. I'm not Kim, for Christ's sake, she thought to herself for an instant, but John had put his arm around the back of her chair and was fixing upon her what appeared to be his total and serious attention, so she chided herself for her paranoia as her self-confidence began to revive under the heat lamp of his gaze.

She noticed his cheekbones, which lifted his solidly sculpted face into true handsomeness, and his dark blond curls, which receded slightly in two indentations on either side of his head, and his remarkable upper body, toned into rounded curves of muscle, tan against his white polo shirt. The blue of his eyes was lost in the semi-darkness, but the colour had startled her in the shadowless, desert-toned twilight during their walk.

Glancing out over the dance floor, Madalyn watched a young black man jutting his knees and elbows in perfect double time to the music. His partner, a fortyish bottle-fried blonde in tight pants, was turning in circles in front of him. Written on her face were her instructions to herself: Have a good time, let loose, meet and mingle, meet, meet, meet, if it kills you.

Madalyn took renewed comfort in John's muscular aura; she cozied up in it, she infused her eyes and her smile with playful affection, she arched one eyebrow, a tic of wickedness, she said nothing and she let John talk.

"Yeah, I slummed it in West Van," he was saying, his tone a faultless mix of deserved pride of place and humility. Upper middle-class WASP guilt worn like a condom—one did not want to catch any criticism, so, just in case.

"West Van's very Iranian now. Not that I have anything against that. Lots of old people too. I'll probably end up back there, at least that's the plan." He winked.

She had found out at dinner that he had two sisters, both older and married, and that his parents had divorced when he was in his early teens. Besides implying that it had been messy, he gave few details on that subject. The way he said the word "divorce," like a door slamming shut, like a reprimand that she could not help but take personally, had scared her off from pursuing it further.

"Do your parents both still live in West Vancouver?" she now asked, her drink providing some daring. She was fascinated by the glamour of his upbringing: divorce and scandal in the highest per capita income suburb in the country, and the things she had deduced and imagined about his mother, namely, martinis at five and lots of them, and the kinds of clothing her own mother would never wear, like high heels during the day and shopping at the West Van Safeway in wonderfully impractical winter white suits with a few pale grey smudges on the skirt, perhaps the result of heedless swipes at carelessly spilled ash from long, lipstick-coated cigarettes. These sorts of things were absolutely foreign to Madalyn's own upbringing, which had been so wholesome and solid that its glitterless, substantive value had been obscured by an almost rancorous boredom in her memory.

"Yup," he said, looking away and taking a slug of his drink. He leaned back in his chair, away from Madalyn. She swept her eyes over the dance floor again. The blonde's torso was held close in the arms of the young man, who grooved in closed-eye comfort, long fingers kneading the woman's back. Just relax, baby. The woman had her arms around his neck, true, but barely, the backs of her hands resting lightly on the very edges of his shoulders. Madalyn could feel her ambivalence. Body language. Needed no translation.

"So you were asking what it was like back East," John said. "Like I said, I went to U of T for undergrad and Western for my MBA. London was shitfully boring, but Toronto was a kick," he went on, finding his stride again and visibly relaxing. "I met lots of oldish money with little sisters." His eyes were twinkling as he leaned on his elbows over his drink, close to her again.

Something like a pinprick, or a match burn, stung Madalyn. A little bit of pain—on the inside. Ignore it, she told herself. She thought of tracing the indentations around John's smile, practically dimples.

The rum and crème de cacao and tequila slow-danced in her bloodstream as John detailed his experience in the MBA program—the heavy chains of discipline required to crank out the heavy loads of work, exams once a month, followed by the treat of a one-night-per-month alcoholic binge he and his classmates doled out to themselves.

"It was rigorous. I have so much fun at work now, it's a piece of cake in comparison. It's much more of a personality thing, even with Jerome, though the guy is relentless. He's got twenty deals going at once. You've got to be totally up to snuff all the time in case he wants to stick you on a plane that afternoon. And God forbid he wants to go with you. With the Japanese, of course, I have to go overboard in the politeness department, to make up for him. I can't tell if they think he's a laugh riot or the most boorish 'ugly American' they've ever known. You should see me with the little slants. I really play the straight man. It might look like groveling in another context, but in the long run, the practice will be valuable."

"No doubt," Madalyn said.

She was enjoying listening to him talk about himself. She envied his obvious and enthusiastic interest in his own life and was more than content not to nurture the instructions she heard in her head, instructions she was supposed to follow but did not, which told her he should be asking her more questions about herself. In fact, she did not want to talk about herself—she found it tiring trying to justify what she felt to be her unremarkable existence, to make it sparkle and snap, to make it draw and envelop. She felt she could do a lot better by just sitting there and looking beautiful.

As he continued to talk, about the resumé-building jobs he had held in Toronto between degrees, about his "overall career plan," about the perks he was only now beginning to enjoy, she felt her heart opening up to him. A sort of emotional image was taking hold inside, of his masculinity being tested, rising to meet all occasions, and being made stronger, its edges honed harder, out in the scary real world. This took courage and must take its toll. And here he was, seemingly opening up to her and needing, perhaps, her soothing touch, the pervasive magic of the sensation she now felt so strongly. *I must have done something good*, she thought.

When he noticed that she had finished her second drink, which had come in a glass the size of a volleyball, he asked how she was doing.

"Feeling no pain."

Drunk and scared, for her editors' had long ago passed out, Madalyn was silent for the most part during the cab ride home. Not on the first date. No. She shouldn't.

John saved her from herself, to her great disappointment, escorting her to the door with gentlemanly conscientiousness, leaving her with no more than a kiss on the cheek. He left her alone, in that place where desire lights up most brightly and what we know we must have is articulated with razor sharpness against the backdrop of its absence.

1-900-370-1010. Madalyn could barely make out the number she had scrawled on a matchbook the night before. Oh, right. Psychic advisors. The coping skills of the drunken insomniac left something to be desired, and she was a frequent casualty of very-late-night television. She threw away the matchbook, along with the contents of a full ashtray.

Rested up, cleaned up, made up, refilled with most of the vitamins, minerals and fluids she had lost last night, she surveyed the apartment, tidied and aired. Time, now, to do some life. At least a bare minimum.

At 4:58 the telephone rang—4:58:11, to be exact. At 4:58:30, she clicked off the television listings channel and answered.

"Hi there, gorgeous," he said. "What's up?"

"Hi, well, um . . ." she said, suffering a personality implosion. "Not much. What about you?"

"I'm calling from the office. Hasn't been a helluva lot of fun. Hey, I heard this joke on the radio. Ask me, if someone offered me a million dollars to kill a stranger, would I do it."

"Ah, okay. If someone offered you a million dollars to kill a stranger, would you do it?"

"No. I don't need the money."

"Ha, ha. Very funny," she said, twisting the phone cord into loops. "That is so sick."

"Yeah, but catchy. So . . . tell me about your day," he commanded with gentle authority, like a psychologist in session, a voice with no need.

"Well, let's see . . . um, today . . ." Her mind raced to create an interesting itinerary. "I had coffee with some friends," she cheerfully lied, "then I went to the market at the Island, and I have a bottle of white wine chilling in the fridge, as we speak," she continued, describing the previous day with conviction.

"Planning on opening it sometime in the near future?"

"The thought had crossed my mind," she said, her stomach sinking into a luxurious quicksand of anxiety.

"Unless you've got plans, how 'bout if I join you?"

Plans. Plans. Nope. Just not quick enough.

"Sure, okay, um, I've got some shrimp and stuff, so if you want dinner . . . Why don't you drop by when you're finished at the office?"

"Okey dokey. I'm outta here. See you shortly."

There was not much to do—check the face, the hair, place a panic call to Tina's answering machine and listen to fear and anticipation taking each other into and out of every possible state of emotion, every possible plan of action. It was a noisy, disturbing strategy session going on inside, but she had her body's agenda, and she had the Good Witch of Romance hovering in her midst, with her pearly, suffused countenance, mouthing benevolent maternal blessings that could not be heard through the rabble chatter in her head, but it was enough that this luminous presence was there, lifting her up and out of danger.

5:35:12. Just checking. The entrance buzzer blurted his arrival. She felt the time it took for him to ascend eighteen floors. She stood by the balcony, as far away as she could get from her door. He knocked. She counted. At ten, she walked to the door and opened it, and her image of him came to life, bearing tulips. They smiled at each other like fools.

My God, I adore that man, she thought to herself, thankful for something to do, the arranging of the tulips in her kitchen. She claimed with resolve a feeling which washed out the years of efficient love from her parents, the intellectual talk and the friendship and the good healthy sex from the small, widely spaced collection of her former boyfriends. She turned her back on that past and entered the living room where John waited, at home already, in a polite but comfortable sprawl on the cushions of her couch, a dark and thick pink upholstery, faded from languishing in the sun.

She sat down beside him. John took the wine and glasses from her and poured, and they drank a toast to second dates. Sunlight from the open balcony door filtered through the dust in the air and into the glass in her hand, making a brooch of lights against her chest. As she raised the glass to drink, the brooch rose into the hollow of her neck.

"That's Grant and Evelyn, my parents," she said, having searched her immediate surroundings for something to talk about, to resuscitate the held breath of the silence surrounding them. She indicated a framed picture on a bookshelf several feet away. John stood up to retrieve it, then sat back down closer to her, studying the picture.

"You've got a lot of your mom's looks," he said.

In the picture, her mother's long, dark hair was coiled and pinned behind her head, her usual hairstyle.

"And from Grant, my restless intellect," she said, slipping John a smile. She talked about her father, about his love of teaching, the innovation and dedication he brought to what she felt was becoming, unjustly, a denigrated profession.

"I don't think teaching is attracting many of the best and brightest anymore," she said, "because it lacks prestige, I guess, not to mention the almighty dollar."

Tears puddled in the corners of her eyes as she thought of her father, of the burden of humility that had settled around him over the years.

"He's a very gentle person. My mother is the assertive one," she said, sponging up the tears with a finger. "She can't handle indecisiveness or ambiguity, so she can really relate to me, as those are specialties of mine."

She expected him to laugh, or at least to smile at her humour, but he did not.

"Sounds like we both have mothers who pretty much do what they want," he said.

She was watching him in profile and noticed his jaw working inside his cheek. He turned to look at her, and she saw in his eyes some well-guarded pain.

"Enough of this seriousness?" she asked.

"Absolutely," he said, his voice soft. Then he looked away, setting down his wineglass, reaching out for the picture of her parents. She watched the curls on the back of his head, glinting in the late afternoon light, and wanted to touch them, to test their spring. He took her glass from her hand and set it next to the picture, which he had turned around so that Grant and Evelyn were taking in the view from the balcony.

"I don't know if Grant and Evelyn should be watching us right now, do you?" he asked, encircling her waist with his arms. "Hmm? What do you think?" She placed a hand on his chest and fingered the fabric of his shirt, a thick finely woven cotton. She felt as if she were privileged to touch it.

"Well, I suppose not," she said, looking up at him, suddenly flooded with shyness, which she struggled to control as their eyes flicked over each other. She entered her own fantasy. He tightened his arms around her and shifted her slightly so that her knees bent, and she slid one leg over his. She felt the firmness of his muscles and let her eyes slip downward.

Waiting, she examined his belt buckle. Then John pulled both her legs over his lap. She put her arms around his neck, and they drew each other into the first kiss, which began the unfolding of their separate visions of what it would be like. They set each other off: both felt something start in the solar plexus and spread out, finding eventual relief on the very surface of all of their skin.

The clock radio read 7:14. They were finishing the wine in bed, her head on his shoulder. She tried following his thoughts with her eyes as he drank in silence. Well, it seems I am also adored, she thought tentatively. So it seems. Another more exuberant part of herself thought, of the love-making moments just past, that this is bloody well what it's all about. This helped her relax. She rearranged the sheet over her chest and under her arms, snuggled into her own pillow and caught his attention by her own self-contained reverie.

"You," he said, relieving her again of her glass, "are quite a find."

"I am?"

"An amazing find," he said, turning and stretching out over her and looking straight into her eyes, his voice faintly self-conscious.

"I want to *find* you again," he said, and their smiles coaxed each other's into the gaiety that comes with security. The second time, just before he entered her, he stopped to check her eyes again, as if confirming her permission.

Hours later, at about three in the morning, she awoke, got up and sat in the living room for a smoke. Her thin, slippery robe slid over her legs as she curled up in the corner of the couch. In the next room, John was sleeping deeply, lying across her bed in a solid sprawl of ownership. She contemplated her exquisite elation and revelled in the stillness and darkness that surrounded her cozy, smoky love nest, scented with sex and containing all she needed to make bearable and meaningful the world that crouched outside, its fearsome contradictions, for a short time, at rest.

For Lawrence, lunch was usually a sandwich in his office or an uncomfortably suit-jacketed meeting over not enough food and never enough wine. That first Friday in August, however, he had allowed for two hours, at least, in the spacious embrace of a padded banquette, and he ordered, right away, a full bottle of wine, the first two glasses of which he drank quickly; he felt them taking him to that state of relaxation between the built-up tensions and irritations of the morning and the place he longed to be, where the cumbersome, life-thwarting bulk of his rational self would be completely dissolved.

While the waiter explained the specials, Lawrence noticed Tina suppressing a laugh over the earnest and dramatic account of how the raspberry vinaigrette would be lightly tossed with watercress and pine nuts, and how the medallions of veal, if the diners should so choose, would be complemented, but their delicacy not impinged, by the equally delicate glaze of lemon and wine.

Lawrence ordered the New York steak. To the waiter's obvious relief, Tina ordered the veal. She was clearly the more sophisticated of the two, judging by the way he ignored Lawrence and assured Tina of the excellence of her choice. Young and obviously professional, he had no doubt been working to iron out of his voice any remnants of the steak house "Hi, I'm Jeff and I'll be your waiter" sort of camaraderie. Nevertheless, his smile bloomed and he even allowed an abbreviated though natural chuckle to escape his lips before he disengaged himself from his interaction with Tina and turned to leave.

"So the New West deal should be tied up by today," Lawrence said, his voice purposefully tapped up a notch or two, to regain her attention.

"Yes. I sent the whole package over this morning," Tina answered. "Renata is reviewing the numbers, then it's just got to be filed." She crossed her legs under the table, nicking his shin.

"Sorry," she said, blushing and gracing him with one of her smiles, which rounded out her translucent cheeks and rose just a smidgeon above her gumline, making her look very young and humanizing what Lawrence considered to be the symmetrical perfection of her face.

Ginger. Toffee. What exactly would she call her hair, Lawrence was wondering. My God, she's a sexy girl, he thought, suddenly realizing that he now knew why some men had a thing for redheads. He had been tapping his fork and knife together on top of the folded linen napkin. Now he suddenly noticed the napkin, unfolded it and spread it on his lap, as Tina had done as soon as they had ordered.

"So. Lunch without Jere, as you put it. This is very nice," she said, looking out over the restaurant, done in pale pine and shades of dove grey and greyed mauve, colours of early morning sleep. The notes of the background music, silver, china and glass, played in soft, sporadic phrases. Two rods of pink began to appear atop Lawrence's cheekbones.

She asked, "How are the kids?" He watched her trail her fingertips down her neck and over the white silk of her blouse, draped so expertly that what might be termed an ample bosom was only hinted at through the thick folds of fabric, smooth as icing.

"They're really cute. The girls are quite blonde, um, I guess they get that from their mother." A second of alarm deepened the pink of his cheeks, making his brown-black eyes even brighter. Then he remembered the picture in his office.

"Yes. Susan was blonde as a child too. The kids are great. Thanks."

"So. Did you take holidays this summer?" Lawrence asked.

"As of Monday, actually. I'll be gone for two weeks. To Texas. Since today is my last day, I tried to finish everything up this morning, and I've basically written off the afternoon." She smiled and raised her glass in a one-sided toast and took a healthy sip.

"Great," Lawrence said, the word clogging his throat until he cleared it up with another try. "Great."

Just then, Barry and Joanna Klammer stopped by the table, Barry's mop of silver hair atop his square red face reaching the ends of Joanne's ash-blond bob, where it grazed her collar.

Lawrence asked how they were enjoying the house. Last year Lawrence had personally taken charge of the conveyancing of the Klammers' modern monstrosity on Marine Drive. He did not usually handle residential deals; it had been a favour to Jerome.

When Lawrence introduced Joanna to Tina, Joanna's eyes stepped back in their sockets, taking in the seated couple. She suggested to Barry, who seemed inclined to chat, that Lawrence and Tina were just about to begin their lunch. The Klammers left for their table, and the salads arrived.

"Bet you'll be glad to get away from this rain for a while," Lawrence said. "It's been one strange August, hasn't it? Used to be you could count on August."

"I'm not sure which is worse," Tina said. "It's terribly hot down south."

We're still on weather, Lawrence thought to himself, sifting through his brain for ideas. Without the security of whatever task was at hand during their meetings in his office, he, at least, seemed to be having trouble finding a conversational stride.

"Texas is certainly an original choice," he said.

"Well," she responded, pausing in a way that caused him to feel so much maddening anticipation. "I have numerous relatives on my mother's side down there—it's a built-in social life. I always have an interesting time, even though my cousins are constantly trying to set me up with supposedly eligible males."

"You're not currently attached to a supposedly eligible male?" he asked, forcing some disinterested incredulity into his voice.

There was that pause of hers again, a firm, unhesitant pause, a statement of some sort in itself.

"No. I'm not."

"Hard to believe," he said. She caught his compliment and bounced it on the lift of her eyebrows and on the wing of a one-sided smile, her lips closed, a skewed bow prettily denting one cheek. She looked at him over the rim of her wineglass, and this prop, this bit of business of taking a sip, muted her look into congruence with their polite conversation. But he had not missed it.

Into the magical kingdom he stepped, extra-conscious, fully alive. The wonder with which he had been toying for months, without really admitting it to himself, slid away, but not entirely. Its mists no longer obscured the reality, suddenly clear, that he was involved in an actual flirtation, starkly and brilliantly lit with possibility.

Lawrence was the kind of married man single women observed with resentment because he was always so oblivious to the sexual charge he unthinkingly inspired. They would attribute his lack of interest to his marital status, which thus became an affront to their femininity. If he had been aware of this phenomenon, he would have been startled by the divergent workings of Tina's mind and heart.

Lawrence drank freely throughout lunch and had less and less trouble thinking of things to say. By the time they arrived at dessert, he was feeling quite proud of himself, laughing easily and heartily at the picture Tina painted of her father and his politics in particular, which, as she described them, seemed to be fomented from childlike Reaganistic idylls which embodied a limitless potential for personal happiness, which Mr. Tyhurst believed to be the natural outcome of the application of rigorous optimism and enterprise to the textbook functioning of capitalism.

"Just a touch to the right of centre?" Lawrence remarked, renewing her laughter, which she tried to hide in her hand as her eyes crinkled and glittered above it.

With their coffee came two double brandies.

"Courtesy of the grey-haired gentleman in the far corner," the waiter said, indicating the Klammer table. Lawrence raised his glass in a toast to the back of Joanna's head and to Barry, who winked.

"At this rate, I'll have to write off the afternoon too," Lawrence said. "But hey, who am I to pass up what is probably the most expensive brandy in the house? Like it?"

"Mmm-hmm. I hope I don't need a stretcher to make it back to the office."

"Well, *I'm* in no rush . . . if you're not."

It was closing in on two thirty, and the restaurant was nearly emptied of the lunch-hour crowd. Rain continued to roll down the windows on the far side of the restaurant, which looked out over the inlet to the North Shore.

"Have you seen the Woody Allen film *Hannah and Her Sisters*?" Lawrence asked, suddenly filled with the sensation the film had inspired in him, of warming himself within a rich, dark, tastefully appointed apartment after a bracing walk in the perpetually autumnal New York air of Allen's films.

"Yes, I have. Michael Caine has an affair with his wife's sister, right?"

"That's the one. I've seen it four times, I think, at least. It's definitely one of my most cherished of Woody's films. The voice-over of his guilt, well, I found the whole thing very entertaining."

"My friend Madalyn, you know her."

"She works for Ross White."

"Right. Anyway, she really related to the third sister, you know, the flaky one who can't seem to get her life together."

"And who ends up marrying Woody in the end?"

"Did she? Oh, yes . . . that's right."

"Anyway," Lawrence said, "I'm a real Woodyphile."

"So is Madalyn. I should get you two together."

At three o'clock he was dropping her off in the lobby of her building. He wished her a good holiday, and she thanked him again for lunch. As he watched the elevator doors close, he was emboldened to keep eye contact with her until the doors shut. Then he walked back to his office, as slowly as he possibly could.

By four thirty the brandy had worn off, he had fought the rush-hour traffic, had pulled into the carport, entered his home through the basement door and tripped over a jumble of small muddy shoes. He was soon enveloped in the beginnings of a family weekend, his children milling and screeching through the kitchen after plopping three heartfelt kisses onto his cheek. Susan turned toward him with a slightly harassed smile when he came up behind her at her post in front of the sink, placing his hands on her waist.

His lunch with Tina had been wound up and hidden away in a projector in his mind, so he could play it back at will, and would, often, later. The quality, in terms of probability, of the thoughts he had entertained during lunch decreased until he truly wondered at himself, and thoughts of infidelity were transformed into static fantasy in the face of the flesh-and-blood domestic scene now playing itself out around him, which revolved around him, in fact. He sat at the kitchen table and fielded all the guess what? and can we? He nursed the beer Susan had offered him, along with her pleasure that he had come home early.

# Chapter Two

Two weeks later it was still raining, and a crankiness pervaded the mood of the city by the sea as hopes grew dim for some sort of summer other than the five spotty weeks of sun enjoyed in June and July.

Madalyn revelled in the rain. It kept her, and John, indoors, and on that Sunday morning it kept them late in bed, a pall of rainclouds muting the daylight, extending the night. Her eyes opened, then closed again as she moved slowly under the covers amidst the warmth of his body. Before she could turn toward him, she felt the blanket of his skin wrapping around her from behind and she cuddled into it, with a sigh of leftover sleep. They rocked together, slightly, like the gentlest of tides, and the warmth between them grew. How could they not love each other in those kinds of moments, feeling the ineffable perfection of the bliss of a baby enveloped in its essential embrace.

When she did turn around, she smelled the pungency of his body odour, fermented overnight—a harbinger of reality—but the sight of his face, whiskery and masculine, punctuated by his startling eyes, only magnified by their sleepiness, cancelled her mild aesthetic cringe. He kissed her. Moments later, the ring of the telephone next to the bed caused her to twitch in his arms.

"Calm down," he murmured teasingly into her lips as she withdrew her hand from the hair at the back of his neck, the softly matted curls she had been fluffing with languid strums of her fingers.

"Madalyn." A male voice spoke into her ear through the receiver she cradled against the pillow.

She turned away from John to prop herself on an elbow. The covers fell away, and he ran his hand over her shoulder, down her side and over one hip. She felt a charge like weighted gossamer shimmering through her body with the instantaneous scurry of static electricity.

"Madalyn? It's Nihil."

Madalyn's ear was pressed tight against the receiver. The depth of Nihil's voice, usually rolling extravagantly with louder-than-average timbre and the assured fluidity of a trained actor, was today tempered with something tentative, falling in dollops into her ear.

"Nihil?" she answered, clearing her throat and half-heartedly imbuing her voice with some wide-awake normalcy. She felt as if she were in bed with two men. John was using her hip as a pillow while his fingers traced with delicious nimbleness the insides of her legs and regions thereabout.

"How the heck are you?" she asked. "I've been meaning to call you since we ran into each other." John's fingers continued to flutter. With perverse enjoyment, she decided to settle in for a bit of a talk.

"I'm cool," Nihil said. "Still living illegally in my studio. I called because I've got an opening at the Crash today, and I wondered if you'd like to come."

"Would I like to come?" She turned and smiled wickedly at John. His fingers continued to dance and her legs slipped and slid beneath the sheets. "Well, um, sure."

"Are you alone?" Nihil asked, hearing the rustling of bedclothes. "You're not, are you? You naughty girl!"

"Well, no," she said. "Um, what time is it, the opening?"

"It's at four, and, ah, bring your friend."

She turned to John and covered the receiver with her hand. "Art show? Four o'clock?"

"Whatever you say, honey," he answered in the tone of a dutiful husband, into her thigh.

"We'll be there."

"Don't do anything I wouldn't do. Just close your eyes and think of me," Nihil said, his voice large and rich.

"See you, Nihil."

"Bye bye."

Nihil continued to nurse a tepid cup of instant coffee and sat staring out of one of the many long, narrow windows that allowed light into his L-shaped studio. A pull-out couch of a stiff, bristly red material occupied the large, otherwise empty corner near a door that led out onto a rooftop, the Asphalt Patio, he called it.

On the wall opposite this door was a large industrial sink with an artfully cracked mirror above it. Beside the mirror was a snapshot in an absurdly oversized frame, much wider than the picture itself. The frame was painted a garish lilac, striped with yellow. The picture was of a barrel-chested man in his late fifties, whose meaty face looked to be sliding off its bones, like melting wax. Beside him was a woman, small and thin. Between these two stood a beautiful young man with long-lashed, gentle eyes. This was Nihil's family.

Unlike his brother, Peter, Nihil had inherited his mother's frame and her grey eyes, which crinkled above the lift of one of her rare smiles. Both Nihil and Peter had inherited their mother's full-bodied, shiny black hair. Only now, Nihil's was a chalky white and scarcely more than an inch long, and his mother's had lost much of its shine and was graded with grey. Only Peter's hair was in its natural prime. It startled against his white skin.

Often, when Nihil was using the sink, he would look at the picture, his eyes resting briefly on his mother and then, longer, on his brother, and a feeling of the bitterest sort of nostalgia, nostalgia for things that would never be, would prod his heart for a moment. He did not know why.

The telephone in Madalyn's bedroom rang again, having given them barely enough time to consecrate the morning to Eros. It was Tina, just in from Houston.

As John wandered naked out of the bedroom in search of coffee, turning at the bedroom door to give Madalyn a boyish smile and a rogue's wink, Tina was saying that she had had a wonderful time, in her usual tone of voice, even and careful, minimizing even excitement, tidying up whatever she was feeling into neat recitations, fluent, pretty, but curiously dry. Flat on her back, stretching and settling under the covers, Madalyn tried to concentrate on Tina as she heard, with an amazed thrill, John begin to putter in the kitchen, and thought of how unnatural a naked man looked from behind.

Tina was reminding Madalyn of the Ma'am-this and Ma'am-that-never-let-you-do-a-thing-for-yourself Texan breed of male, which had flabbergasted them both when they were eighteen and Madalyn had accompanied Tina on one of her trips down south. Apparently they had not changed. There was this one guy, Tina said, at this gala charity event, very Town and

Country, who kept appearing every hour or so to ask her to dance, and who had to have been at *least* forty, she said, and yes, he was attractive, but he didn't talk much. Tina confirmed Madalyn's assumption that her aunt still believed something was drastically wrong with the combination of Tina's age and marital status.

"So what are you doing today?" Tina asked. "Why don't you come over?"

"I'm still in bed," Madalyn whispered into the phone, "working on my marital status."

"Pardonnez-*moi*," Tina said, and they quickly steered the conversation to a close, making arrangements to meet for dinner the next evening.

"Don't hang up on my account," John said, reclining on one elbow beside her.

"I will if I want to," Madalyn said, eyeing the towel around his waist.

"Coffee's almost ready if you are," he said. "Want to check out the televangelists?" He placed the palm of his hand on her forehead. "Heeyul!"

"Is that the best you can do by way of a plan?"

"Well, what did *you* have in mind?" he asked as she ran her hands over his chest, sculpting his muscles.

"Not getting saved, anyway."

"Do you remember Emil Nolde, by any chance?" Nihil was asking Madalyn. "I took a certain amount of inspiration from him for this stuff, his use of colour, the jarring aspects . . ."

Madalyn was standing in front of a painting entitled *Jealousy*. A five- by eight-foot canvas, it was a wide-angle perspective of a room. The floor was green, an ugly green, "a sick, urine green," as Nihil had described it. Partway up the walls, the colour clomped in rectangular slashes. Flowing down from the ceiling to meet it was a rosy pink, tinged and warmed with pale yellow in the mix, Madalyn could tell, and a touch of blue. It was a beautiful pink. It flowed into the green with large, fat, tearlike drips.

"I wish I'd done this," Madalyn said, and John looked at her quizzically. "It's so sad. Not jarring so much as . . . well, it jars sadness from me. The pink, it's so hopeful . . ."

Madalyn looked at Nihil with admiration. Then she teased him. "Besides switching mediums, you appear to have left behind your broad political themes for the personal."

"That juvenile shit," Nihil said.

John rolled his eyes as he turned away.

Dressed up for his opening, Nihil had donned his black leather jacket, which hung heavily on his bony frame over his T shirt and shorts. He wore red flip-flops and sported a pair of evil-looking, black wraparound sunglasses on his white bristled head.

Nihil's new group of paintings covered two long walls on the main floor of the Crash Gallery, a black-walled space for alternative art in an old Gastown building. The gloomy quality of the light in the gallery, punctuated coldly with choreographed track lighting, matched the light outside on the cobbled streets, slick with rain.

*Jealousy* was hung at the end of the hall-like room so one could see it from a distance. It was the last of Nihil's paintings upon which he had commented for Madalyn and John on their private tour. Now they stood near the desk by the door, refilling their glasses once again.

"John, whadja think?" Nihil asked.

John took a sip from his water glass and worked the water around his teeth, his closed lips stretching in apparent thought.

"You don't have to answer," Nihil said.

"What would you call your style?" John asked, and Madalyn noticed a flush rising above his collar. "I'm not up on modern art, I'm sorry to say."

"Madalyn?" Nihil deferred.

"Um, let's see, um . . . how about, Lite, as in L-i-t-e Germanic Expressionism?"

She and Nihil laughed.

"Thank you, Madalyn," Nihil said. "Gosh, I feel artistically vindicated."

"Are you selling much?" John asked, and Madalyn's heart became spongy with tenderness for both men.

"Not usually. But they're all ticketed with hope and prices, and today's only the first day of the showing, so we'll see. But that's the idea."

"Is it?" John asked. "Not Art for Art's sake?"

Nihil's eyebrows rose and he shot a bevelled glance at Madalyn, seeming not to believe that John had ever heard the expression.

"That too, naturally," Madalyn blurted out without thinking. She moved closer to John and willed him to put an arm around her. He heaved a sigh as he looked at her and returned her smile as her eyes rolled slightly in Nihil's direction.

"What are you doing these days?" Nihil asked Madalyn. "Ah, yes, thanks," he said, pulling a cigarette from her proffered package. "Artwise."

"Nada. Rien. Mea culpa," she said, tossing smoke from her mouth over her shoulder.

"You seen her work?" Nihil asked John.

"I've asked, but she's chosen not to show it to me . . . yet."

"You mean you haven't snuck a look at that stash of canvases behind the couch?" Madalyn asked, feeling a mix of fear and embarrassment settle heavily and with great discomfort onto her shoulders, as if she were balancing upon them two coin-filled sacks of slippery leather. She breathed deeply through her cigarette.

"You'll show me when you're ready," John said.

"She's good," Nihil said, and went on to elaborate upon her drawing technique, deliberate in process and astounding in result, her lyrical use of chiaroscuro, her affinity for the layering of oils.

"Well?" Madalyn asked Nihil a few minutes later, after John had excused himself and headed toward the men's room, making his way through thickets of the Alternative Art Crowd, black-booted to a noticeably large extent, deliberately thin or at least pale, and sharing with more conventional patrons everywhere their enthusiastic and conscientious consumption of the free booze that thankfully accompanies these sorts of events.

"A Symbolist, by George, you're sleeping with a Symbolist!" Nihil answered.

"Nihil!" She hit his arm. "Sex for sex's sake," she whispered emphatically in his ear. "Not really," she then said out loud, her voice wobbly, embarrassed to elaborate upon what she felt, feeling as if she had to apologize to Nihil for being in love because he'd think it wasn't cool, because he would think John was less than spiritually equipped for big L love, just because of the way he looked, just because he was ensconced and expert in the workings of the material world.

The short walk back to the car after receiving Nihil's quick kiss on the lips, his hands grasping her upper arms, a cigarette held between his fingers, then the short ride in John's rain-coloured BMW and the short trip with him up her elevator, seemed to take forever and had the effect of stirring up her Art anxiety and other vague and nameless insecurities, to such an extent that when they arrived at her door, these things were surging through her body with flu-like effect. Weak and sweaty as she entered the apartment, she felt an instant easing of her symptoms when she saw, through the open bedroom door, the corner of her duvet in a soft splash on the floor.

Especially in those moments when the urgency of the passion was suspended, devolving and evolving at once, when time was stretched, not tight, but in slowed-down contours around them, and his hands on either side of her face brushed away imaginary hairs, and she held his vulnerable sides below his arms, which supported him above her, and they kissed with supple, suctiony kisses, it would be safe to say there was no need or desire for discussion.

Thus the talk they were to have about her Art, prompted by her preemptive query as to whether he *really* wanted to see it, and her inevitable display of her "body of work," as she would jokingly introduce it, was delayed until after their champagne-assisted foray back into her wrecked bed.

"Syndication," Barry Klammer was saying, "it's the way to go with this product in this market. Tell Pickard it's a sure thing. It's no skin off my nose which way he goes, but any friend of yours . . . anyway, you've got 'til December to talk him into it."

Barry and Jerome were emerging from Jerome's office in a cloud of smoke—from Jerome's cigars and Barry's cigarettes. Passing by, Tina blinked through the fumes. Barry's doctor had told him he must quit, so he did not actually smoke his cigarettes, just lit one after another and chewed each one into a pulpy, acrid mess.

"Talk to you later, oh, and Jere, get your girl to call my girl and tell Phil to wait," Barry said. Since no secretary was in sight, Jerome's eyes apologized and pleaded above his back-slapping smile, and Tina glared and picked up a phone. When Barry had left, and as she spoke with Barry's "girl" from the secretarial desk outside Jerome's office, Tina could hear Jerome on his own phone, asking for Lawrence Pickard. When she finished her call, she pretended to be studying the contents of the file she was carrying, and listened.

". . . it's a first-class development, Lawrence, Klammer's got the O.M. going out to the Commission for vetting at the beginning of December . . . so the time to line up the inside capital is now . . . I know . . . I understand it's not your personal policy to tie yourself up in these sorts of deals, but it's a solid, first-class setup . . . yeah, I don't doubt you're not keen on hearing a spiel from Klammer, but I wanted to give you the opportunity . . . yup . . . and I've got one of my young guys seriously interested . . . yup . . . he's probably gonna do twenty-five K, leveraged, mind you, but you could go fifty or a hundred, that's how confident I am . . . let me send you Klammer's package, yeah, no, don't worry, I won't send Klammer . . . okay, do this for me, Lawrence, I think you owe it to yourself to at least take a look."

Back in her office, Tina sat at her desk, burrowing in her purse, preparing to leave for lunch.

"You just back, or going?" John asked, a hand on each side of the doorframe, ready to shoot himself in either direction. Since both were planning on picking up something from the mall beneath the office tower, John volunteered to buy. When he returned, they started in on their six-dollar croissant sandwiches in Tina's office.

Madalyn lurked behind their crenellated conversation. John confirmed that they had been seeing quite a bit of each other, which Tina said she had gathered, making sure her remark was well buoyed up by enough formal disinterest in her tone of voice.

"You know Barry Klammer," Tina said.

John rolled his eyes. "Know the man, hate the scam."

"Oh, really? He was in with Jerome just now. I think they were discussing some new deal of Barry's. Sounded like real estate—something about syndication. But Barry doesn't *do* development, so I wondered . . ."

"Oh," John said. As his eyes lowered, a flush rose under the shadow of his shave. "Well, I'm aware that somehow Klammer's got his slimy fingers into a big condo thing in Arizona, and yeah, it is a syndication deal. I can't say I like the idea of his name all over the O.M., but the group he's in with is only one of the general partners. I'm actually thinking of the deal for myself. It looks pretty solid, but I wish to Christ Klammer wasn't yammering about it all over town. Kinda takes the distinction off the thing, because the other partners and investors, to date, are a respectable group."

"You've seen the info, obviously."

"Yeah. Like I said, I'm ready for some serious investment."

"And you think this *is*, I mean, it's safe?" Tina asked.

"Well, of course the market down there in three months is everything, but I've looked into that too. Seems good. And the timing's not bad—people are looking for tax shelters. But still, it's a risk. I mean, everything's got some, and this definitely has its factors . . . I'd only invest what I could cover or carry comfortably."

Tina's upper lip felt moist. She dabbed at it with her napkin. John took the last swallow of his Perrier and stretched in his chair. He was looking at Tina, watching her wiping her lips— feathery motions with a paper-covered index finger. She ran her fingers under her eyes and made a few delicate pokes at the hair around her face. Then she met John's gaze. The conversational lull between them bloomed.

John cleared his throat, began to gather up the remains of his lunch, and said, "Well, I'll clear out now. By the way, I do admire your taste in friends. I owe ya one."

Then he was gone. That wink of his turned up the volume on Tina's thoughts, clattering bits of worry about safety—Madalyn's, Lawrence's, hers.

That evening, Madalyn brought the wine and Tina provided dinner, after which they sprawled for hours on Tina's pale leather furniture, inhaling the details of Madalyn's love life, getting high, as if on the incense of the Religion of Romance, its rich history promising so much. A dangerous practice, perhaps, the lull of religion, which can make for lazy brains, disguise evasion and attenuate the future if left unquestioned. But it feeds the heart of the passionate adherent and can sharpen shades of grey into the absolute abyss of black or into white, pure and blinding.

"On Darvon and champagne," Madalyn was saying, "that's essentially how I feel most of the time. But I cannot concentrate, naturally."

Tina responded with a certain amount of effort. "Naturally."

Madalyn was twisting her cigarette against the sides of an ashtray, gently rubbing away the ash. She gave it a final twist, tapped it briskly with a finger and brought it to her mouth, drawing energetically. She blew smoke through her lips in a long, steady stream. She was half sitting on the couch next to Tina, and the length of her free leg leaned crookedly against the coffee table. Against the light carpeting, her black hose gave her leg a spidery emphasis. The energies of a heart in love, feeding upon themselves, reproducing themselves in order to stoke the highs of love, ricocheted through her, with nowhere to go. They threatened to rise up through her throat, and she had to swallow them down. The insecurities of love, of course, gave these energies their heat and steam.

"But I have this sense that he doesn't quite know what to make of me," Madalyn said. "I'm not sure we share an interest in things intellectual.

"You mean he doesn't find 'the naïveté of your insular, first-world, middle-class politics to be egregious'?" Tina asked, and they laughed.

"You deliberately memorized that comment of Walter's and just would *not* leave him alone." Madalyn's voice was bouncy and teasing.

Walter Bara—they had met him in London on their post-university graduation trip. A Nigerian PhD student studying at Oxford, Walter had teamed up with the two of them on part of their holiday. During their three-week Portuguese bacchanalia, Madalyn and Walter had become lovers. Tina and Madalyn recounted this time to each other, flipping overlapping remembrances into the conversation, a growing commotion of memory revived.

Portugal . . . red wine throughout the afternoons, and still more in the evenings, lubricating their conversations . . . . Madalyn and Walter getting all revved up over theories of art and politics and philosophies of life, and jabbing holes, good-naturedly, through each other's sociopolitical frames of reference. Once when Walter was complaining, again, about the evils of colonialism, Madalyn stunned him by stating bluntly,

"You should read more. Ever heard of Shaka Zulu"

One evening, after a week of this, when Tina had gone to bed after dinner, pleading excessive inebriation, on the beach in front of their cottage, against the backdrop of an orange and purple sunset besmirched with long wisps of charcoal cloud, Madalyn and Walter first made love.

The friends recalled how Walter's generosity of spirit and humour had prevented Tina from feeling left out, had helped to spin those weeks and the three of them into a capsule of time, isolated, rare, and rendered more precious by the protective layering of each passing year. Madalyn, to herself, recalled Walter—tall and thin, with long, gentle hands and a face made handsome by a slightly ponderous sensuality. Yes, Madalyn remembered Walter, to whom she had entrusted the deficit of her virginity, and the nights he had credited her with enough new knowledge to carry her into the black of womanhood. And she remembered, like a particular question still in her mind, when Walter had discovered, and mused upon like a poet, a beauty mark of hers, hidden in the sunless fold of her inner thigh. She could still feel his cool, elegant touch.

"So I finally showed my paintings to John," Madalyn said, breaking a long pause, plunging ahead into a troublesome topic she had been debating whether or not to bring up with Tina. With herself, really, she had to admit.

"He thought they were wonderful, of course," Tina said, with long-held admiration for her friend's talent.

"Wellll . . . I think he was a little confused, actually."

"What's the deep inner meaning?" John had asked when she showed him a large double panel.

"This one here is my fourth-year piece," she said, leaning the bulk of the canvases against herself so he could get a look.

"Oh, yeah?" he said, hmming a little. "Boy, you sure like the colour pink." Meaning, perhaps, her tastes in decorating—the burgundy of the living room curtains, the faded rose upholstery of the couch, the frankly feminine pastel shade of the curtains and duvet in her bedroom. And meaning the slightly brownish pink she had mixed for that particular canvas, the splotches she had made, amorphous and translucent, tubular in shape, with pinched ends, through which thin black figures could be seen scattered, some upended, like pick-up-sticks after the fall.

He was standing behind her, his hands on her waist. She felt his belt pressing into her back and had an urge to lean back against his chest; concrete, permeated with his body heat, which she knew could steam away the wrinkles of her discomfort. He spoke into her ear, kissing it first.

"What's the deep inner meaning?"

She turned her head around to look at his face, at his half smile.

"How should I know? I called it *Her Harrowing Dreams*," she responded, blushing. She abruptly let go of *Her Harrowing Dreams* and of all the other canvases and let them fall against the wall. They fell with a loud slap as she turned around to put her arms around his neck, to kiss him. When she let him up for air, she saw she had successfully wiped any kind of smile off his face.

"You are very talented," he said.

"He all but admitted he didn't know enough about art to say if they were good or not. Which really makes me wonder about the whole point of my painting if what I do is that inaccessible. Though granted, it's not representational stuff. I mean, it's not *The Swing* by Fragonard. Oh, and we were at Nihil's opening on Sunday . . ."

"Oh, boy, I bet John just loved *him*," Tina interrupted. "Are you sure that was a good idea?"

Madalyn was deliberately unresponsive and busied herself with topping up her glass. There was no point getting into the subject of Nihil with Tina.

"Well, we went, in any event," she said. "Then we went back to my place and had great sex for the rest of the afternoon."

"The three of you?" Tina asked, and they exploded into tension-leavening laughter, Tina's upper gum flashing pinkly as she bent over her terry-covered knees to deposit her sloshing wineglass with an unintentional clank on the glass coffee table. Then she refolded her legs under the white plushness of her robe and curled back up into the wide, smooth embrace of her corner of the couch.

"And another thing: John doesn't think I'm very ambitious," Madalyn said, lighting a new cigarette and pulling at the neck of her black wool dress to air herself out. She'd arrived at Tina's straight from work, and the day's stale sweat felt gummy under her arms, and her bra was pinching below her breasts.

Tears came to her eyes, and she hoped Tina would notice. "What do you think he meant? I took it as a criticism."

"In what context, in general or artwise?"

"Well, I guess artwise. He asked why I haven't kept up with my painting, the big question, the one everyone's so bloody interested in. Maybe he thinks I should be having openings like Nihil, or something, although I don't think he liked Nihil any better than you do." She smiled weakly at Tina through her tears.

Tina sighed heavily. "I don't know why it would matter to him one way or another, if you're ambitious or not."

"My thoughts exactly. Anyway, I'm all screwed up about the comment. It's something my mother would say." Now she was really crying, having a good alcohol-enhanced bawl.

The conflicts she had about Art and Ambition, separate but intertwined, tightened in a tangle inside her. She had a vague, skewed notion that excessive ambitiousness would render her, ten years down the road, as someone dry on the inside and grey on the out, who had sacrificed the most alluring of her feminine attributes upon the altar of the Feminist Agenda. She preferred her pink-collar limbo to such a scenario. And although she had a few private theories as to why she was not painting, she had yet to attain much insight into why this condition made her feel so distressingly paranoid. Sometimes she explained her frightening immobility to herself as a stubborn refusal to do what was expected of her, and at other times supposed she was an all-or-none type of person, and until she found herself compelled to become an Artist, or anything else, with an uplifting, joyful sort of compulsion, she would refuse to try.

During the insulated years at university, she had painted because that had been her major, and had enjoyed it because it was something she had always done. And she was good. However, once released into the real world, where choice gnawed at her from every side, she had drifted away from making a commitment to "her Art," as her classmates would term it—"my Art," they would say, as if it were an internalized shrine to which they were enslaved in ecstatic, sacrificial worship. Many of them had embraced Art As A Lifestyle, living out a phenomenon that appears generation after generation in certain segments of the young. But she had not shared their darkly conspiratorial ideologies concerning the cancerous properties of The Mainstream, which, if one lacked vigilance, would eat into your soul until there was nothing left, until you were little more than an automaton like all the other automatons who populate the malls, the office towers and the transit systems on a daily basis, empty indicators of the success of consumerism, puppets of the evil technicians who program into them their safe and banal appetites.

In truth, Madalyn was terrified of the existential vacuum, out of which art offers but one means of escape. If taken, it leaves us no choice but to demand of ourselves that we call upon that most concentrated and consecrated part of ourselves, and insists that we, God-like, create.

Even if our ennui is utter and all there is, the only available material, we must use it. But that kind of elemental struggle took more courage and strength than Madalyn had. She needed something different, more substantive—some deeply felt passions, rich and gelatinously smooth, like gobs of bright fingerpaint. She needed something that would cause her fingers to twitch and hum with the urge to touch it.

"I just don't understand," she said, as Tina moved to sit beside her, shaking out a dinner napkin and placing it on her friend's lap. "This fucking *ambition* thing. I don't understand why I don't have it. Why I'm expected to have it. And why I don't want to have it. Maybe I'm just afraid of it, I don't know, but I'm so sick of being harassed about it . . . I'm just so sick of it . . . ." She swiped the napkin vigorously across her face.

"I wouldn't worry about it with John," Tina said. "I'm sure he adores you."

"Well, on one level, we get along like a house on fire . . . as we've discussed in lurid detail."

Seeing that Madalyn had recovered enough to smile with reassuring lasciviousness, Tina went to the kitchen to rustle up their customary carton of chocolate Häagen-Dazs and two spoons, as Madalyn mopped up her face.

Reclining in front of the graceful licks of an artificial fire, buoyed up by supple puffs of upholstery, surrounded by the pale walls and carpeting of Tina's white cocoon, her throat soothed by the cold sweetness of the ice cream, her brain diffused by the buzz of wine, Madalyn wondered if her emotional dramas were very likely interchangeable with those of so many others, and agonizing over them in a setting of such luxury and comfort was, well, surreal. With no frame of reference other than themselves, she wondered if the machinations of her heart were of diminished value in the greater scheme of things. But then she riled at the politicization of context so pervasive in modern thought. Besides, the life of her heart was all she had that made her feel alive.

Like flipping a record, she refocused her mind on John, on the eruptive glow of their chemical attraction, on the effect of his caresses, on the power of a lover's touch, the kind that makes one's hand ache with the effort to be gentle yet affirmative. For the recipient of such a touch, the fact that it is voluntary, and thus the possibility that it may be capricious, raises the nap of the skin, densely packed fibres of nerves—both sponges and flints of sensation—and each of their corresponding places in the heart. Such exposure cannot help but allow release of the fear of loss, heightening feelings of love with the tinge of desperation.

Madalyn settled into the comfort surrounding her, trying to enjoy it and trying to absorb as much of it as she could. It compared, in its quality of unreality, with the way she felt at just a certain point on those mornings when she drifted out of sleep and into the realization that she was waking up with John.

During the final snuggle, they would talk about who should shower first, with the happy, solicitous gravity that people suddenly out of danger use when discussing a practicality that is not yet, again, taken for granted. After she had showered, if she went first, and if she felt confident that the towel would stay up around her chest, she would go and lean over John, still in bed, and he would chuckle and tease her about having cleavage, happily reminding her of Linda Tyhurst.

After school, in the late springtime, she and Tina used to find Mrs. Tyhurst on her sundeck, in a bathing suit with big pads lining the bra, which Linda hardly needed. Five children, after all, and this was before the horrifying era of aerobicizing oneself back to "normal" while still in the hospital. Linda had the height and personality to carry off her extra weight, and she certainly still curved in and out in all the right places. Squeezeable Barbie.

Even her suits had cleavage. Like the one she had worn to the Grade Twelve Girls' Graduation Tea. Blouseless ("a showy dresser," Evelyn had said), the inside edges of the suit's lapels crossed just in time, an inch or two below the crack of her bosom. The suit was a warm pink fabric, with a sheen the colour of a lipstick called Flamingo Flame. Mr. Tyhurst was constantly touching his wife, patting her rear in passing, making a show of looking down her top, which made her laugh and blush and "Honestly, Don" him away.

When John showered first, she would lug his wrinkled clothing from the floor, heavy clothing, his pants further weighted down by the belt still in them. A man's clothing in her bedroom, where she had the two little white china lamps Evelyn had bought for her when she was nine. She would shake out the clothing and watch the dust from her floors, never as clean as Evelyn's, sprinkle upward. She would sit on the bed and try to smooth out the wrinkles, nuzzle his pillow for a whiff of him, or study herself in her mirror, yesterday's makeup worn away, her face buffed to pinkness by his beard, Linda Tyhurst's smile on her face. She would revel in the so well-used look of her room, in the remaining sensuality, in the same kind of day-old, messy glamour that a certain Mrs. Savory had evoked in her clean-scrubbed child's heart.

If Mrs. Tyhurst was the softness and whiteness of unbaked, braided bread, Mrs. Savory was a browned little bird, overdone to the point where the fat had evaporated from under the skin. Mrs. Savory's skin looked like a piece of tobacco-coloured tissue, crumpled then smoothed out again, where it disappeared into the mystery of the vee of her red, lacy slip. In her early teens, Madalyn had babysat for the Savorys. The Savorys and their household were such a contrast to the Pauls, and Madalyn had been fascinated.

Cars, for instance. The Savorys drove a white Oldsmobile four-door, which always seemed to be covered in a layer of dust—good for writing in, the kids had found. The Pauls drove a clean, wood-panelled station wagon, long, with a third seat intended for a large family but used instead by Grant for his books, or for three or four of his students when he drove his teams to their games. The station wagon was equipped with curb-scratchers, coiled pieces of thick wire that stuck out over each wheel and let you know if you were going to hit. While Grant and Evelyn were already careful parkers, Mac Savory was the one who could have used the curb-scratchers, the way he flew up to the curb, the kids bouncing around inside the car like eggs. Then he would slam the door, his job done, and stride to the house, leaving the kids to disentangle themselves and follow.

When Madalyn arrived at their house, Vivienne Savory would greet her in her "almost there, Mac, we're almost there" state of dishabille as she struggled to get ready to go out for the evening. Madalyn remembered particularly the red lace slip, Mrs. Savory's long white cigarettes with the lipstick marks and her red fingernails tapping a glass of something helpful. To oat-filled, plaid-clad Madalyn, Mrs. Savory was Womanhood. If it meant the nails, the underwear, the cigarettes and being called "Viv," Madalyn wanted it. In truth, Mrs. Savory was, like her children, somewhat grimy and marginally nourished (chips and Smirnoff's, Froot Loops and Koolaid, yet how this family appeared to thrive!). Mac would be waiting for his wife and often sat at the kitchen table and talked to Madalyn.

"So, you're not married yet, are you, Madalyn? Don't do it too soon. You've got lots of heartbreaking to do first!" he would tease.

"Mac, for heaven's sake! Don't listen to a word he says, sweetheart. Listen, there's half a chocolate Sarah Lee cake in the fridge for you. Don't let the little monsters near it, okay? Mac, will you get the zipper?" She would take a deep menthol drag and suck the ice cube at the bottom of her glass to get the last sustaining bit of vodka. "Okay, okay. Calm. I am calm. I am ready."

Mac and Vivienne's three children would be in the den with Gilligan and Alphaghetti, lying in wait for Madalyn, who would get little homework done. They were wiry and tough, like their mother. Mac was round and balding and amiable, and would drag Mrs. Savory out of the house like a sheaf of siding, his arm around her waist.

"So, are you sure you didn't meet anyone with potential in Houston?" Madalyn asked, calling out from the kitchen, where she was emptying the ashtray and uncorking another bottle.

"What about that one guy, the one at the dance? He seemed attentive, at least."

Tina smoothed the ends of her terrycloth sash between her fingers. "Mmm, thanks," she said, as Madalyn filled her glass. "He was, and maybe there was a bit of chemistry, but he lives down there, and I live up here . . ." She gave Madalyn one of her that's-about-it smiles, and Madalyn could hear the closure in Tina's tone of voice.

"Okey dokey," Madalyn said, stretching out flat on her end of the couch.

"Did I tell you who I had lunch with the week before I left?" Tina asked after a moment.

"No, who?"

"Lawrence. Pickard. Do you see much of him around the office? I've probably asked you that before."

"Not really. Separate floors, different departments. But you're right about him being a real gentleman. He seems it. Compared to some of the excuses for humans who work there. By the way, I just do not know how Lawrence puts up with that horrific secretary of his, although I was thinking more of some of the other lawyers. I've told you about the head of securities, His Highness, C. Mark Downton. Now there's a first-class jerk. Did I tell you what happened the other day?"

"No," Tina said, with the lilt of a question.

"Well," Madalyn said, sitting up, "I was helping him with this big negotiating session, the board room was full of clients, a.k.a. disgusting pigs, and Downton had me running in and out, photocopying stuff. Anyway, I was in there, and he gave me some documents and told me how many copies of each he needed, and this real cretin piped up with, 'Do you think the Kelly Girl can remember all that?' Everybody heard, including Downton, and naturally, I only thought up an appropriately stinging reply after I had left. But I refused to go back in. I sat at my desk with the copies until Downton came out looking for me. I told him that if he required any further assistance, he would have to come out and find me, because I was not going back inside that board room. I know he knew my reasons, but he did not apologize for his client. Lawrence would never do anything like that, at least that's the impression I get."

Tina hmmed sympathetically.

"What about that Renata?" she asked. "She does seem to have a bee in her bonnet all the time."

"*Please* . . . let us not be so polite. The woman's got a giant carrot up her ass. But she positively worships the ground Lawrence walks on. So what was lunch like, where did you go?"

"Montenegro's."

"Mmm. Such a romantic place. On your pricey side too."

"We had a three-hour liquid lunch," Tina said, each word suspended with emphasis. Madalyn caught some import.

"Nice," she said, examining Tina's face.

Not one to become easily flustered, Tina nevertheless betrayed herself by suddenly looking away, seeming to become remarkably preoccupied with something on the floor in the far corner of the room.

This is big, Madalyn thought with a shock, but she did not probe further, out of respect for her friend's penchant for privacy, and because of the enormity of what she saw in Tina's eyes—the golden green of her irises dilute with a vastness of feeling. Fasten your seatbelts, folks. It's going to be a bumpy ride. Oh. Yes. Madalyn felt her sense of daring gathering itself about her, the same sensation she had had on the plane to Europe, because she knew Tina was quite possibly contemplating a profound adventure, something very adult, something requiring the skill and appetite for sin of a Margo Channing.

They were well past the point of deciding to stop drinking and therefore to retire sensibly, so on they drank. Madalyn's earlier reverie about Linda Tyhurst, still one of her favourite feminine role models, prompted her to ask Tina how her parents were, and eventually they found themselves rambling backward through their lives together into the mythologized shadows of their childhoods at school. Madalyn reminded Tina of her girlish regrets concerning Tina's wardrobe: black velvet hair bows, lots of lace, not an Oxford shoe in sight, so dressy and impractical in comparison to Madalyn's sensible jumpers. This fashion inventory took them naturally into another double-versioned bit of oral history, this time a recollection of Pants Day . . .

"Tyhurst Cadillac, No. 3 Road, and Tyhurst Cadillac, Broadway near Oak. *You* can't afford to miss Don's deals!"

As usual, Madalyn thrilled to the fame of her best friend's father, flogged by the hyperactive baritone on her transistor. But that day she was distracted only for a moment. Pulling a pair of leotards on under her Black Watch jumper, she was concentrating on the dramatization of her resentment toward Evelyn, who, safely true to form, was forcing her to be a mere spectator at Pants Day, which would turn out to be one of the highlights of grade five.

Last night, Cheryl Reiss had called all the girls in their class and said she and Wendy and Alanna were all going to wear pants to school the next day, because they didn't think it was fair there was a school board rule saying girls in elementary school could not wear pants. *All* the grade five girls were going to wear pants. If their mothers would let them.

Evelyn said that until the rules were changed, Madalyn would wear a skirt. Besides, she didn't have any pants that were appropriate for school, just her blue-jean bellbottoms.

"Well, I'm not Mrs. Tyhurst, am I?" Madalyn repeated to herself in front of the mirror, hand on her hip, head bobbing from side to side, her body imitating Evelyn's tone of voice.

At 10:30 that morning, grade five was in Miss Riley's class for Art. The principal, Mr. Meakin, came in and had a few words with Miss Riley before addressing the class. He said how disappointed he was that some students of Howe Elementary had seen fit to take the school board's dress code into their own hands. He spoke of the students' responsibility to obey the rules and respect the process of school board policy-making, which was, in the long run, for their own good. He said that all those girls who had broken the dress code were to accompany him to The Office. He looked to Miss Riley, perhaps for some thin-lipped nod of support, but she, pant-clad, looked away. The next day, everyone would seek out each of the seven skirted radicals to find out her version of what happened next.

The gist of it was that all the mothers had been called to take the girls home, and everyone had been milling around the outer office, waiting for the private consultations to begin, when Mrs. Tyhurst arrived, slightly disheveled, glamorous, a fur coat slipping and sliding around her shoulders.

"Mr. *Meakin*," she said as he came out of his office, list in hand, squaring his shoulders, "you know my husband, yes, that's right! Don told me about the *excellent* choice you made, was it last year? *Tyhurst Cadillac!*" she finished, as if making small talk at a dinner party. She did not mention that Mr. Meakin had selected a Ford from the pre-owned section of the Oak Street lot.

"Mr. Meakin, the girls are just expressing themselves, making a statement, if you will. I thought it was such a cute idea. They're just little girls. I'm sure you understand. I'll take my own little revolutionary home now and have her back after lunch. Thanks *so* much. Lovely to talk to you."

Tina left smiling as her mother's coat swished out the door, leaving Mr. Meakin with the other mothers, a secure group now, vindicated followers, and he had little choice but to suspend all sentences and soothe his smarting ego by taking Mrs. Tyhurst's tone as if it had been his all along—a bit of fun, no harm done, merely routine, you know the board.

Taking part in Pants Day was the only conscious political act of Tina's life. "The politicization of every damn thing" was how she later summed up feminism and environmentalism and every other kind of –ism that everyone, it seemed to her, jumped on and rode to death in the twenty years between the two. Above all, she hated conspiracy theories; one deluded group venting their collective personal resentments upon what they imagined to be the colluded wills to power of their enemies of the moment, chuckling evilly over hidden agendas.

Tina's father, on the other hand, believed himself to be a very political man. Don Tyhurst's political acts were one hundred percent rhetorical; opinion was all that was necessary in his nicely padded bunker of a world. Reading the paper after dinner, when the boys had gone, chairs left askew, their smells of sweat and clean dirt still in the air, he would editorialize all of the news for his wife, and Linda rarely entered into debate, although she was the one with the education and the knack for conceptual thought.

During the 1968 federal election, when Pierre Trudeau was entering the fantasies and stealing the votes of more than enough Canadian ladies, Don warned of the evil to come and asked how Canadian was this Trudeaumania?

"You mean the sexualization of politics, dear?" Linda asked.

What he meant was, he was shocked that his wife could be attracted to a communist Frenchman balding away in a white suit. Tina and Linda would listen at these times, exchanging protective smiles, and Tina would trace an invisible line between the freckles on Don's big, blond arm.

# Chapter Three

On the November long weekend, Lawrence slept late, for him, dragging himself out of bed at a quarter to eleven. He heard the rain as soon as he awoke, and from its metallic, staccato ping on the broken piece of gutter he had been meaning to repair since summer, he could tell it was coming down thick and heavy. He could picture the padding of cloud that would squeeze out a dense and steady downpour all day long. The light of day would have but a few hours to weakly illuminate the hillside suburb of West Vancouver, already darkened by its shroud of evergreens. He thought to himself that he might as well just stay in bed.

On the edge of awakening, he had felt a deep thrill of guilt pounding through his heart, but could not remember any of the dream from which the feeling must have come. He was still wondering about it when, in a haze of detachment, he shuffled into the kitchen, an old, stretched-out sweatsuit of navy velour bagging about his body. Susan looked up from the countertop she was wiping and gave her husband a tolerant, caring smile, worn soft by the years, but still evidencing a certain attraction.

In a way peculiar to rainy days, Lawrence felt as if he were living in his past as he poured himself a glass of orange juice and sat down at the kitchen table. A *Time* magazine lay open to the article he had been reading the day before. He scanned once again the forecasts of the pundits who predicted the priorities of the newly elected Bush administration. The words rattled through his brain and he regarded them without interest.

He flipped to the letters to the editor and read the elegant arguments of an obviously highly educated Arab on the subject of U.S. Middle Eastern policy. The next letter was another well-argued statement, this one on the Israeli position. Lawrence admired the grace and fluency of the language, but the substance of the letters left him cold.

He had been feeling a profound disinterest in things political lately, and his especial interest in American politics no longer held him in its thrall. He had watched the election returns the previous week without much of his usual excitement. And he was finding that his favourite PBS rightwingers, William F. Buckley and John McLachlan, who usually kept him highly entertained and nodding in agreement, to be increasingly irritating and dilletantish.

Lawrence kept himself unusually well read and loved to discuss, often arguing both sides of an issue for fun and for the intellectual exercise. He had been a top moot court participant in law school and had practised as a litigator for more than five years in Toronto, before the lure of Lotusland had finally proven too strong, and he and Susan had come out for a look-see. That had been twelve years ago, and they had been in Vancouver ever since.

Lawrence attributed his current mental lethargy to the endless coastal rains, something he was still not completely used to, and which had been almost constant that fall, and to a bit of professional burnout, perhaps. His workload for most of the past year had been staggering—big development deals, fancy and rich and complex, landing on his desk with escalating regularity. For several months now, he had not had much contact with the Stackhouse people and other of his longstanding clients, having had to parcel out their work to more junior lawyers while he babysat the new Asian money.

"Want to watch the services?" Susan asked. He followed her to the family room and sat on the worn corduroy couch, nursed his orange juice and wondered if the schleppy start to his day was an indication of the general state of his life. He noticed tears forming in Susan's eyes during an interview with a World War I veteran. The old man's shrunken body stood heartbreakingly straight in his dark suit. The war medals on his chest gave him the nobility common to any man in uniform. His eyes were diluted with tears and age, and his voice was dramatic in its soft, halting, unrehearsed delivery. "There was no hope," he said. "Paschendaele . . . was . . ."—and here his tears pooled heavily—"it seemed at the time . . . so many men . . . a folly of sacrifice."

When the half-hour Remembrance Day service was over, Lawrence looked at Susan again and saw that she had regained her composure. Sometimes she would cry during commercials for long-distance telephone plans, which always surprised him, and he would tease her. She would shrug off her outburst with practical cheer, her gift. "Exercising my heart," she would say and sigh a recuperative sigh and amaze him with her ability to slot unreasonable emotion into the paradigm of a healthy psychology.

"Remind me," Lawrence said, "do we have children?"

Susan looked over from where she was perched on the edge of the couch, in her trim denims and white shirt, tucking stray hairs into her short, blonde-streaked ponytail.

"It's so quiet," he said by way of explanation.

"They've gone to the Robertsons. Doreen is renting a whole lot of videos, and apparently she's going to have quite a troop on her hands today. Very kind of her."

"I should go for a jog, or something, but this weather . . . what are you up to today?"

"Let's get drunk," Susan said.

"What?!"

"Not really. It's a euphemism," she said very quietly. Then she brightened. "But why don't you light a fire in the living room, and I'll make some lunch and we'll open a bottle of wine?"

"Uh-*huh*," Lawrence said, looking at his wife with something akin to embarrassment.

"Don't look so shocked," she said, and slipped the elastic off her ponytail. "How about it?" She stood and walked to the door. "Meet you in the living room in half an hour?"

"Sure," he said, trying to ease up on the incredulity in his voice.

In the shower he thought to himself, is this some sort of romance-reviving maneouvre? Do we need a romance-reviving maneouvre? It struck him as a little forced, and he really wondered about his embarrassment, could not understand it, and he chided himself for his bloodless analysis of Susan's invitation.

Feeling revived and a little overdressed, he knelt in front of the fireplace in a pair of khaki pants and a clean dress shirt.

The cannelloni, stuffed with spinach, ricotta and garlic, was delicious. And hot. He burnt his tongue on the first bite. He grabbed for his glass of cabernet, which Susan had thought might be too overpowering for the pasta dish, but she had opened it anyway, knowing he much preferred red wine to white.

"This *is* nice," Lawrence conceded in a noncommittal murmur after they had eaten, resting his feet on the coffee table, which they had pushed up close to the fire along with the loveseat.

He noted that the wine was almost gone and asked if he should open another bottle. Susan looked at her watch.

"It's one thirty, the kids'll be home by, say, five, well, um, I guess, okay, yes."

That *was* the idea, was it not? Lawrence thought as he perused their stock in the dining room cabinet. Granted, she doesn't want us to be completely useless when the kids get home, and she does do the bulk of the dirty work around here.

With the new bottle of wine, they continued their discussion about what to do for Christmas. Both sets of parents wanted to fly out from Ontario for the holidays.

"They'll all expect to stay here," Susan said. "We can hardly put them up in a hotel. Why don't we have Nora and Denis out in August instead? It's a real feat that I talked Mum and Dad into flying in the winter, and I had no idea your parents would want to come out two years running."

"What to do," Lawrence responded, his eyes half shut, his head resting on the back of the loveseat, the fire and the wine relaxing him, warming him and stimulating him, to a point. He could go either way—sleep or sex.

"I'll call them on Sunday," he said, "and try to weasel out. They'd *love* the full house, though. Compared to the house in Thunder Bay, this place is massive. And we could squeeze everyone in. The girls could double up."

"And you and I could move to the family room."

Susan groaned, and Lawrence had to admit he also did not relish two weeks on the old pullout.

"And I could cook for six adults for a solid two weeks," she said with a light laugh, but Lawrence could hear the tang of resentment in her voice, and he supposed it would be a bit much.

"Don't worry, I'll take care of it. Even if I have to emphasize your mother's fear of flying, her noise intolerance, her generally fragile state?" He sat up straight to look at Susan.

"Even if," she said with a smile. "Because it's true."

Lawrence reached over and placed a hand on her knee.

"Okay," he said. "Your people at Christmas, my people in August. Call me, let's do lunch, love ya, don't ever change."

Susan laughed. She loved his teasing—it still made her feel like the envied, chosen one. She leaned over and kissed him on the lips, and his hand slid from her knee to between her legs. For a few moments, they kissed softly. The stimulation he had been feeling seemed to have evened itself out—he noted this with mild surprise—and as Susan stroked the side of his head and her hand nestled into the back of his neck, he knew she would begin very soon to squirm into his lap and give out those little high-pitched hmms from the back of her throat. He pulled away slightly, just enough to break the kiss, and cleared his throat.

"Perhaps we should take this upstairs," she said.

"Right."

"Meet you there in five minutes."

She found him, ten minutes later, when she came down the stairs in search, asleep. Deeply asleep. His mouth was open, and she heard the rumblings of an embryonic snore as she sat down beside him. She reached out and closed his lips with her fingers. Then she ascended the stairs once more, to change back out of the ivory lace robe he had given her last Christmas, and which she had scarcely worn.

The restaurant looked half full to Madalyn, rather an over-estimate, but her claustrophobia was acting up. She spotted him right away, diligently reading the menu at a corner table, secluded by the empty tables around it, which would, she hoped, stay that way. She made her way toward him, trying to decided between wine or a Bloody Mary.

He's looking quite crisp today, Madalyn thought. He must have just had a haircut, and that must be a new sports jacket. She could tell by the stiff, grey suede elbow patches being broken in on either side of the menu. He sat back and looked out over the restaurant, then cocked his head back slightly and smiled, and Madalyn knew he was saying "Ah" to himself.

Grant Paul's face looked as if it had been aged by hand. The slight sag of flesh over his jawline had been tidily tucked under his chin, and the lines around his eyes were spaced evenly and not too deeply, splaying onto his temples in symmetrical wings. He had the look of someone who has filtered all experience through a good and capable nature and has never had a clog. Grant had had his debit of sadness, but his tragedies had never caught him short of practical solutions, and he seemed content to bunt all the philosophical explanations around his accepting, magnanimous mind, without pronouncement. Daddy.

When Grant was ten years old, his parents lost their younger son, which was how Mrs. Paul Senior always expressed it when someone she did not know well had occasion to compliment her on Grant.

"Yes, we certainly are proud of him," she would say, as if trying to disguise the fact that they had no choice, followed by, "We lost a son, you know," as if to say they had extra pride available, which naturally would go to Grant, and as if four-year-old Daniel Paul had, horribly, disappeared around the end of an aisle in the Red & White Superette, never to be seen again.

Daniel had died of aplastic anaemia. Those were the days before the hope of a bone marrow transplant. Grant had read up on it recently and had told Evelyn that siblings were far and away the best bet for a match, statistically significant, one article had said. The realization that nowadays he very likely could have saved his brother's life sharpened his memory of Daniel's face, white on white against the hospital pillow, seeming to waft cell by cell into heaven before their eyes.

The Pauls had allowed their only remaining child to care for them in their daily grief. When Grant grew older, he decided to move out of their North Shore home to be closer to the university. There had been some laden looks from his mother, but he knew he had to do it and not just for school.

After the cash-poor four years it had taken him to obtain his bachelor's degree and teacher's certificate, he had been thrilled, in the first month after graduation, to be hired on the West Side and, shortly thereafter, to fall in love with an aristocratic-looking brunette.

He had at first assumed Evelyn was far too beautiful for him, but she had actually liked him, had not even appeared to mind at all that he was shorter than she. His mother had at first seemed daunted by Grant's fiancée (rather sudden, don't you think, Kathleen Paul had said to her husband). When she later saw Evelyn in her nurse's uniform, her dark hair folded over and over in back under her starched white cap, Kathleen felt some relief. Evelyn presented a competent and sensible picture; her strong-boned good looks were less threatening to little Kathleen.

After the joy-filled first few years of marriage, Grant found himself again tending sorrow, this time his and Evelyn's. Each of the three miscarriages Evelyn suffered before Madalyn came were, for him, a familiar and singular loss.

"Well, here we are," Grant said, getting up while his daughter sat down. "I guess I can't say Happy Remembrance Day, but it's nice we have this Friday for one of our lunches."

Madalyn settled herself on a chair against the rain-washed glass wall of the same oyster bar where she and John had eaten on their first date. With both hands, she smoothed her black turtleneck up under her chin, elbows on the table, and waited while Grant discussed the long list of available beer with the waiter. The weather pervaded the restaurant, which was warmed by a large fireplace in the middle of the tiled floor. Madalyn watched the fire's reflection in the window, flickering over the marina outside. She watched the white boats, battened down, waiting, bobbing slightly in neat rows on the sky-coloured water.

"And the chardonnay for the lady," the waiter confirmed to Madalyn, Grant having finally decided on a pint of Rickert's Red.

"Um . . . yes," Madalyn said, turning her attention from the water back to the indoors. Mentally she dimmed the light that shone like summer through the windows of her eyes. As usual, every unattended moment was given over to soaking in a pool of still, narcotic excitement, fed by thoughts of John.

Madalyn took a sip from her wineglass after clinking it against Grant's beer mug. She was already anticipating the second and possibly third glass of wine she would need in order to ease the effects of her feelings that stiffened her breathing into shallow, anticipatory breaths.

"How's Mum?" Madalyn asked. "I haven't talked to her for several weeks."

"Well, she's right into the new term, putting those RNs-to-be through their paces. The new curriculum seems to be taking well, which she's happy about, since her name's on it. And she had a heck of a shift the other night. The ward was packed, one crisis after another. But she handled it with her usual aplomb."

Madalyn asked how Grant's own term was going. He said he had a few bright bulbs in twelfth-grade History, but his eighth-grade English class sported an inordinate number of tragic illiterates.

"It never ceases to amaze me," Grant said, "how it cuts across all lines of social and economic class. Even more disturbing are the ones who have been ignored so absolutely by whoever is supposed to be raising them. What chance have they got?"

They veered off into literature, a shared interest, and although Madalyn said she had not picked up much in the past year, she listened to Grant, enjoying his graceful analysis of his latest newly discovered author.

"How's John?" Grant asked, about an hour into lunch, his eyes on the breaded oyster he was spearing with his fork. "I gather you're still seeing him," he continued, stealing a quick glance at his daughter.

Grant and Evelyn had met John at Thanksgiving dinner. Madalyn smiled as she remembered how John had told her mother, his voice a balance of respect and sincerity, that she and Madalyn could easily be sisters, that he now knew where Madalyn got her good looks.

"Oh, yeah," Madalyn said. "We have a 'big date' tomorrow night, as a matter of fact. Some friends of his he really wants me to meet. I hope they're not as stiff as some I've met so far."

"Stiff?"

She related to her father the time in September when John had escorted her to the Vancouver Club for drinks after work. They had gone to meet two of his high school buddies, now grown up into their business suits, which they seemed to Madalyn to have been born in.

"The *Vancouver* Club. Well," Grant said.

"It's as dark and oaky and formal and politically abhorrent as you think," Madalyn said, leaning over her plate toward Grant. They laughed together.

"If John moves in such circles, then I suppose he can afford to be a young Republican," Grant said.

"He can't help his economic status."

"But does he give anything back?"

"As far as I know, his noblesse oblige extends as far as participating in a corporate relay to benefit Children's Hospital. He did that in August. His team came first."

Grant chuckled. "And I'll bet it was a good opportunity for a little networking."

Raised by rote-voting Tories, Grant had evolved into a self-described nineteenth-century conservative, a label derived, correctly, from British politics. This translated into rather left-leaning voting behaviour, much to the dismay of his parents. Madalyn had grown up with Grant and Evelyn's practical politics of thrift and service (they had begun to recycle fifteen years before it became the thing to do), their partisan politics of liberal safety-netism and Grant's intellectual politics of the duties of privilege.

They were not wealthy by any means, but Grant and Evelyn saw themselves in a global context as recipients of the privileges of the Western industrialized world and of their educations. In addition to working in the hospital, Evelyn was a clinical professor of nursing at the university. Grant had obtained his Masters degree in history over a period of several years when Madalyn was in her early teens, and talked of working on his PhD, perhaps taking an early retirement to do so.

Living out his political philosophy gave a larger meaning to Grant's life, and while Madalyn found her parents' lifestyle severely lacking in glamour, something she had always secretly and desperately desired, she appreciated her father's generous heart and his thoughtful mind. He had given her at least a starting point from which to differentiate among the myriad political ideologies she would encounter and from which she had refrained from choosing.

Madalyn, also, from a global and historical perspective, knew she had the best of everything, arguably. The best era, the best country, the best parentage, education, health. No apparent handicaps, perhaps some talent. Body, heart and mind, all tended, nurtured, loved. Except there was a part of her that seemed to watch all of this from a corner, always hungry, always afraid, always wondering, when will I get mine? A soul in a state of karmic retardation.

She had not been brought up with much religion, other than the occasional United Church service. Religion was a personal thing, her parents had said, and Grant in particular was leery of the organized form. It was not until she met Tina and had become ensconced in her friend's family as virtually a second daughter that the glamour and emotionalism of religion had presented themselves to her and had drawn her in for some years.

She had begun by accompanying the Tyhursts to Redeemer Baptist, a big old downtown church, a little scary from the outside with its massive, muddied granite walls. Inside it was all polished wood, high-vaulted ceilings and stained glass. And there was a wonderful pipe organ—its huge tones reverberated within her little girl's body and sometimes brought tears to her eyes. The grandeur of the old hymns was something she missed in her adulthood. She loved especially the heroic musicality and strangely sensuous lyrics of "The Battle Hymn of the Republic":

"In the beauty of the lilies Christ was born across the sea,
With a glory in his bosom that transfigures you and me,
As he died to make men holy, let us live to make men free,
Our God is marching on . . ."

The Tyhursts took great social satisfaction from church attendance and were happily unperturbed by the evangelical rumblings that emanated from the pulpit, but which Madalyn pondered with earnestness, and which produced within her disturbing germs of guilt and confusion.

There are a great variety of Baptists in the world, and for those who adhere to the traditions and leadership of the more theologically sophisticated British seminaries, the subject of money can be a problem. If one has a great deal of it, or even a fair amount, it can be a burdensome blessing, and God would want one to be as subtle about it as possible.

Tina came from a family of outgoing, cheerful and extremely liberal Baptists—perhaps a contradiction in terms—and due in part to Mrs. Tyhurst's Texan heritage, the family had a guiltlessly American and decidedly expressive attitude toward money. What they had, which was somewhere in between a great deal and a fair amount (depending on what sort of Baptist was doing the counting), they spent conspicuously. Mr. Tyhurst's late-model Cadillac stood out cheekily among the dark sedans and wagons in the church parking lot. But it was there every Sunday.

In their teens, Tina and Madalyn had been caught up briefly in what Madalyn would later term the cult-like propensities of Christian evangelism. During the summer they were both sixteen, the friends spent two weeks at a resort up the coast, owned and operated by a U.S.-based group that had come to the high school to show a promotional film. The film highlighted the part about tanned young people sailing and waterskiing, but left out the parts about the sermons at breakfast and the hysteria of emotional connectedness, which caused one of Tina's and Madalyn's campmates to literally try to throw herself from the ferry which took the campers back to the city.

Tina had been encouraged by her parents to go to this camp, really a resort, as her equally Baptist cousins from Texas were being sent. Madalyn was allowed to go after some pleading despite skepticism from Grant and Evelyn. They knew how close she was to Tina. Of course, Madalyn could not confide in her parents her most compelling motivation: the possibilities inherent in all those American boys. Madalyn could not recall the exact words, only the sense of what she had written in her diary one night at camp. If she still had that diary, she might have seen that particular entry as a summation of the peculiar thirsts of her soul back then.

During Quiet Time and before Lights Out, Madalyn had written:

"*What* a day it has been!! I stood up tonight at the Joyful Assembly and gave my heart to Jesus. It was hard to stand up, but I *did it! And* on the way out, Mark put his hand on my shoulder and smiled at me. I sort of smiled back, but I wish I'd smiled more. He was with a whole group, so no chance to talk. Midge, our counsellor, said tonight during Girl Talk that a new life in Christ is better than being *in love!* He is always faithful and will never leave us. And we must be faithful to Him. I've seen Mark a lot in the last few days. He's usually with the other Texans, which includes, of course, Tina's cousins. He has such a sort of lost, quiet look in his eyes. I *know* he needs someone to talk to. It could be *me!* But I don't seem to know what to say to him. I am so (underline, underline) shy, it's pathetic. I love Mark. I have only four days left. I want so much to get him on Blind Date Night. Dear God, if it is Your will, please let me get Mark on Blind Date Night. I don't want to be selfish, but I really ask that I get Mark. But Thy will be done. I will sleep now, in your care, and dream of, oh Lord, I can't help it, of Mark!"

On Blind Date Night, God's will for Madalyn was a guy named Jim—attentive, accessible, Canadian.

Brougham House was just the kind of restaurant John loved. An old, elegant house, beautifully refurbished, it was a rarity on the streets of the West End near Stanley Park, streets lined solid with high-rises. Purchased a year back by a Californian restaurateur who had given his new acquisition an English-sounding name that he just thought up and a Continental menu, Brougham House was perfect for Vancouver, where tastes were eclectic and little valid snobbery existed. Since the prices were high enough, the cuisine good enough and reservations almost impossible to obtain on short notice, Brougham House had quickly become *the* place to dine for those for whom artificial snobbery served their purposes just as well as the real thing.

Madalyn was finally meeting Geoff and Mia Sarkissian, relatively new friends of John's, but obviously valued, the way he coached them and at the same time deferred to them over every choice that needed to be made: seating arrangements, cocktails or wine, then, when wine was agreed upon for pre-dinner drinks, red or white, Californian or French.

Mia was seated between the two men, which put Madalyn on one end of the curved banquette, opposite John. She had said she would rather sit on the end, which was true. There was her claustrophobia, the matter of her small bladder and the fact that she felt obligated to keep her smoke as far away from the other couple as possible. You could never tell. But Geoff and Mia seemed friendly and comfortable with everything, Madalyn was thinking after the wine had arrived. Geoff had even lit her first cigarette, and Madalyn had seen John visibly relax.

John's ingratiating manner had rankled, but now that he appeared to be rewrapping himself in his usual mantle of confidence, she could relax also. The charge she always felt when she was out with him in public snapped to life as he regained his luster, and she settled in to enjoy another evening of basking in the light of being his.

The restaurant was pleasingly dark, and tiny halogen lamps spaced discreetly at various points along the walls coolly diffused their colour and cast a bottle-green glow over the group. Watching John across the distance of the table, Madalyn felt herself growing deaf to even the gentle burble of restaurant murmur around her, elongated into softness as it was absorbed by the padded panels of the walls, the carpeting and the banquettes— firm and generous, upholstered to within an inch of their lives with the same green of the walls, shot through with irregular lines of nubbly royal blue thread. The black velvet she wore, drawing light into its dull surface, made her feel solid, rich and luxurious. She crossed her legs under the table and felt her thighs brush against each other above the silky slide of her gartered stockings.

No idea in the world could stir her soul as did the sight of the creases in John's face when he smiled his sly smile, or the blue of his eyes, blackened and inky in the dim atmosphere. She felt the heaviness of accessible ecstasy filling her entire self and, with the grace afforded by such happiness, she willingly turned her attention to their guests.

Mia and Geoff look more like brother and sister than anything else, Madalyn thought to herself. They were both small and sandy-haired and looked about nineteen years old. Mia ran a hand over the back of the banquette and commented on the raw silk, which she and Geoff had chosen for one of the occasional chairs they had bought to furnish the Shaughnessy estate gatehouse they had moved into a year ago, after their wedding.

"It's quite a deep ochre," she said, "and we used the same fabric for our front window side curtains. We wanted to add some richness to our basically white-on-white theme. Well, it's really cream, the chesterfields and the carpeting and so on. We have the most marvelous divan, which my father found for us. We thought of using the ochre on that, but it was too much.

"Basically, we tried to keep the darker tones to, um, an accessorizing function, so we didn't want to go overboard with the ochre. And we had to absolutely *force* ourselves to stop shopping for wood, or we would have gone mad, we both love it so much. Our favourite pieces are the cherry with walnut inlay nesting tables. John, I know you asked, but please tell me to shut up if I'm boring you. You two should come over and tell us what you think of our attempt at being grown-ups."

"We'd love to," John said.

"Yes," Madalyn said in response to John's glance.

"We'll see you at the Snow Ball, of course," Mia said, a bit of a question in her voice.

"Well . . ." John paused, hoping to be rescued. He was.

"I can't imagine why you wouldn't have received an invitation by now. Leave it to me," Mia assured him. "Worry not."

Madalyn could feel John's embarrassment at not being quite a part of the In Crowd who attended the annual event, although now it appeared he could consider himself included in the select group of the city's thirtyish professional set who hailed from the right neighbourhoods and whose names mysteriously appeared on the Snow Ball guest list, or not, depending on who they knew or who their parents were.

Madalyn had never been invited to the Snow Ball. She felt distinctly piqued that she actually felt honoured to be included now. Geoff and Mia's social circle was not one that held much attraction for her. Over the years, she had attended several private parties given by one or another of their set, usually in parents' homes, and after the last one, some three years past, had vowed to herself, never again. "Been to Whistler lately?" had been the most common refrain, and she had wanted to let loose with a slew of truly dirty jokes, although she had not possessed the wherewithal to do so.

Geoff, who had been quiet, letting his wife talk, suddenly piped up. "So, Madalyn. John tells us you're an artist."

"Well, um" she said, taking a swallow of wine, "I guess you could say that, although I haven't produced much lately. I sort of grew up with painting, and it was my major, but . . ." She deplored her lack of sparkle, her less-than-scintillating delivery, her usual dull angst when compelled to speak of the subject.

"But it's hard to make a career out if it, I'll bet," Geoff said.

"That's true," she answered.

"Maybe you can give us some advice on a certain 'work of art' we have," Geoff said, exchanging a knowing grimace with his wife.

"It's very abstract," Mia added. "We don't know what to do with it, but Geoff's sister gave it to us—you'd probably like her. Anyway, it's mostly white and black, which actually does go with the living room, but it's got a lot of shocking blue and orange, and I don't know, you can't help but notice it, although I'd rather not. I mean, I'm sure it's got some meaning, but aesthetically it's atrocious."

"I know what you mean," John said. "I don't understand the point of a lot of so-called art. I mean, if you can't stand to look at it, what *is* the point? I don't mean yours, of course, Mad," he said, and she could see him struggling to maintain a balance of discretion.

"Why don't you just put it up in the middle of whatever your style is," Madalyn said with warmth, "and just let it be itself, let it say something about the two of you, that you are so confident in your taste that you can afford to be completely nonplussed by a bit of a shock."

She was smiling, largely at Geoff. She included Mia with a quick shift of her gaze, then returned to Geoff to more fully punctuate her remarks with plenty of humour, which she hammered out through her eyes.

"Could do," Geoff said, warming to the idea. He chuckled after a slow start, steering himself into the new tributary that the conversation had obviously taken.

Madalyn chomped vigorously on a mouthful of honey-mustard–coated watercress. After their salads and appetizers had arrived, and after the obligatory comments and comparisons and offers to taste, Geoff proposed a toast.

"Here's to bad art and good food," he said.

As John touched his glass to hers, Madalyn detected in his eyes a defensive embarrassment whirlpooling in the blue. Now, as she chewed her greens and washed them down with great gulps of golden, perfumy chardonnay, she felt a gathering sense of power and daring, and wondered what further gilded perversities might flower from her lips.

It was at the end of the main course, some time after she had given up gamely trying to do justice to her lamb chops without any assistance from her non-existent appetite, that the subject of art as a career came up again. Mia apparently dabbled part-time in interior decorating, and John asked Madalyn if she had ever though of painting on commission for private homes, "maybe work with a decorator and do stuff people could hang in their living rooms to complement the décor." Madalyn suddenly decided it was time to entertain Geoff and Mia with a description of Nihil's opening.

She was in the thick of it, describing one by one Nihil's paintings. She happened to catch John's eye—he had disassociated himself from the Crash experience. As his eyes roved over her, leaving tracks, and her stomach collapsed in on itself, she could only bring even more style and drama to the telling of her tale. She acted her heart out, gesticulating dramatically with a newly lit cigarette.

"Sounds like a different guy," Geoff said.

It was all she could do to smile at him and keep her pooling tears at a safe level within the sockets of her eyes. She took one deep breath. She took many sips of wine. She would not allow herself to look at John. The conversation suffered from a lull until she reached out for her glass, without looking, and knocked it over. Because John's face was flushed, giving him a look of feminine weakness, and because of his immediate apology to

Geoff, under whose dinner plate the invisible stain was spreading, Madalyn wished with oblivion that the wine had been red.

She was now drunk. And this was good. Through the remainder of dinner, through the remainder of the wine, through the brandies, her anger toward John, her feelings of hurt, would become ever more diluted by her lovesickness, and hours later when she was finally alone with him in bed, he would then profess, with conviction, that he was glad she and Geoff had had such a good time.

When she spilled her glass of wine, it was obvious Geoff was not feeling much pain either. He and Madalyn laughed as if possessed. Geoff declared, between choked giggles as Madalyn lifted the tablecloth from his lap and inquired as to whether she had done any damage, that the least that could be said for those employed in the legal profession, as were he and Madalyn, was that they knew how to get a party off the ground. He flagged down the waiter and ordered a round of brandies for the table, specifying that Madalyn deserved a double.

"Guess I'll be driving tonight," Mia said a few minutes later, as she placed her own brandy in front of Geoff. He seized upon it with a display of mock thirst and continued his account of a now infamous scandal that had taken place at his firm's last Christmas party, apparently involving a very young secretary and a very married lawyer. Madalyn interjected briefly with a description of Renata and her tight-assed approach to office socializing, which Geoff found highly amusing. He and Madalyn had their heads together, empathizing with vigour over their common observations, feeding each other delicious bits of gossip. John had his arm on the back of the banquette, his hand resting just behind Mia's head. Mia and John exchanged looks of indulgence—Mia's a natural look of wifely good humour, John's an imitation, disguising a visceral disapproval.

"The gist of it was," Geoff said, "that after only three months with the firm, the poor girl was let go with a substantial severance package. I mean, what choice did they have? They had to compensate her somehow and shore up the guy's reputation."

"Poor girl," Madalyn clucked.

"She was manipulated pretty badly," Geoff agreed.

Later, at his place, John said "Geoff really has it together." He grunted up into another pushup.

"You think so?" Madalyn asked. They were in John's brown-on-brown living room, and Madalyn lay on her back on the leather couch, which, under her slip stockings, was slippery and cold.

"Well, uhhh! . . . phew!" John rested on one cheek and looked up at her. "Yeah, I mean they've got that great house, at his age, and Mia's dad gives Geoff probably two-thirds of his client base with his *own* shit, and the rest in referrals. He's got it made." John collapsed his jutted elbows, rolled onto his back and slapped his chest with both hands.

"The guy doesn't have to do a thing," John finished. There was a whine in his voice, Madalyn noticed unwillingly, like a child denied what the other kids got to do. Madalyn waited, eyeing him through the jiggling spiral of smoke she tapped out of her cigarette.

She asked, "What do you think Geoff sees in Mia? She looks like a boy."

John laughed, crawled over to her and ran his hand up her shinbone.

"Checking for nicks?" she asked.

"Maybe."

"But what do you think he sees in her?"

"I dunno . . . eye of the beholder, I guess." John got up and went to the kitchen for a glass of water. Madalyn followed him.

"No, really, John, what . . ."

He had scampered sideways the length of the hall, then braced his hands on either side of the doorframe, ready to shoot himself out. She called him back.

"I'm serious," she reiterated. "I want to know what you think."

His eyes tagged hers and dashed away. He stepped behind her, put his arms around her waist and sighed into her ear, "Audited financials."

He took her hand and led her back to the living room couch. He walked backward, pulling her with him, a seductive look in his eyes—mocking and authoritative. He sat her down on the couch, lifted her legs off the floor and stood looking down at her. Madalyn leaned over the ashtray on the floor to stub out her cigarette. When she turned back, John was in pushup position above her. His eyes cackled with the satisfaction of having gotten whatever it was he wanted, after all. He lowered his body into their perfect fit.

Madalyn thought *Cosmo* would have described last night's sex as athletic. This was a word Madalyn herself would never use in reference to something she found to be just the opposite of the cheery, broad-daylight sort of health that "athletic" implied to her. She would have conceded to *Cosmo*'s description only in that last night was, yes, *sustained*. (John had not snuck off into sleep, as he often did, as soon as her back was turned, leaving her, a frustrated insomniac, to get up and smoke and try to be grateful.) But as always, the sex had felt clandestine.

In the mornings, she loved feeling as if she had just been released from a certainly unhealthy internment in a fire-flicked room, where the wicked count had lured her with the proverbial rubbing of hands, anticipating getting them onto the body of the quaking but willing virgin, and him getting excited all over again later when he watched her legs, so white against the velvet of his port-coloured jacket. And the newly empowered young girl would smile a perfectly sly, unpractised smile as she sauntered toward him, carrying the jacket now, and would press her nose into the cloth, marinated in the cigar smoke and the same kind of scent John left on his pillow.

Madalyn sniffed up the memory of some of the more stimulating details of last night, until a car's honking caught her attention.

She felt blessedly unanalytical on most of these drives home; sleep deprivation usually allowed her euphoria to seep into her brain. Today she had chosen not to push it and had defaulted into daydreams, to try to dispel a disturbing grumpiness. After the honking made her reprimand herself about the dangers of fading out when she was driving, she tried to think out the cause of this feeling that was taking some of the rush out of her morning-after high.

Even though last night's extra dosing should have been enough, Madalyn was still plagued by an insatiable need for the elixir of skin. But then she almost always felt this way, a common enough condition—people had all those years of deprivation after babyhood to work up a thirst. So if this wasn't it, maybe it had something to do with that revolting bit of dream tooled onto her mind when she woke up, an image of herself spitting teeth into her hand. Teeth from only half of her mouth had come loose, some singly and some attached to each other, like chunks of pop-apart plastic baby blocks. She remembered feeling the teeth in her mouth, like stones, and how ugly she had felt after she had spit them out.

After showering and changing, Madalyn puttered around her apartment, noticing the dust bunnies that would be safe for another week, and wondered what to do with the gulf of Saturday. She thought up some activities to tell John about that night, being lenient with herself upon the realization that she was winding her life in tighter circles around him.

In the late afternoon, as she dressed for the evening, the bulb in her bedroom lamp crackled out. She unscrewed it with a towel to protect her fingers from the heat, and before she threw it out, she shook it, like Evelyn used to do, to see if it wasn't perhaps the lamp. There it was, the tiny coil that makes the difference between light and dark, dancing around on the inside of the GE Soft White stamp, sounding like bug-wings against the glass as she shook. Yup. It was really out.

# Chapter Four

L awrence had felt chronically tired for weeks, he realized while driving home one December evening, the wipers beating away the rain that rinsed down over the windshield every time he had to brake in the bumper-to-bumper lineup for the bridge. The lights of the oncoming cars jiggled in front of him, the way things do before the first tears are blinked away.

Christ. How long have I been spinning my wheels? he thought. He fiddled with the radio station dial and paused briefly on "C-F-I-X morning show, don't miss . . ." then scratched through some dead reception space, then paused the dial again, for a minute this time, on a young, male, British-accented voice that described the work, the production values, the profound, reworked influences, and said what a thrill, akchully, it was, to finally get to work with . . . Lawrence passed him by too, irritated by the description of a rock album that sounded, inappropriately, like the words of some respected art historian dwelling on the exquisitries of a consummate example of genius. He whipped through ". . . dillac, ten point nine percent financ . . ." and finally stopped on some relieving saxophone—melancholic, filled with regret for things not done, like a home-town main street lit and empty in the dark, a stretch of the highway sped through without a stop to avoid the forward wash of the wake of memory.

Lawrence sat watching a bouillon cube eroding in the bottom of a mug. He chopped at it, unsuccessfully, with a spoon. The hard, concentrated spice was not yielding easily to the water, which was slow to take on colour. Must have been in the cupboard for quite some time, he thought.

"You'd better get warmed up," Susan had said when he finally arrived home. He had been thinking more along the lines of a healthy two inches of scotch after that drive, but decided to do penance with the bouillon she offered, thinking he'd work in a casual beer or two while he ate. Susan was slicing something by the light of the open fridge. That and the plastic ball over the breakfast nook were the only lights on in the kitchen, which rested in the vapours of detergent and the remains of dinner, now tidily refrigerated, stowed away in tidy Ziplocs.

It was, what, ten o'clock! Which meant he had missed the kids too, although Michael could still be around somewhere, unless it was his night for band. Susan set a practical-looking sandwich in front of him, roast beef on brown. He dipped the dryish crust into his mug. Mondays and Wednesdays, or Tuesdays and Thursdays, Lawrence could not remember which, were the nights for Junior Band. He had had Renata red-ink her own calendar as well as his for next Thursday's city-wide high school Band Concert.

"With your father's erratic schedule, I'm not really in a position to commit myself as a driver," Susan had said over dessert several weeks ago. She and Michael and Lawrence too, supposedly, were discussing the form from high school requesting parental availability for chauffeuring students to school and back in the evenings during the final two weeks of practice.

"Somebody has to be here with the girls."

Lawrence faded out, to sneak a peak at the letters to the editor in *Time*.

. . . to know how your reporter thinks that Mrs. Quayle's hair, stiff or not, impacts on the very serious issue of Mr. Quayle's *present* suitability, which, notwithstanding his "bolstered past," is, I agree, a "ticking liability one hopes can be muffled, defusion not an option at this late date." So leave Marilyn out of it. Mr. Quayle must stand alone, without qualification. Which he appears to be doing, heaven help us.

P. Bosnan
Baltimore, Md.

"Michael's at band," Susan said.

Ah.

The next afternoon at four o'clock, Renata stuck her head into Lawrence's office.

"Tina Tyhurst," she said, her tone implying that Lawrence had done something wrong and Renata was owed an explanation.

"Be right out," he said, not looking up from his work. Renata sighed.

At his desk, Lawrence put his face in his hands and took a deep breath. He ran his fingers through his hair, which had gone cubist in the shiny brass surface of his desk-lamp shade. Oh, well. He unrolled his sleeves and scrambled around on his desk for the cufflinks he had tossed somewhere after lunch.

"Hello, Renata," Tina said as she passed by the secretarial desk, her big round eyes holding Renata's, daring her to do any damage while she was under the protection of Lawrence, who held open the door of his office, embracing the air around her with his arm.

"Tina," Renata said, with grudging softness.

Lawrence closed the door in the middle of an anecdote he had been relating, in the middle of Tina's laughter, a low-pitched bubble of sound deep in her chest, rolling up through her throat with the ease of intimacy.

Lawrence's door opened again just after five, as Renata, sweating in her winter coat, was tying up her tennis shoes while her small, bespectacled husband stood by, his hands full of Renata's plastic bags stuffed with sweaters, magazines and the remains of a week's worth of lunch. She sat up in time to see Tina's high, patent-leather heels pivoting down the hall, in synch with Lawrence's loafers.

Renata hurried her husband to the elevator in time to see Lawrence and Tina standing together beside the lit Down button, to catch an unintelligible exchange between the two, to hear that same laughter of Tina's, and in time to see the elevator door close, Tina inside. Lawrence turned and met Renata's eyes.

"You just missed one," he said, pressing the Down button again. "Tim, how are you?" he said to Renata's husband.

Tim shrugged and held out his plastic bags. The two men laughed. Lawrence's laugh was big, full of relief. As he walked back to his office, he found himself deliberately putting off thoughts of the impending weekend lest they dampen the high of the tag end of his Friday.

"My lips are numb," Madalyn said, stating the discovery with deadpan self-consciousness. She rubbed her lips with her fingers, which were cold from the glass that held her fourth double vodka tonic.

She was smoking a black Russian cigarette with a gold filter, a Sobranie. The two women sat on the floor of Tina's living room, imprisoned within the soft padded cell of comfort that glinted with bits of glass and brass. The artificial fire burned perfect, eternal, smokeless flames.

They were discussing John, neither seeming to tire of endlessly analyzing Madalyn's relationship, or of their projections for it, which they lobbed into the future—intricate scenarios fleshed out down to the details of children's names.

Madalyn was drawing deeply, tasting the perfumy sweetness of her "fun" cigarettes. Tina was smoothing the carpet with her hand, collecting fuzz.

"I'm jealous, quite frankly," she said, and they both laughed, Madalyn—a winner at that moment—magnanimously. Tina, who rarely betrayed any need, teetered on the edge of tears. She could fall back into just laughter, or fall the other way and risk revealing the fantasies that leapt and licked at her heart. She almost confided her growing sense of certainty, fed by the last hour of her work day on Friday. She wanted to believe that the look in Lawrence's eyes yesterday, as the elevator door closed, was a validation of her hopes.

Next Friday, perhaps. Next Friday would be Jerome's famous annual Christmas party. Tina thinned out her hopes and lined the conversation with their plastic excitement. They discussed the upcoming party, agreeing they should wear their most elegant silk blouses, under suits, and bring extra jewellery, thus enabling themselves to go from day to evening in the Four Seasons ladies' room after work.

A week later, they stepped off the elevator at the nineteenth floor of the Stackhouse building, smack into Jerome's party. And smack into Jerome. And Lawrence.

The party was being held on one of the three floors occupied by the Stackhouse Developments offices. The large board room, its double doors open to the lobby area, was clotted with people pressing to get near the long tables draped in white, which lined the far wall—the bar.

Jerome had been drinking since four. It was now seven o'clock, and he was completely immersed in his role as host. His small blue eyes, alive in thumbprint-lock sockets in his round face, were laced with red.

"Tina!" Jerome said, putting an arm around here. "You look ravishing as usual, doesn't she, Lare? And who is your charming friend? What can I get you ladies to drink?" Jerome was on send-only; his reception often jammed when he drank. "You've gotta have champagne—I'll getcha some myself," he said, bowing, and turned to barrel through the crowd, stomach first.

"I'm Madalyn," Madalyn said to empty air, and she, Lawrence and Tina rolled their eyes and smiled with good humour at the waylaid Jerome, who was making frequent stops to tease and cajole one guest after another on his way to the bar.

A pair of arms encircled Madalyn's waist, and she turned to receive a kiss from John. He waltzed her into the crowd as they exchanged whispers of greeting, leaving Tina and Lawrence momentarily unto themselves.

To have arrived at the party and to have run into Lawrence so immediately had not been part of Tina's ideal scenario. Her nervousness increased as she recalled their meeting last Friday. For some months, a more junior lawyer in Lawrence's department had been handling Jerome's day-to-day business, and she had therefore been surprised when Lawrence had called to set up a meeting to review what they both well knew was very standard paperwork, of the sort the other Birk & Samuels lawyers had been handling with competence throughout the fall.

"We've been summarily abandoned," Lawrence noted, and Tina's nervousness betrayed itself as she smiled in agreement but found herself unsuccessfully searching for something to say, as if his observation required a response of careful and unusual erudition.

Then Renata swooped down upon them, infusing the meager conversation with efficient questions and comments about Tina's drinkless state, and the less-than-reassuring statement that Jerome would never make it back from the bar.

"Yes, Jerome is a hopeless social butterfly," Tina said.

"Allow me to escort you to the bar," Lawrence said to Tina. "Renata, can we get you anything, or is that very tall drink going to do the trick for a while?"

"I guess I'm just *fine*," Renata said, quick on the uptake and dangerously insulted. She watched them walk away, Lawrence's hand hovering ever so lightly on the back of Tina's waist.

They finally made it to the bar. All around them, the other guests appeared to be having no trouble doing their best to make a substantial dent in Jerome's enormous liquor supply. Business acquaintances networked without the usual workday inhibitions, rehashing the past year's accomplishments and mistakes alike (no failure that night—it wasn't the season). Magnanimous best wishes were exchanged for a new year that would be just as lucrative as the last, or a damn sight better, depending.

Tina requested white wine and told Lawrence she would meet him "out there," motioning toward the lobby.

"I've got to get rid of this coat," she said.

In her office, she removed her coat and stored her purse in a desk drawer. She arranged the draped folds of her blouse, pearl-coloured satin, as she moved toward the window, which, with the blinds pulled up and darkness behind, mirrored her.

"Thought I might find you here," she heard from the doorway.

She turned, but not before giving her curls a few pokes, hoping this gesture would signal that she had not been embarrassed to be caught primping in the window. Lawrence appeared not to notice, however, and handed her a glass of wine, commenting on what a relief it was to get away from the crowd.

Tina's blouse reminded him of the colour of his youngest daughter's hair, when she was two. Her name was Megan, but Lawrence called her Mite—she had always been such a tiny thing.

The lights of the city sparkled behind Tina, framing her. She moved around to one of the two client chairs and sat down. Under the fluorescent lights, her red hair showed single strands of light, all over. Lawrence felt a sudden nostalgia. He thought of streetlamps on snow from his childhood days. He felt something gear up inside and shatter his recent malaise. The redemptive possibilities of risk and adventure presented themselves to him once again, and this time everything clicked.

He made a decision and felt his heart begin to hum and purr as his rational mind kicked out the last of his indecisiveness. The very real danger inherent in his decision no longer mattered; it served, in fact, as a sort of quick-burning fuel. He took a large swallow of scotch. It flared at the back of his throat, then sank with a liquid singe on its way to his blood.

Madalyn and John poked their heads into Tina's office. Lawrence said, "John," John said, "Lawrence," and the two men raised their glasses in a salute. Madalyn swung her long hair over her shoulder with a snap of her head. Her face was already coloured with wine, her eyes dark and reflecting. She sat in the second client chair beside Tina and crossed her long, black-sheened legs.

"Jerome is such a riot," she said. "He's so completely loaded, but he's *so* funny! I *love* him! What's he like at work?"

"Tina, we've got him pegged, haven't we?" John remarked. He was leaning against the door frame, his arms crossed over his chest, one leg crossing the other, a foot propped on the toe of a fine, slick, chocolaty Italian loafer. His conspiratorial gaze pointed straight past Madalyn and into Tina's eyes. Tina smiled at Madalyn, then passed her smile along to John, like a tray of hors-d'oeuvres.

"Well, let's just say that Jerome's manageable, once you know how," Tina said. She rose from her chair and walked right through the line that John's eyes had left, to stand in front of Lawrence.

"Anyone want to go out and mingle?" she asked, rounding her eyes into spheres of innocence, thus cancelling her talk of managing men. Lawrence fell for those rounded eyes, unaware of the grip and release of anxiety that had caused little beads of sweat to form at his hairline.

"Sure," he said. Again he rested a hand on the small of Tina's back, briefly, and steered her past John and out the door. John and Madalyn followed, and the two couples were soon stirred into the celebratory cauldron of Jerome's party, and eventually lost track of each other.

Two and a half hours later, Tina and Lawrence were standing in a circle with a group of brokers and lawyers who had coalesced around a growing tower of one-upmanship stories. Close calls was the theme—brushes with death, the law, embarrassment. Lawrence noticed Tina, who had moved away from the group, wilting a little. She was leaning against a wall, her drink on the floor beside her, her eyes downcast. She looks a little pale, he thought, and edged around the outside of the circle to speak into her ear. The laughter surrounding them was deafening and claustrophobic.

Tina listened to what he said, then appeared to revive. She looked up with a grateful smile, and the two slipped away from the group slowly, a nod here, a wave there, a handshake or two. After a wordless walk to Tina's office to retrieve her things, they slipped into an elevator, which had arrived with merciful speed. Saved by grace.

They decided on coffee and brandies, and ended up in a dark corner of the Peacock Lounge at the Hyatt. The Peacock had been Lawrence's suggestion to himself; he had determined that it was far enough away from the party and would be nearly empty as it was.

OPHIR

Tina's chair, dark pink, soft, with huge arms like upholstered pillows, held her like Thumbelina cradled in the eye of a ripe rose. She was almost as tall as Lawrence, but seeing her nestled in the chair made him feel big. Big and protective.

"Feeling any better?" he asked.

"Much," she said, smiling a curved little smile that expressed its fullness and intention through her eyes. Knowledge—sure of itself without being presumptuous—beamed thrillingly into his eyes as she raised her glass of brandy, waited for Lawrence to raise his.

They talked about the party, who they both knew. Lawrence asked about her friendship with Madalyn. As Tina related an abridged version of their shared history—"The fourth grade!" he interjected. "That's amazing!"—she was playing with her watch strap, a gesture that caused him to notice her wrists. So tiny, he thought. Such little bones supporting such a figure—modeled smooth and tight, but rounded. He wished dearly for a cigarette, though he'd quit ten years ago.

"What time is it?" he asked after a while. While Tina had been speaking, he had slipped in a number of questions and comments, softly spoken and cadenced with sincerity, noises indicative of a genuine interest in Tina and Madalyn's long, steady past together.

"Ten to twelve," she said, easing her legs out from the cuddle of the big pink chair. She crossed one leg over the other toward Lawrence and smoothed the pillowy chair arm, caressing it.

"Time for another drink?" he asked.

"Yes," she replied without hesitation.

The waiter slid silently across the room. Lawrence ordered, then settled back from the edge of his chair into its comfortable spaces.

"Done your Christmas shopping?" Tina asked, her chin in her hand, her elbow dimpling the chair arm.

"I'm sort of last minute with that kinda stuff," he laughed. Susan always bought the children's things, and every year he blazed through Holt's on Christmas Eve afternoon, amassing his collection: satin robes, leather purses, even dresses on occasion, when he could get the right saleswoman who could translate his vague descriptions of Susan's build and "personal style" into something elegant, quiet and appropriate, which Susan would thank him for with a quizzical How-could-you-have-known? look. She always seemed slightly incredulous when she opened those silver boxes and found herself inside.

With the mention of Christmas, Lawrence asked Tina what hers were like, consciously trying to avoid a prolonged discussion of his family life. Fifteen minutes later, new brandies half sipped, Tina was tying up her Christmas schedule for him.

All those brothers, Lawrence thought, she must get loads of stuff. God. They must *adore* her.

"The witching hour has come and gone," he said, indicating his watch: 1:21.

"So it has."

No mention was made of heading for home, and they eventually ordered coffee. The anxious edge of Lawrence's excitement had become somewhat diluted. He swam in pleasure as deadlines drowned around him, he revelled in the real perfection of the super-oxygenated bubble of the present moment, and he began to talk about himself.

The anecdotal descriptions of his childhood, which now in its goodness and cleanliness sounded so quaint, had the sand coloured shadings of nostalgia. Then he spoke of his present existential quandaries. He couched them in terms of a general need for a rethinking of goals, a consideration of what might have been left out of his life, his desire to prevent the unintentional omission of anything crucial. He was veering precariously close to expounding upon the meaning of life when he caught himself. With a note of paternal care, he suggested that perhaps they should be getting Tina home.

They talked of catching a couple of cabs or, Lawrence suggested, they could take just one. Tina was not that far away, a five- or ten-minute ride at most, and he would like to make sure she got home safely. Tina thanked him for his concern, both of them fully aware, of course, of the very slight possibility of danger that might exist for her during a ten-minute cab ride alone, but they did not say this out loud, risking certain laughter. And neither wanted to do that—to risk wrecking the fragile net they were weaving.

They had not settled on two cabs or one by the time they stepped outside the hotel. No doorman was in sight—perhaps he was on only until midnight—so Lawrence hailed a taxi from the lineup parked thirty feet, or so, from the hotel entrance. Tina disappeared into the cab without saying goodbye, without turning around. Lawrence, right behind her, did not wait to hail his own taxi.

Had she not had such small wrists, Lawrence would still, perhaps, have had a chance. To back out, to rethink. But he had been thinking for the last hour only of picking up one of her wrists, of circling it with his thumb and index finger. Another thought, which he had been pulling up and letting drop like a yoyo: he had been wondering if both of his hands would fit around her waist.

His thoughts in the past months had not been much more graphic than these. He always imagined new female bodies, bodies that weren't Susan's. He imagined them, in high-gloss, crotch-swelling detail, all the time. But with Tina, he could not seem to orchestrate his fantasies past the part where her blouse was off and she was stroking his Hero's head, just under her chin.

He would go blank if he tried to conjure anything further, the whole shebang in its clinical completeness. Whenever he tried, he failed, and frustration flowed in, darkening his heart. His head would throb with blank thought. He knew what he would find if he was right up against her, inside, in her darkness. He knew what it was. It was just that he could not name it.

But it was too late. They were both in her cab, she had given the driver her address, and Lawrence had not said there would be two stops. He stayed where his plunge into the cab had left him, in the middle of the seat, shoulder to shoulder with Tina. He wondered if he was truly feeling her leaning into him. Like an idiot, he commented that the coffee would probably keep them awake all night. She sat up a little straighter and looked at him. Then she said, right into his eyes, yes. Then they both looked straight ahead.

Lawrence suddenly became aware of taxi etiquette and how this might affect the situation. The big silent driver, smushed into his seat, looked as if he had been sitting there, in the same position, for years. Lawrence started to try and work things out, how he should handle it once they got to Tina's place. He looked down at her lap. Then he picked up one of her wrists and whispered, "Tiny." Tina hmmed ever so softly, and yes, she was definitely leaning into him now.

All of a sudden, it seemed, they were in front of Tina's place, and he was on.

"I'll, um, walk you in," he said, thinking how embarrassing if, at the door, she asked him in and he had to come back and pay the driver, the driver who would think to himself that Lawrence had scored. This cheap analysis that Lawrence thought up for the driver disgusted him.

"Come on in for a few, if you like," Tina said, halfway out of the cab, but where the driver could still hear her. She made it sound like she and Lawrence were friends and that it would be natural for Lawrence to come in for a while.

"Thanks so much," Lawrence said to the driver, handing him ten dollars for the five-dollar fare.

"Thank *you* and Merry Christmas," the driver said very pleasantly. Perhaps he wasn't as coarse as Lawrence, in his paranoia, had thought he looked.

Tina's townhouse was at the end of the block. The entrance, she said, was around the side. As they walked around the corner, Lawrence noticed the park across the street, dark and still above the beach. He could hear, faintly, the rhythmic surf.

Tina's door was at the top of a winding staircase, built against a tall white wall that curved with the stairs. Lit by a floodlight, the pale stucco glowed with what seemed to be a Mediterranean ambience. Lawrence followed Tina's winter white coat up the stairs and inside. On the outside of the door, as it closed, a big gold Christmas bow jiggled on its hook.

A light in the living room shone down a short hallway, which was open on one side to the kitchen. Everything seemed white, even in the dimly lit hallway where they stood just inside the front door. After helping him out in the cab, Tina now seemed to be leaving everything entirely up to Lawrence. She did not fling off her coat, snap on lights, stride to the living room and ask about the proverbial drink, as he imagined she might. She just stood there, looking at him. Her purse on its long, skinny strap dropped with a light thud to the floor.

Lawrence lifted one of her arms with his hand and found her wrist under the sleeve of her coat. He had no idea what to say. The roar in his ears was too loud for thinking; blood gushed through his heart, which beat with alarming force. He looked at Tina's wrist as if it had all the answers, as if it had asked him to come in. Still, she said nothing.

He lay her wrist on his chest and held her face, her waist, his breath. Then their arms were around each other and there were kisses—real and redemptive. For a long time they stood there, just inside her door. Slowly, gently, aware of the net they had made, and of what it was made, how fragile but now finished and cast, they let the first magic suffuse them.

It was a matter of audience: dinner at Mia's parents' place, sort of a precursor to a black-tie fundraiser her mother was chairing, for Mia's Junior Committee and a few friends.

"Sort of dressy, but pretty low key," Mia had told John. This invitation was a coup, and he wore at least nine hundred dollars' worth of silk-weight inky wool, the most threads per inch you could buy.

But Madalyn. Black angora cuddled her up the front, from mid-thigh to collarbone. Then, down her back, the dress took a startling plunge, draping just above the waist. Her glossy black hair was piled on top of her head, scrunched into bunches of gold-dusty tulle, leaving the white tongue of her back to carry the rest of the accessorizing burden.

She liked to dress up and away from the sartorial sameness of these events, the women all muted and buttoned up into *Vogue* wardrobe builders for the Conservative You, of obvious French-seam quality.

John had looked slightly baffled when he arrived to pick her up. But he complimented her on her gorgeousness and ran his hands all over what there was of the back of her dress, petting her like a kitten.

"Cozy," he had whispered in her ear, causing her to undo his single jacket button and browse lightly underneath, until he held her wrist away and croaked that they were now fashionably late enough and should get going.

The party was as stilted as she had expected, the guests looking like younger, pinker versions of their parents. There was one young man in particular: the combination of his hair, prematurely grey and smooth as the underside of a sterling gravy boat, and the babyish, expensively fatted look of his face, buttery lips dolloping out words chosen carefully from some sort of aristocrat's thesaurus in his mind. Madalyn wanted to slap him. She needed some release for her gassed-up critical streak, which was accelerating steadily toward full throttle.

After dinner and before Madalyn had done anything John might regret, like putting her dress on backward, which of course she'd never do, but it relieved her to think about it, she started a conversation with Mia's father. When she saw him approaching, she rewound her pre-recorded response to the usual question about what she had studied at school, and prepared to press Play.

Mr. Stoller had surprised her—there is a God, she thought—by remarking that she looked very lovely, artistic and quite *original*, giving a nod to the room full of flat-slippered women. Madalyn responded that art was her thing, as they say, and, smoothly lying, said she tried to keep up with her painting, but with working full-time, it was hard.

Thankfully, he didn't ask about the work, but picked up on the art part, and it turned out they had a common interest. He was horribly well read on the subject, but Madalyn held her own nicely. After all, she had studied it, piquing his genuine interest with a description of Schnabel's broken plates, which, no, he hadn't heard of, but wasn't it intriguing. To keep the momentum going, she followed this up with the one about Picasso's fishbones, which made him laugh. Mr. Stoller had the kind of laugh Madalyn liked in a man, coughed out in a deep staccato, noticeably louder than the level of normal conversation—like John's.

John laughed out loud at the oddest times, like when she had told him she was nervous about meeting his mother. But the unexpected bite of his laugh had shocked her into courage. Then she felt silly for having worried, as *he* made *her* laugh with stories about Patricia Smilie Hazeldine's second husband and their powdered yellow Buick and gin-soaked home in the Properties. That was John's private laugh. In public, his laugh was more subdued, a polite heh-heh-heh pecked out in a tone flush with the talk.

Madalyn was telling Mr. Stoller that her dad was a great reader too, and his latest interest in fiction was V.S. Naipaul's work. She herself was *addicted* to Oscar Wilde, although she understood he wasn't really taken seriously in an historical sense. She had heard him referred to as a literary scamp, not really grounded in any one a particular style or period. She realized these were unnecessary qualifiers when Mr. Stoller pounced on the author's name with me-too glee and engaged her in a quiz on Wildean aphorisms.

They were off, again. Mr. Stoller's laugh certainly didn't go with his slight build and the eyes, a watery grey, which turned down at the corners behind his glasses, making him look like a socially backward, perpetual academic when, in fact, he was a Chief Financial Officer, of the province's second largest forest products company.

Mia came around and offered to bring them fresh drinks. Mr. Stoller took both when she returned and sheltered Madalyn's hand with his until she had the glass firmly in place. He paused for a Thank you, dear, and seemed relieved when his daughter had gone.

Madalyn was thinking that Doug Stoller (it was Doug now—he didn't want to hear one more Mr. Stoller from her) was probably about her father's age, maybe five years younger, and she realized she found him attractive, really quite—something about the exercised look of his solid, oblong face that seemed to belong on a more athletic body. She felt a thrill of synthetic guilt when that Bible verse she had learned in Tina's Sunday School popped into her mind: that a man looking on a woman to lust after had already committed adultery with her in his heart. She assumed this worked both ways and wondered how Baptists could even dare breathe, there not being much to get away with if you took this verse to heart.

She flirted as subtly as she knew how, occasionally grasping his forearm to steady herself from laughter, leaning into most of the personal space surrounding this open-minded, thoughtful man who suddenly remembered something he had meant to ask her when they were on Art.

He escorted her down a hall that felt as if it was carpeted with layers of fuzzy bedroom slippers. He wanted to know what she knew about the technique of two eighteenth-century first-print etchings, which had been quite a stroke of luck for him at an auction in London last year, and which now hung under their little lamps in the sanctuary of his study. As she bent toward the wall to examine them, Mr. Stoller stepped back, appreciating fully the black-on-white aesthetic of her back.

John and Geoff found them a half hour later, giggling over a couple of brandies, Madalyn's high heels bouncing some inches above the rug and several feet below the top of Mr. Stoller's desk, where she sat.

"This is quite a young lady you've got here," he commented to John, getting up from his chair to usher the men into a conversational circle.

"I thought you'd quit smoking, Dad," Geoff nitpicked at his father-in-law, who had just finished enjoying one of Madalyn's naughty cigarettes. John glared at Madalyn, as if she had not asked Mr. Stoller if he minded her smoking, and had not assured her host that she never smoked in someone else's home unless she was absolutely sure they did not mind and were not just being polite.

John knew the routine by now. She usually didn't bother asking at all; his social set was becoming increasingly, mysteriously allergic. Ignoring the coffee-table ashtray that held Doug Stoller's extinguished cigarette, John picked up an ashtray from the desk—something green and pinched that Mia had made in school—and held it out to Madalyn, who glared back, flicked some ash into the dish and took another puff.

"Here, I'll help you down," John said, evidently noticing just how much thigh Madalyn's skirt was revealing.

"I think Madalyn enjoys the view from up there." Doug winked at her, a conspiracy: Let's see if we can get under the skin of these young fuddy-duddies."

"You boys have a seat—the party's in here now."

John moved away from Madalyn to sit down dutifully beside Geoff on the sofa, of the old kind of leather furniture with piping, medieval-looking tacks and sculpted wooden legs.

Geoff got into the swing of things. "So, Dad, you weren't showing Madalyn your etchings, were you?"

Doug Stoller laughed. "Actually, Madalyn was able to fill me in quite a bit on the artist and his technique. You two must get out to the galleries fairly often."

"Actually, not all that often," said Madalyn, "but I have a friend from art school who John's met. He paints and does very weird quote unquote sculpture, and actually, he's had a few showings, and I think he's starting to be taken seriously. Though John wonders why." Madalyn gave John a grin designed to make up.

"His name," she went on, "his pseudonym, actually, is Nihil Asso, and he has the most *cynical* explanation for how he came up with it!" Madalyn watched John out of the corner of her eye. He was unwilling to let his brief, straight-across smile part his lips. He had the look of a father who has just washed his hands of the crimes of a denfull of manic children, resigned to letting the damage be done while he waits for the wife to take over.

Later on, when they said goodnight to all the Stollers at the door, Madalyn and Doug held eyes for that deliberate, unmistakable moment longer that dares anyone to notice and confirms something mutual and private, to be dealt with later in fantasy.

The poop didn't really hit the deck, as Geoff would have put it, until Madalyn and John were inside John's car.

"I actually had a great time tonight," Madalyn said, buckling up while she watched John's profile.

"I don't want to argue," was all John said in response. It wasn't like him to be so, what was it, Oh yes,—anal retentive? Madalyn thought, feeling vindictive. Fuck, she thought—this is just sickening. They drove the rest of the way in silence, each strapped in place by a different tension. By the time John parked in front of his house and met Madalyn halfway out of the car door he had intended to open, she was in tears.

"What? . . . ah . . . *jeez*," he said when he noticed.

"What is your problem?" Madalyn retched out the words, part of a sob, when they got in the door.

"What, what's my problem?" John appeared to slit his throat with his tie as he yanked it off. "You're the one who was advertising all your assets to Doug Stoller." He volleyed his backside into a chair, arms and legs flopping about, landing wherever. "And why do you always have to rave about that fucking weirdo?"

This attack was absorbed by silence. Madalyn was barely into the interrogation, and already she was doubting her own innocence.

"What have I done? I've done nothing!" Madalyn exclaimed, lighting up. "Mr. Stoller and I had a great conversation about art and literature. We *killed* ourselves laughing . . . it was great." She was kneeling in a corner of the couch opposite John's chair, one hand moving back and forth from the ashtray to her mouth as she worked on a thickening screen of smoke. "And about the leg issue—that *is* what you're choked about—do you think Mr. Stoller has never seen a *leg* in his life? Why are we all of a sudden the ever so modest one? I thought you liked the dress."

"I do like it, Madalyn. But don't you think maybe you should stop to think if something you're saying is appropriate . . . for your audience? I thought you were going to go into the homoerotic details of that idiot's name."

"Homoerotic! That's a new word for you! Been working on your vocabulary?" She was stung by his obvious lack of faith in her discretion, which really was such an insult, considering the great time Mr. Stoller had had.

John wasn't responding, and they stared at each other. To her disappointment, her real anger began to dissipate under his look, and she tried to manufacture some more, but it felt too much like a cheap imitation, and all of a sudden she was afraid. Don't, whatever you do, she told herself, be one of those shrill, emasculating creatures. I love him.

And now it felt real, not like when she'd first told him, when it had seemed like something done by people with real lives. Madalyn had a sudden urge to laugh—the laugh of a madman in a movie after he has committed some dastardly crime, his cocked eye filling the screen, a laugh to alleviate his own nausea over his sickening lack of control.

John was leaning on his elbows, which were planted on his knees. His forehead was wrinkled to hold up the top half of his face, and he looked sweet and confused to Madalyn, who was staring back in the same way she had stared at Mr. Stoller. But John held her eyes much longer, in a look that was fully a part of this talk game which he was winning. He looked at her the way a snake charmer looks at the snake, which undulates like ribbon, upward, charmed by the pipe.

"I'm uncomfortable when you are so blatantly sexy . . . sexual . . . God, this sounds ridiculous," he said, losing some advantage.

"Can't stand to be outshone?" She couldn't help it, but good, not shrill at all, a teasing sort of purr. She cuddled herself in the offending dress.

"I don't want my wife to be that obvious and flirtatious," he said, a vision flashing in his head of his mother, Patricia, drunk and glorious, fluttering her eyelashes, squeezing the arm of one or another of his father's friends.

"So now I'm your *wife*."

"No."

He moved to her side of the couch, gently unfolding her legs, then drawing them up over his, closing the door he had left open for interpretation. He held her face and gazed into her eyes with a look that told her nothing except that it was time to go to bed. She let him take her there—Yes, I don't want to think. You're right—and that night her hands did a lot of sculpting of the bones of his face and the muscles of his chest, memorizing.

The next day, the drug of morning love shooting through her sleep-weakened body left her with limbs too limp to realize her urge to stretch. She felt handicapped and defenceless. Just don't say a word. As John readied his day voice with some throat-clearing, Madalyn forced herself up. She didn't want the feeling of watching him walk away, leaving her a well-used crumple under the sheet.

"It's okay to walk around as if you belong here, y'know," John teased, referring to the breathless way she had of tiptoeing around when she was naked.

Madalyn cried a little in the bathroom, the tap running. She had nothing else to wear home except last night's kitten costume, which felt like the hands of someone who appreciates the exquisite, hovering on a cushion of air above her skin. He asked if she wanted to wait while he made some coffee, then he'd drive her home. She said no, just please call her a cab. At the door, John was generous with the best kind of dry kisses, lips making slow dabs, like someone gently tending a wound.

# Chapter Five

By February, Lawrence and Tina had established a routine. Thursday evenings from six to eleven. This was their regular time, although more often than not, they spent at least one more evening together each week. Lawrence was always a little more anxious before and after these unscheduled trysts. Any more time carved away from his regular life—family and business—only added to the pressures he already felt to keep up to speed, to maintain normalcy. These areas of his life were becoming ever more burdensome, a duty-driven routine. He wanted to be with Tina all the time.

He had rigged Thursday evenings thus: He told Susan in early January that he had joined a squash league at his downtown racquet club. He said he needed the exercise. He suggested that Susan make a point of giving herself some personal time too—hire a sitter during the week, maybe take a class. Susan had not taken him up on his suggestion, saying she felt she had her hands full at home at the moment, with all the children's activities.

The first few hours of Thursday evenings were spent on Tina's pale, roomy couch with a bottle of very good wine, the room around them lit by a few candles. The parameters of their relationship were slowly and delicately established. They talked of the business they had in common, of their childhoods, high school and university years, of their young adulthoods. Lawrence's story stopped at the murky moment when he married. But he spoke of his children as if they had just suddenly appeared in his life one day, to be his friends, creatures of imagination come to life.

Those weekly conversations, rarefied by anticipation of the hours of lovemaking to follow, were the most perfect of times, and they would live on in memory the way happy endings of requited love live on, undiluted, in the pages of a book.

Their last half hour together was sweet drama. Lawrence's deadline was scrupulously observed by both, Tina slipping with ease into the role of co-conspirator and, at the same time, co-protector of Susan. Tina knew this consciously, and somehow it did not bother her, nor did the fact that, she assumed, Lawrence continued to have sexual relations with his wife.

Susan was, to Tina, a static entity and of little interest. Tina herself was so obviously the object of Lawrence's rich, ragged declarations of love, pulled from his gut and breathed onto the warm skin of her neck. In them she could hear the crack in his self-control, his emotion bleeding out, hot and messy.

Lawrence had done one other thing after Christmas and before the new year. He had taken out a second mortgage on his vacation property, a winterized home of warm, varnished cedar and glass on two ocean-front acres in the Gulf Islands. This money, and the proceeds he received from cashing in a twenty-thousand-dollar term deposit, he invested in Barry Klammer's Arizona condo deal. The frantic energies of love had stopped up his usual sober thought processes and sandbagged this part of him sky-high and tight with rationalization. He was *moving*. His *life* was moving. Oh, what a feeling. What a rush.

Nihil called Madalyn on Friday night, Friday the thirteenth that February. He was surprised when she said she had no plans for the fourteenth. John had been in Toronto for two weeks and wouldn't be back until Sunday, she said, looking at the embarrassingly pert arrangement of pink roses in their little round vase, which had been delivered to her at work earlier that day. So no, she was not busy and she'd love to meet him on Saturday evening at what sounded like a most interesting event.

The taxi pulled up in front of the warehouse. A very young man, in tails, opened the door and helped Madalyn out.

"Welcome," he said, appraising her long black legs, the form-fitting mini, the short leather jacket. He flipped his long hair, which fell over one eye and flowed past his shoulders, away from his face with a white-gloved hand. He gave Madalyn a dazzling smile and opened the heavy metal door.

Madalyn wandered through the crowd, searching for Nihil. She felt nervous not knowing anyone, as if she had entered a high school dance at the wrong school. The atmosphere did not help to put her at ease. The music was deafening industrial-strength Euro techno-pop—the sort of music that suits the aesthetic tastes of nose-ringed youth forced to while away their teens in Mannheim, sustained only by their premature cynicism.

Madalyn found herself surrounded by a collection of partygoers who, for some reason, she found intimidating. Perhaps it was because of Nihil's description of the guest list: the warehouse owners/organizers, some media types and local artists—some older and established, some young, who, like himself, hoped to encroach from the fringes by sheer impudence if not talent. This party, Nihil had said, was an example of disgusting I'll-do-you-if-you-do-me mutuality.

The event had been organized by a group of "yukkies," Nihil's term of endearment for people in their prime who had actual careers and made money. This group had recently purchased the warehouse as an investment. It was to be redeveloped into upscale condos, which they would sell, and artists' studios—living and working space combined—which they would rent. Some sort of deal had been worked out with the city. So the artists had been invited; not, Nihil said, that any of *his* cronies could afford the yuppified studios, even with the city's help.

A number of the younger artists had spent the past week in the warehouse, first whitewashing the walls, then "making art." The interior was scheduled to be torn apart by construction crews starting Monday, and so with these people and many of the guests in mind, the artists had covered the walls with such images as a wolf-like dog's head with a fifteen-foot jaw span, open to devour a smiling Mr. and Mrs. Howell. Someone had taken up on this theme on the wall behind the bar by painting Gilligan, naked and with a huge erection.

"We're just a bunch of jerks acting out," Nihil said into Madalyn's ear, his hands at her waist. Nevertheless, she couldn't take her eyes off Gilligan, such as he was, sexualized out of all proportion, making up for all those years as a goofy castaway who never got any. Gilligan's wall was titled in huge, childlike lettering, "Hey, little buddy!"

Nihil and Madalyn wandered down the wide hall that joined the bar and bathroom area (bar on one wall, Porta-Johns on the other) to the dance floor. Nihil grabbed two glasses of wine from a passing tray.

"Drink, my friends, drink!" said the bearer, a skinny blond kid in a sleeveless shirt. He had bruised, waxen-looking arms, ropy and hard. "I'll be back with food—the catering is *won*derful. *Derek* did it." He kissed the air in front of Nihil.

"*Fabu*lous party." He left, forging his tray right into a group of suits whom he chatted up in the same fashion without batting an eye.

Standing next to Nihil and Madalyn was a prosperous-looking couple in their late forties. She, in her round-necked dinner dress, clapped reservedly in time to the music.

"It's quite a mix," Madalyn said into Nihil's ear. He smiled and steered her out into the hall where it was marginally quieter. A man with the pasty, exhausted look of a deskbound journalist approached them.

"Ronny. How's it hangin'?" he asked Nihil.

"Eric. Nice to see you. I'd like you to meet Madalyn. Madalyn, this is Eric Abernathy of local art media fame."

Eric extended a hand. "I'm charmed," he said.

"I read your work," Madalyn said. "Your new film column in the *Weekend Review* is to love." She hesitated to add that she loved his humour, his chronic crankiness, the way, in print, that he begged to be inspired, disarmed, surprised and not manipulated.

"Eric here is my one great hope," Nihil said. "He did the only 'straight' review of my Heden exhibit. What was that one part, I memorized it,

'. . . the usual derivative presentation of popular culture, "politicized" by refraction through the artist's own clichéd psychology. But saved, in this case, from being abysmally irritating by Asso's detached, almost innocent sense of ironic humour. He manages to float on his own flatulence.'

God, I love that line."

Eric laughed. "I've told Ron he should get into film. And I am serious. I know you've got the maturity, though God knows it's hard to see," he said, giving Nihil a gentle prod with the three free fingers of the hand holding his glass.

"If I go into film, Madalyn," Nihil said, "you have to promise to take up the slack in the visual arts department. My departure would leave a huge, gaping space. She is seriously talented." Nihil nodded toward Madalyn. "I've got to get her producing."

Madalyn felt herself blush, her tiresomely familiar, crushing lack of confidence dropped suddenly and heavily onto her shoulders.

"Well," she said, "all in good time."

"That's right," Eric said. "Artists produce, as you put it, Ron, in their time. Madalyn, may I interest you in a dance, if not now, then perhaps a little later?"

"Um . . . sure. Now would be nice," Madalyn responded, managing what she hoped was an interested smile. She and Eric handed their glasses to Nihil, who juggled them along with his own. With a wink for Madalyn, he said he'd catch them later.

In the dark, with the music pounding against her, strobe lights blinding her, she felt graceless, too tall, tense. Time to head back to the bar, she kept thinking, as she was spun around in Eric's hands, which felt warm and dry.

"Mad . . . Mad!" She heard Nihil's voice coming from a clump of black backs just to the right of the bar. Nihil emerged with a young man in tow. Madalyn recognized him as Nihil's brother, Peter. A young, startled Adonis of a deer, Peter shone amidst the black surrounding him; his white shirt and skin, his navy eyes, took Madalyn's breath away when Peter stepped under a light as he came toward her.

Peter smiled.

Some of Madalyn's sadness, a bile that tasted like tragedy, filled her throat as Peter's smile broke over her. And as she met his eyes, whose light snuck shyly out from under an innocent, bewildered brow, she felt that sweet, clean ache that comes with imagining oneself as a child before anything has gone wrong.

Nihil, his cheekbones drawn up tight, his eyes sharpened with purpose, put an arm behind each of Peter and Madalyn, who waggled her fingers and mouthed a goodbye to Eric, in

conversation with a colleague by the bar. As Nihil shepherded the
two of them into a dark corner, the gaggle of youngsters, from
which Peter had emerged, stared after him. They were mostly boys
and two girls with blackened eyes like stabs of darkest charcoal on
their white faces. There was much giggling amongst this group,
extravagant displays of feigned weakness, much pawing at each
other for support.

Nihil had stashed a bottle of tequila under a sawhorse
and had purloined three tumblers from the bar.

"Oh, goody," Madalyn said as she and Nihil seated
themselves on the sawhorse, Peter finding space on a pile of old
newspapers. A tight little group, they cozied up together, kids
around a campfire.

Later, unburdened by the constraints of sobriety, Madalyn
danced with Peter, her jacket off, her hair bouncing off her bare
arms and shoulders with silky slaps. She could feel an audience of
eyes watching from the sidelines.

Peter, a vision turned out from a mould of teenage
imagination, tender and firm, his long denim-fitted legs anchored
by cowboy boots, moved in slowed-down time to the beat, which
Madalyn could feel in her stomach. At intervals, they rested by
the side of the dance floor, drawing little crowds.

Madalyn felt ebullient, talkative, in control of her high.
Hungry for expression, thirsty for attention, secure in the simple,
easy social cachet that comes with being a tall, leggy, good-looking

woman, she simply had to stand there—it did not matter what she said. People enjoyed her, and Peter, the sort of celebrity spell they cast for a few hours at the height of the party.

Sometime after one thirty, Madalyn went to the bathroom. She held her compact up to the weak light entering through the ceilingless top of the Porta-John along with the throbbing music from the next room, thinned out by the warehouse walls. Blotting some perspiration from her face, she looked into her own eyes, barely, briefly. Then she snapped the compact shut and opened the door. She felt a tremble of snug excitement, tequila freedom quickly regained.

She had no luck finding Peter again. Finally she spotted Nihil in a dark corner of the dance area, leaning against the wall, evidently enjoying the earnest, quasi-seductive attentions of a thin-faced woman who was fondling a long black scarf that fell from her neck. Madalyn caught the drift of the conversation—the woman was grilling Nihil on the life of an artist was, verbally trying to palpate the mysteries of his creative process. Nihil was smiling, his eyes half shut. His attenuated responses to the woman's questions only deepened the mystery for her. He enjoyed these sorts of ministrations when he was drunk.

Nihil stood up straight and extended a hand to Madalyn.

"Looks like I'm about to hit the road," he said to the woman. A look of disappointment scuttled across her face, then some quickly gathered pride coalesced into a meaningful smile for Nihil as he and Madalyn edged away.

"Would you and Peter like to come back to my place?" Madalyn asked. "I was looking for him, but I don't see him anywhere."

They began to comb the warehouse. In the hallway by the entrance, Nihil nabbed one of the girls who had been so taken with his little brother.

"Oh, he's left . . . with Derek," she said. "We're all going to Derek's. He's having a after-party."

"Great," Nihil said, the word turning him around. He pulled Madalyn away from the girl.

"Who *is* this Derek?" Madalyn asked.

"Derek is a restaurateur, owns Monty's—y'know, black, white, trendy all over. He's a touch flamboyant, if you know what I mean. Those kids are his waiters slash groupies."

"Well, do you want to go?"

"I'm not really up for one of Derek's energetic little soirées, but I'm not sure I trust that crowd with Pete." Nihil ran a hand over his forehead and across the bristles of his hair. "Got a cigarette?"

"Well, I for one have got to sit down," Madalyn said, sinking into a stray folding chair amongst the noise and press of departing guests. "I'm pretty wrecked." She handed Nihil her pack.

"Yeah, I'm fairly bagged myself. Let's get out of here," he said, an unlit cigarette in his mouth. He heaved the heavy shoulders of his leather jacket. "Maybe some fresh will revive us." He pushed open the heavy metal door with his back.

They walked for blocks through Gastown, gulping the cold air, Madalyn's high heels tapping, Nihil's boots making a softer, broader sound on the dirty pavement. By the time they had hailed a cab on Water Street, they did indeed feel revived and had decided on Madalyn's place, her stash of cheap champagne, and the two big, fat hydroponic joints in Nihil's pocket.

"God. It *sounds* so trite," Madalyn was saying, her feet up on the back of her couch. She had taken, so far, only two tiny tokes. "I'll be either comatose or unbelievably horny if I do too much at once," she had said, to which Nihil had responded, "Interesting odds."

"Great sex is great sex—don't knock it. However, he seems a most conventional lad," Nihil said, squinting as he took a few quick, delicate sucks on the joint. "And," he inhaled the word with a squeak, "you," he paused, holding in the smoke, "my dear, don't really want to be a conventional girl, do you?" he finished, exhaling, clearing out his lungs with an extra puff of smokeless breath. He leaned over the coffee table to carefully carve the ash tip of the joint on the edge of the ashtray. In profile, his strong lower jaw, his high brow, his straight long nose stood out—the first broad, defining strokes of an artist sketching a face composed of bone.

"But I *am*. Horrifyingly so . . ." Madalyn said. "If you knew how I thought . . ." She was feeling good. She wanted to talk about herself. She wanted a fresh perspective from someone like Nihil. She anticipated the effect he might have, like seeing a European film where the people love without bourgeois guilt, do it fully clothed with a stranger in the hall, wake up wearing day-old eyeliner and light a cigarette before their feet hit the floor, drive themselves literally mad with obsessive love and show up in the last scene as crazy, eccentric, wise old existentialists. Or young and dead. She anticipated Nihil's words reaching inside her to turn the sod of her mundane self, packed down by routine and the clean, rigid, puritan grid of her North American world.

"Babies, burbs and hooked on Valium when you're thirty-five?" he asked.

"The Valium part sounds great," she said, wiggling two straight fingers at him, signaling for drugs. She sat up, took another toke, a big one, what the hey, gulped down a large mouthful of champagne and lit a cigarette. "Look at me," she said, laughing. "Drugs everywhere. Did you want to call Derek's or anything? I mean, are you worried about Peter?"

"Nah," Nihil said, "I thought about it, but he came down to the coast to have a good time, to check it out here . . . and anyway, I don't want him to feel like I'm monitoring his every move. God knows he gets enough of that at home. But I wish he had let me know he was heading out to Derek's." He sat back, rubbing his chest with one hand. He exhaled with some force.

"Ah," he continued, "I guess those kids are pretty harmless. And Derek's cool. A nice guy. It's not like Pete's going to find himself at an exclusively gay party, though I doubt he'd even recognize it if that was the case . . . he's pretty naïve, y'know, small town."

"Does he have a girlfriend?"

"He's *always* got a girlfriend. Pretty and bossy, all of them, they love to mother him . . . he's the sensitive, lost puppy dog type . . . attracts that kind of girl."

"What about you? What have you got in the way of a love life these days?"

Nihil laughed. "It's sporadic . . . and eclectic." He told Madalyn about a little romance he'd had the previous summer with a seventeen-year-old private school student. "She was desperate to rebel with style," he said.

Then he told Madalyn about the love of his life.

"I guess I was sixteen when I knew her. She was a Mennonite, not allowed to date *at all*. So I asked if I could walk her to church on Sundays, but even that was a no-go with her father. A real stiff. Anyway, I cornered her at school whenever I could, and sometimes I'd walk her partway home. She was so sweet . . . I knew she shouldn't really be seen with someone of my ilk."

"Was she pretty?"

"Beautiful. I mean, it's not like she'd start any riots, but let's see . . . she was very petite, quiet, with these huge grey eyes. I don't know what it was about her . . . something . . . and God, I was this long-haired greaser, telling her my wild ideas and nothing seemed to shock her, as protected and religious as she was. She was just this serene creature . . .

"I remember once, getting mad. I asked her how she could accept all the subservient shit in her religion—I didn't call it shit—and she said she didn't feel subservient, she said she felt taken care of—by her parents, her church, by God. Anyway, Christ, she had *something*, it was mesmerizing. Her eyes. Her voice was so soft I could hardly hear her sometimes. And she was so off limits. The combination was very sexual."

Madalyn felt jealous as she listened to Nihil's description. Jealous of someone who did not need to project herself. Someone who contained within herself such a peace, such certainty, without any need to sell it to others, without any need to express it, over and above a natural look in her eyes, a natural response from the heart, spoken in a voice with no compulsion to impress, underscore, convince or convert.

"I wonder why we make these connections when they don't *go* anywhere," she said. "A friend of mine is madly in love with a married man. She says she can't see him getting divorced, but she's worried that the time will come when she'll want him to."

"Yeah, that's pretty dangerous ground. But no more dangerous than the ground you're treading on," Nihil said, filling her glass.

"Meaning? . . . Meaning my relationship with John is hopeless and perverse . . . right?"

Nihil didn't press the issue.

"Well, I live for perversity," Madalyn said, summing up, swimming in a temporary perfection of feeling, convinced of her ability to live up to the exquisite rigours of self-destructiveness, European style. She took a swallow of champagne, ran a hand through her hair and down her neck. She took a deep breath and curled up her legs. She was enjoying that transcendent state of drunkenness when alcohol swooshes cleanly through the brain, when, with an aerating action, it gives life to empowering emotion usually bound by restrictive thought.

Nihil stood and walked across the room to the stereo. He tapped up the volume on Joan Jett—"I Want to Be Your Dog"—and slid open the door to the balcony.

"It's all experience," he said. "You never know which one will be pivotal, which one will crack you open and let out all the gods and demons."

"But I'm getting so *old*. God. I'll be twenty-eight in November. I want and need a pivotal experience."

Nihil smiled, sat down beside her, reached out a hand and massaged her neck for a moment.

Nihil laughed softly. He lit the second joint and handed it to Madalyn. She inhaled and coughed as the strong smoke hit the back of her throat. She took a drink and then another toke, this time enjoying greater success, holding in the smoke for an admirably long time.

There was a long silence. Madalyn hiccupped, and grabbed Nihil's arm.

"Omigod . . . do you remember paisley? That is very Emil." "What a scream!" she hiccupped. Her voice was falling all over itself. "Decorative sperm-like shapes. Rather phallic. I wonder if the shape of paisley has some meaning from mythology or something, some ancient religion. I really think it probably does." Her babbling stopped abruptly. She looked at Nihil with all the guilelessness of his little Mennonite. She was perfectly stoned. Nihil gave her a hug. She burst into tears.

For some moments she cried quite violently into his shoulder, surprising them both with the force of her outburst. Then she pulled away and attempted to dry her face with her hands.

Nihil said softly, "You're crying as if you really mean it."

This produced a small smile. Nihil got up, turned down the music and jogged to the bathroom, returning with a handful of Kleenex. Madalyn mopped at her face. She needed a cigarette in order to breathe.

"How worried about you should I be?" he asked.

"Don't mind me. Tina and I used to have a saying about parties, that unless one of us cried or threw up, we weren't really having a good time." She blew her nose.

"What brought this on?"

"Oh, I don't know," she said, then paused to fight back some emotion that threatened again to wash up through her chest into her throat and pour out of her eyes. Her voice sounded shaky and congested. "I'm fine. Really. But I think I'm going to need to lie down . . . very soon."

She walked Nihil to the door. He held her up.

"If you ever need a shoulder, you know how to reach me."

"Thanks. You too. Are you sure you want to walk all the way home?"

"I'll be fine," he said. "But I mean it. Call me if you need me."

"I will," she said, pressed against the door frame like a damp rag.

As soon as Nihil left, she dropped her body, fully clothed, onto the bed. Her head was filled with a multitude of thoughts that darted and zoomed like protozoa through her liquefied brain.

Any attempt to focus made her queasy. Almost immediately she passed out, and for many hours her head was packed solid with sleep.

Gently, Madalyn placed the naked baby boy in the arms of her father, who lay in bed.

"Here is your baby," she said.

"Where is your mother?" he asked.

Madalyn answered, "She can't talk."

Then she was startled awake, nagged from her dream by the telephone next to her ear. She had no time to savour the feeling of triumph she had found deposited on the doorstep of her consciousness. She answered. It was John. He had arrived back from Toronto earlier that morning, wanted to see her.

"Just a sec," Madalyn said. She lay the receiver on the pillow beside her head and sat up, testing the extent of her hangover. Slowly, she stood. No nausea, a little weak, slight headache, very thirsty. A leftover of relaxation from the pot, like a lining of soft dryer lint, cushioned her nerves and the inside of her head, leaving her with only a trace of her usual hypoglycemic anxiety. She lay down again and picked up the phone.

"Give me an hour," she said, and hung up.

On his end of the line, John pondered her tone of voice. He bounced his keys in his hand, then tossed them onto the kitchen counter. He was dressed and ready to go; a bottle of champagne tied up with a ribbon sat by the door. He picked up the package propped against the champagne and ran a hand over the wrapping, made lumpy by the paint tubes and brushes underneath. Someone he had met in Toronto had taken him to a major art supply store and had helped him choose some colours—brilliant jewel tones, of green, blue, red. He put down the package and walked to the window. Looking out, his thoughts pingponged between Madalyn and the destiny he was *almost* certain he could see looming up behind her.

She answered the door with a cigarette in hand. As he kissed her, John smelled perfume in her hair and last night's smoke. She wore a long black T shirt, her legs white against it, as beautiful as ever as she walked through the pink-grey living room sunlight.

"I had quite a night last night. I'm still recovering," she said, sitting on the couch, stretching out her legs and crossing them—a familiar position that would look posed with anyone else's legs, John had often thought. He noticed the dark smudges beneath her eyes when he looked up from stroking her shin.

"Let's open that champagne, shall we?" she said.

"You eaten yet today?" he called from the kitchen, two long-stemmed glasses clinking together as he drew them out of a cupboard with one hand.

"I had a bite, thanks," she lied.

"What were you up to last night, anyway?"

"Nihil invited me to this very chi-chi party. Lots of arty types. You would have *loved* it. Oh, and thank you for the flowers. That was very sweet."

"I might have. Enjoyed the party. You never can tell," he said as the cork popped, the sound satisfyingly round and rich.

John handed Madalyn a cold glass, which she rested against one temple. He sat down and put an arm around her shoulders, picked up swatches of her hair and let them filter through his fingers.

"So. How was Toronto?" she asked, intrigued by the serious tone of his voice, the sincerity in his blue eyes, which looked somehow sad.

"Everything went fine, not much to tell . . . did you miss me?"

"Maybe. Did you miss me?"

"Of course," John said. I miss you now, he thought.

"Mmm, this tastes wonderful. Vieux Cliquot. Old widow. Can I open my present now?" she asked, reaching for the package.

"Well, I don't know. Do you think it's safe?" She smiled at him as she pulled off the ribbon and paper.

"I have it on good authority that those are the very latest colours of that brand—European—and the brushes are top of the line," he said, watching her fingering the tubes. Her hair had fallen over her shoulder and obscured her face. Softly, he drew her hair back with one finger.

She looked at him, tears forming in her eyes.

"Thank you," she said. "They're great."

"I've been wondering when you're going to start painting again. I thought maybe you could use some encouragement."

She was silent.

"God knows, I'm no artist, but I know you've got talent."

"Alright! Enough already," she said, feeling something knot her stomach. "When I have something to express, you'll be the first to know. And as my good friend Oscar Wilde once wrote, 'Ambition is the last refuge of the failure.'"

"I'm not quite sure I follow . . ."

"Don't trouble yourself, my dear . . . what about you? I'm starving."

For food, he realized with something of a start, having expected her usually rampant libido to have taken care of the first several hours of the afternoon. But she wanted to go out for breakfast—bacon and eggs and pancakes.

Afterward, they walked down Denman Street to the ocean and onto the seawall, through the thin sunlight, into the wind, past the murky, rusty sea on one side, the evergreen fringe on the other. The seawall skirted the famous park—one hundred acres saved from development, protected by the sea on three sides, the gate of the city on the fourth completing the enclosure.

Madalyn breathed in great gulps of air and took long strides in her flat boots. John teased her about how quickly she walked, how perfect she looked.

Clouds were banking over the north western horizon, packed thick and down low over the North Shore mountains; they slid in spotty clumps over and past the sun. The spoken preoccupations of two lives travelled only as far as each other's ears, undetected by the forest, huge and tangled, keeping the silence of its old secrets.

They were forty-five minutes from home when the rain broke. There was nothing to do but get wet. Holding hands, they showered in the dictates of the day. Back at her apartment, they swiftly shed sodden clothing and crawled into bed. Blanketed by the premature darkness, Madalyn fell quickly and surprisingly, asleep.

May turned out to be a sunny month that year. Madalyn felt only a little of her old, creeping dread of summer when light finally broke over the city, which sucked up the brightness until everything was warmed and smoothed and twinkled with a Disneyesque prettiness.

But this year she *was* happy. During the past three months, this happiness had sunk in slowly. She felt herself in a sort of stupor of disbelief, a refugee granted asylum after years of effort and misery. December and January had been ragged months. Tensions between John and herself had worked up a fair head of steam, always threatening to peak and explode. But they never had, quite. These tensions had been transmuted by sex—a raw, sad, exhausting kind of sex, bodies rubbed and wrung of their juices, leaving her weak and stretched and dry inside.

But things had changed, ever since February, when John returned from his first trip to Toronto. He had begun to show such consideration—the paints and brushes, weekends at Whistler with just the two of them, which she truly enjoyed, free from the stress she felt with the Geoffs and Mias of John's crowd. Except for the monthly trips to Toronto, John spent almost all of his free time with her. Sex was softer, sweeter. And she had noticed something new in him, a lack of urgency, as if he had picked up the tail of time and pulled it backward, forcing it to stay put until it suited him to move on.

This happiness, she thought, walking with John along the seawall on the last Saturday in May, was not something she could have fabricated in her own mind.

"Why don't we turn around, go back to your place . . . there's something I want to talk to you about," he said.

"Oh, yeah? Is it serous?" Her voice sparkled with gentle sarcasm.

His hands were in the pockets of his shorts, and she slid her close arm into the perfect buttonhole of space between his arm and his body.

He was watching his feet. "It is serious, actually."

As she drew herself closer to him, he turned to look at her. In shadow, her eyes, defined by dark brows and lashes, her cheekbones flowing up into her hairline, her closed lips curved in a smile, gave her that kittenish look he loved: her soul expressed in her face as something pretty and compact. In her eyes he could see the focus of excitement and satisfaction, blurred at the edges by dreamy detachment. His heart took a tumble in his chest. His body stiffened.

"Let's pick up some beer," he said as they hit Denman Street. In the beer and wine shop he added to the six-pack two bottles of their favourite Chardonnay.

It was three o'clock when they entered her apartment. As she lifted her white cotton sweater over her head, John had an urge to reach out and touch the indestructible body that filled her black tank top and walking shorts. Black on white, like the day they first met.

He unloaded the alcohol into the fridge, cracked a beer and walked through the very familiar, always dusty, pink living room, out onto the balcony. Madalyn joined him after a few minutes, barefoot. With one hand she held a wet, cold glass of wine to her chest, between her breasts. With her other hand she aired the back of her neck, dark hair drizzling down from the casual chignon held in place with a large clip. She looked like a chic Italian, taking cocktails on the Costa Smerelda, all line, classically unadorned.

"So," she said. "Do tell." Her heart beat like a drumroll announcing one of Life's Big Moments.

"Let's go inside," John said.

# Chapter Six

Tina's toenails, Santa Fe Rose, wiggled above the bed, her legs flung over Lawrence's body. He slept with the authority of a boy—on his back, arms spread out, no fetal fear. Tina was sipping champagne and thinking about summer cottages. What a blessing they were. Lawrence's wife and children were in the Gulf Islands, and he was in her bed. On a Saturday. This was the first weekend they had been able to spend together, and they were taking full advantage. After stocking up on food and wine on Friday evening, they had sequestered themselves in her condo. Her answering machine kept the world at bay.

At three o'clock in the afternoon, Lawrence stirred. He opened his eyes and she smiled into them. He rolled over on top of her and looked up from a vantage point below her breasts, taking in her hills and hollows.

"Hi there, Lare," she said. Lawrence pulled himself up, planting an elbow beside each of her shoulders. He gazed at the freckles on her chest, playing connect-the-dots with his eyes.

He kissed her. Their eyes were open and the kiss was long. She felt herself rising up to meet him where he was pressing himself against her, coaxing her legs apart.

Once inside, Madalyn sat down. John paced. Finally, he sat down beside her. She could feel his fear.

"Mad." He exhaled the word with what sounded like the fatigue of stress but could as easily have been distaste. "I don't think, I mean, it's just not going to work out with us."

"Pardon?" she said reflexively before she could absorb this piece of information.

"I met someone. But, ah, she really has nothing to do with us. It's me, Mad. I've *changed*. God, this is hard, Jesus. How can I explain?"

She moved to sit sideways on the couch, facing him. She brushed her hair away from her face and smoothed an eyebrow with a finger. She removed a cigarette from the package on the table in front of her and rolled it between her hands.

"I don't get it. What are you saying? Spell it out. Are you telling me you're a complete asshole, or just a partial asshole?" She said this evenly, holding her shock in check on a leash of disbelief with the powerful, serene self-control of the professional victim, absorbing abuse and storing it inside for later, when she could really enjoy it.

She wanted to put her arms around him. To curl up in his lap. To stand before him in the black lace merry widow she had worn to bed on New Year's Eve and watch him melt in the face of such a sight, as he surely would. But instead, she took several large swallows of wine. In the same flash, she noticed that her glass was almost empty, thought of going to the fridge for the bottle, wondered if this would appear too degenerate. She lit her cigarette. How much of the tension woven so securely into her muscles was she able to dispel, how much of the miasma of anxiety oozing out of her was she able to stop up, temporarily, with these things—sex and drugs?

John hadn't said anything further. He was studying the beer can in his hand. She rose, glided through the silence into the kitchen and poured herself another glass. As she reentered the living room, she did not look at him until she was standing in front of the open balcony door, facing him, and had begun to drink.

She was lit from behind, flat shadows masking the look in her eyes. After a minute, she made a sound, a scarcely audible sigh giving birth to a sob.

"Madalyn, I want you to understand. I . . . when I first met you, I thought, I mean, this girl has class. This girl is exciting. This girl is a beauty. And then we started seeing each other and it was so great and I thought . . . well, anyway. But now I know it can't work. Mad."

"When, exactly, did you make this incredible discovery? And how long have you just been going through the motions? What, the last six, eight months?" It was better, she felt, standing while he sat.

"No. I mean, no. I've enjoyed every minute with you, Mad, in a way, but there has been a lot of tension, wouldn't you say? It's because we're too different. But that's not it." He paused. "It's not *you*."

He paused again, and then, elbows on his knees, hands placed in prayer-like fashion over his nose, eyes fixed on some particular point on the coffee table, he said through his fingers, "I find you so damn exciting. I'll probably be thinking of your merry widow when my bride is walking up the aisle." He removed his hands from his face and looked up at her, a cough of laughter escaping from his open-mouthed smile.

As she walked toward him, she saw his face change, fear and chagrin making pathetic his features, scuttling the usually self-confident look in his eyes, colouring his cheeks and neck with a deep embarrassment to which he was not at all well suited.

She sat down. She put her face in her hands. The smoke from her cigarette in the ashtray wafted into her hair. He placed a hand on the back of her neck.

"Mad," he said.

How kaleidoscopic he was. It took her breath away. With admiration.

She wanted to tear herself from his touch. Wasn't that how it was supposed to be done? Anger and recriminations? But she wasn't moving. His fingers felt like those of some disembodied hand. Comforting. Not his.

As if he had pressed a button on her neck, she began to cry. She looked up at him. He removed his hand. She wanted to throw her arms around him, suffocate him with her mouth, feel his fingers in her hair as he held her head to return her emotion so roughly and strongly that she would feel his teeth grate against hers. These thoughts fired up her crying, and she covered her mouth to stifle the sounds of purest frustration. Above her hand her eyes streamed tears, and all her emotions coalesced in her eyes.

He stood and walked away. At the balcony, his back to the room, he raised his arms and gripped the top of the doorframe. His shoulders hunched forward, his head hung down, making a dip across the top of his back. His body blocked out the light.

"I *do* love you," he said.

She heard these words, uttered in a soft croak, and for a brief moment wondered who had said them.

"Oh, good Christ," she said sucking on her cigarette, drying her face with one hand. "Tell me what the hell is really going on."

"I love you, I love you, love you, love you, love you."
Whispers into each other—shoulder, neck chest, stomach—
the message was absorbed. Tina placed a kiss in the palm of
Lawrence's hand. He looked at her, astonished. The body he was
wrapped around was still a source of fresh sexual trauma, even
after almost twenty-four hours of intimate contact, during which
he had revelled in every curve and corner, imprinting her into his
muscular memory.

"Larry," she said, to lighten the look in his eyes that
suggested he was out of his depth.

The first time she had called him Larry, he had had a
surge of queer delight, a sort of rotting succulence of feeling.
His mother was the only other person he knew who ever called
him Larry. His quiet, spiritual mother, with her soothing voice,
so light it skimmed the ear, the merest current of sensation. He
had guarded his full name throughout his life, protecting it from
the deterioration of informality. Larry sounded somehow wrong
coming from anyone other than his mother, from whom it would
always be the sweetest of maternal adorations, murmured into
the soap-foam softness of infant skin. From Tina, the name had
become a benediction, absolving him of the costs of duty.

"Tell me what happened," Madalyn said.

At this rather businesslike invitation, John sat down again, several feet away from her, in the corner of the couch. He bit the inside of his lip for a moment, then smiled. He had that aggravatingly attractive, open-faced look that always got to her. His blue eyes had regained some of their usual sly composure— an orchestrated innocence, the questioning, slightly baffled cheat of a gaze that he always unsheathed during their arguments and that always made her feel as if any explanation was hers to make. Because *he* just didn't get it.

His blond curls, cut short where they passed over his ears and settling into an immobile froth just above the collar of his shirt, glinted in the sunlight, bouncing back into place as he ran his fingers through them. When he smiled, his cheekbones prodded those worldly-looking crow's-feet into bloom around his eyes, and his lips lost their fullness and became brackets of the slightest sexual sneer around his truly perfect teeth.

She was vaguely aware that now she'd have to do battle with his every gesture, with every part of him—the back of his hand below his low-slung watch, the hair peeking out from above the open buttons of his shirt. And his shoulders and arms—as wonderfully developed as they were, the worst part for her was knowing their scent so well. Why all these things could put her at such a disadvantage, she'd never really considered, until now. Unforgivable.

"I've changed, Mad. It's as simple as that. Yes, I did meet someone, and I got that innocent, first-time-you-fall-in-love feeling, but I didn't plan it! And I think it *is* the first time for her."

"Ah." Madalyn sat back, leaning away from him. Through the smoke of her cigarette she contemplated John and what he had just said, and sure enough, on clicked the light, and things were clear and oh, so bright. Her pain cast sharp shadows.

"Let me guess," she said, her words liberally coated in sarcasm. "She's very young. And Daddy's rich."

Much more sickening than the humble "yes" he could have uttered was the prideful smile in his eyes, which she could see him struggling to control.

"But you just said you *love me!*" She swept with what she hoped was drama into the kitchen for the wine.

"I do," he said over the safe distance between them. "And I *will* miss you. Very much." He paused until she came back into the room. "Your moods, your wit, your legs."

"You sound like a bad movie script." She tried rather ineffectually to snarl the words as she set the bottle with an unintentional slam upon the glass tabletop. "What is it with you? Do you think I drink too much? I'm not uptown enough? I have weird friends? I'm not domestic? I'm too old? No trust fund?"

"I said. I just changed." Now it was John's turn to go to the fridge. He crushed his empty beer can and threw it into the sink. The sound startled Madalyn. Her body, rigid with tension, flinched suddenly, and tears jolted from her eyes.

"I hate you," she said, not looking as he reentered the room. But as he approached—she just couldn't help it—she searched his face. To see if her words had hurt. At all. John raised the palm of his free hand, his shoulders shrugged slightly. He walked toward her and set his beer on the coffee table. He relieved her of her glass of wine. He held her face between his hands and, incredibly, she let him. Then she sensed him about to move in for a kiss, and she ran.

She slammed the bedroom door behind her with such force that it scared her stiff and dried her eyes.

She lay on the bed, curled up on her side, frozen.

In the living room, his feet twitching on the edge of the coffee table, beer galloping down his throat, John tried to figure out what to do next. His hidden agenda was exacting a bit of a price from his conscience, it seemed.

Sometime in his early twenties, he had decided it would not do to be single much past thirty. At thirty, he would start to be taken seriously in business and would want to apply himself without distraction. By his late twenties, he had figured, he would have had a chance to complete his education and get his career shit together and then, in the last half of his twenties, he would try to cover as much ground with it as possible. Really spread it around.

In addition, during these last years before the big three-O, he'd decided it would do him good to indulge in a few exciting, colourful, improbable love affairs—something to reassure himself that he'd *lived*, as he watched his bride marching toward him and, even if he wanted one, which he wouldn't by then, there would be no way out.

He would be twenty-nine next month. Time was awastin'.

He filled Madalyn's wine glass yet again. Jeez, she'd had almost two-thirds of the bottle already. He knocked lightly on the bedroom door.

"Mad," he said softly. "Let me in. Please. Maddy. Come on . . . I *am* sorry . . . Think of it this way," he brightened. "Now you'll have something interesting to tell your grandchildren about, warn them away from people like me. Ah, jeez. Mad . . . remember those stories I told you about the black-haired baby who flew around the world, magically picking out hearts to break when she grew up? Well, you've gotta get out there and start breaking! And at least this is an experience, right?"

Nothing he had said thus far had provoked the slightest sound from behind the bedroom door.

"This is the only one I can give you . . . you know I'm right. I'm really an incredibly boring person, I'll be balding in an office tower while you'll be 'off in Paris, in a sports car, with the wind in your hair.' You will . . . let me in, Mad."

On the other side of the door, Madalyn thought, It's the warm wind, you idiot. Hearing John's recitation of her favourite line from Marianne Faithfull's "Ballad of Lucy Jordan," Madalyn felt new tears starting, soft and relaxing. Her theme song, John had called it, because she played it so bloody much, cranked up loud when she was drunk. She felt herself surrendering to the crushingly sweet, premature regret she seemed to have always carried within herself—an old, old familiar sense that she had no power over a fate she so often felt beckoning her, to follow, follow, like the hopeless sailors lured by the Sirens' songs.

She opened the door.

John sat down beside her on the bed as she sat up. He gave her the glass, which she held with both hands. She drank the wine gently and quickly, as if it was medicine.

"More, please," she said, looking up at him with a weak smile, taking the tone of their baby-talk sessions late at night and in the early mornings, when she'd wake up and feel the furnace of his chest against her back and he would draw her hair away from her face and whisper into her ear another of the adventures of the Flying Raven-Haired Baby.

"I'll be back," he said. In the kitchen he opened the second bottle of wine and brought two full glasses back into the bedroom, where Madalyn was now propped up against the pillows of her bed, trying to breathe deeply.

"Cigarette, ma'am?" he said, one eyebrow cocked. He bowed when she said "yes" and went to the living room to retrieve her cigarettes and ashtray.

He sat down again beside her. She lent him a pillow for his back. He lit her cigarette.

"I just feel so sad," she said, moving her head from side to side, as if in pain, crying again. "*I love you.* And I *don't* understand. I *don't!*" Her crying surged. She tried to gulp it down with the wine. John put an arm around her shoulders and pulled her head down onto his chest.

"Don't go. Please don't go . . . I can't stand it." She cried into his yellow linen shirt, leaving dark mascara smudges. He stroked her head, over and over. His hand moved down to caress her back. He curved both his arms around her waist and held her tight.

"I've only known her a few months, Mad. I mean, who knows? I might be moving out to Toronto, anyway—a great opportunity, businesswise, has opened up for me there."

Yeah, like Daddy, Madalyn thought.

"I just thought it was best to end things now. I know I must seem like a jerk. Okay, a real prick. Why don't you yell at me, throw things? Madalyn." He lifted her up to face him. "I

OPHIR

have to do this. It wouldn't be fair to you if I let things go on any longer. I've always had this sort of plan for my life, and . . ."

"And I don't fit," she said, starting to enjoy the almost constant balm of tears, definitely enjoying the shackle of his arms.

"It's not, well, I honestly can't explain. You've got better things coming to you, Madalyn."

"Don't you dare disrespect me," she said.

She sat up, dried her face, took a slow tremble of breath to try and ease the grip of the muscles of her back and ribcage. She reached over John and stubbed out her cigarette in the ashtray on the bedside table.

"One more smoky kiss," she stated, looking into his eyes, her voice getting caught in the strained tendons of her throat. In that moment, she began to imagine John's regret already starting, which he would carry around in his heart forever, she was thinking, beginning to create the rest of the drama as she went, painting his future in her mind, with the thick mix of sorrow and despair and addictive misery that sloshed heavy and rich and smooth as oil in her chest.

And then he did weave his fingers into her hair, and he did kiss her. And it began again. For close to two hours they lost themselves in a kind of ceremony of the flesh, an erotic liturgy without words, which suspended the logic of what had just

193

happened. They carried each other off into another round of the dance of sex.

For Madalyn, sex was the chink in the wall, a gap through which she could see past her inertia, into a place where it was perhaps possible to melt into, and move with, her own will. For Madalyn, the object of the dance was rapture, which means two things: ecstatic delight and the art of transporting a person from one place to another. As it had always been with her, the transport was the thing, the art and act and state of being *in* transit. The destination was enjoyed so fleetingly, it always seemed as if it never really arrived. It must be a chimera. But she had not learned this yet, and so once more, into the breach.

"I'll call you in a couple of days," he said at the door.

"What for?" she asked, stricken for a moment with genuine wonder. Then she recovered her badly battered sarcastic sensibilities. "To see how I'm surviving?" She said this with a small smile as she leaned against the wall by the door, her hands behind her back.

John was silent. He reached out a hand and picked up one of the ends of her sash. He looked at the pink ribbon, rubbed it between a thumb and forefinger. Then, as if finally realizing that he did, in fact, possess the necessary mere ounce of honesty, he looked into her eyes for the long moment she would try many times later to recreate, and said a silent goodbye.

It had taken ages to make dinner. Hungry, but not really feeling like food, high on champagne, disoriented by the skewed schedule of the last day, Tina and Lawrence had shuffled around the kitchen in their bare feet and bathrobes in a kind of slow, fumbling, distracted dance. The pasta pot had boiled over several times when they had not been paying attention—when they had been giggling into each other's terrycloth lapels, holding each other up, talking each other out of just scrapping dinner and heading back to the bedroom.

Looking at Tina, her red head bent over her meal, the sleeves of her bathrobe pushed up past her elbows, watching her eat with the great, healthy appetite of a child who has just come in from play, Lawrence said suddenly, "We should be doing this every day."

"I didn't think I was so hungry," Tina said, seeming to interpret his remark as a sort of light, rhetorical expression of enjoyment. "But I sure was." She nabbed her last shrimp between two fingers, tossed it into her mouth and then, still chewing, took a large swallow of wine and burped. Her eyes smiled at Lawrence above the fist she had placed over her lips, a precautionary gesture meant to catch and muffle any more renegade bubbles of air.

With his fork, Lawrence toyed with strings of linguini, then sat back and just stared at her as she stood up and walked away from her empty plate. In front of the window looking out over the park, she raised her arms above her head, twined her fingers together and stretched. He stood and went to her, wrapping his arms around her, tight and strong and secure, right below her breasts.

"God, I wish we could," he said. At this, he hugged her tighter with one arm, his free hand running over her breasts, then down, lightly, back and forth between her hipbones until she leaned her head back onto his shoulder, wedging it into his neck.

"I'll work on it," he said.

She turned around in his arms.

Hours later, Lawrence lay thinking in the dark, enjoying an exhilarating insomnia he had not experienced since the pre-dawn Christmas mornings of his childhood. He glanced over at Tina, sleeping on her back, her arms up over her head. He savoured the sight of her, the darkness and quiet around them, the secret, suspended perfection of the moment.

He rose from the bed and went to the kitchen for a glass of water. The digital clock on the stove ready eleven forty-five. He wandered slowly through the open, connected rooms. He examined the dinner plates and utensils that still lay on the dining room table as if they were objets d'art, as if the food left on them was drying plaster or paint.

As Lawrence began his quiet pacing, Nihil was dropping in at Monty's. His creative funk of the last six months had yielded few usable ideas—he felt stymied, frustrated, dead-ended. He had decided to treat himself to a few five-dollar martinis. He could afford to eat *or* drink, not both. Just as he was sucking the olive off the toothpick of his second martini, Derek walked up to the bar.

"Christ, Derek, you look terrible!" Nihil blurted.

Derek had always been round and ruddy-cheeked. Nihil had not seen him for some months, and the Derek he now greeted was so thin and sallow, almost decrepit-looking, that Nihil had not recognized him at first. Behind the bar, Deanne, one of the girls who had been at the warehouse party in February, shot Nihil a look. A creepy sort of embarrassment smote the sarcastic smile from his face as he stared back and forth between Derek and Deanne, whose eyes were targeting him with serious but unintelligible instructions. He felt inoculated with a sense of dread. Derek laid a hand on Nihil's shoulder and smiled a sad, benevolent smile as he passed by.

As soon as Derek was out of earshot, placing a call from the telephone at the other end of the bar, Deanne hissed at Nihil, her oxblood lips close to his face. She had a tiny, childish, chalky moon of a face, accentuated by the wound of lips and by an excessive intensity of black eye makeup that rimmed her close-set, washed-blue eyes so darkly it looked as if she had run amok with a thick felt marker during her toilette.

"You going to the Tile Room later?"

"Yeah, thought I might."

"Meet me there at one thirty. At the front bar. I'm off at one. We have to talk."

I am very drunk, Madalyn thought as she danced with herself at one in the morning to the songs on the radio, each of which seemed fraught with meaning. The station was doing a Tina Turner retrospective. Damn right, what *does* love have to do with it? Damn right. She twirled and lurched. She threw a leg high into the air.

She was feeling almost happy. It's over. And I had this perfectly dramatic time. The farewell scene. It was perfect. I enjoyed a spectrum of emotion. She took a swig of John's beer. It was warm. Yes, it had been perfect, perfect, perfect.

But minutes later, when the second chorus of the next song began, Tina Turner's loaded voice tore into her and everything changed.

You're simply the best

You're better than all the rest

Better than anyone

Anyone I've ever met.

A synapse exploded somewhere inside, and Madalyn picked up the phone and punched in his number.

"Are you going to marry her?" she asked, no, demanded of him, in a voice full of self immolating courage.

In the short ensuing silence, imagining the sleeping John as he would have rolled his beautiful body over to pick up the phone, she began to lose her bravado. Now she was afraid.

"Mad? Mad, go to bed. We'll talk later."

"*Are* you going to marry her?"

Silence. The silent yes.

"I see," she said. "Well, *FUCK YOU*, my darling." All of the control she had over her situation went into the crash of the receiver. Hope you go deaf, she thought, her hand still clenched around it. Panic hit, and she shook all over from the inside out. She picked up the phone again.

I've wrecked it. God in heaven, I was so gracious, and now I have just *fucked* it up.

She waited to dial, immobilized with indecision. She tried to organize her thoughts. She went over all he had said, exactly what he had said—"You've got to get out there and start breaking"—and then it dawned on her. He *gave* me away. The realization blindsided her and it hurt, so terribly.

She was in big trouble now. Oh, God. She placed her call.

The telephone in the living room startled Lawrence, who was slumped on the couch, his legs stretched out on the coffee table. He had been floating in a wonderful Valiumesque sort of relaxation, almost asleep. The machine picked up the call after three rings. Lawrence listened as the message began.

"Tina? It's Mad. Sorry to call so late. I know this is your 'big' weekend. I'm sorry, but I really need to talk to you. I'm in big trouble, I, please call me, I really need to talk to you *tonight*, I'm in big trouble . . . John, um, well . . . he . . ."

There was an implosive silence, then Lawrence heard the sob.

"Madalyn?" he said, picking up. "It's Lawrence. Hi. I'll get Tina hold on . . . no, Madalyn, it is more than okay.


It took Nihil until about two that morning to make contact with Deanne at the Tile Room. Because of the decibel level, and because the club would be closing in half an hour, Deanne suggested they go out the fire exit at the back and talk in the alley.

"It's about Derek," Deanne said, lighting a cigarette. She took several long drags and then inspected the tip to make sure it was well fired up. She exhaled long—her pursed lips moving up and down as if she were playing an invisible flute—she flicked the filter with her thumb, she cleared her throat, she fluffed her spiky black bangs, all with maddening patience. Nihil waited, fragments of insight and past observances toying cruelly with the worst-case-scenario gut feeling that had begun at Monty's.

"And your brother," she finally said.

"What? What? What about Derek and my brother?"

"Well." Deanne's tone became intimately conspiratorial. She clutched at Nihil's arm with a small, stubby hand—nails bitten down—that wore a fingerless black fishnet glove.

"You know that month your brother was here? Well, he spent a lot of time with Derek. *A lot.* That night, after the party at the warehouse, 'member? Do you know what time Peter got back to your place?"

"Yeah," Nihil said, remembering the flash of pinky blue sky when he'd opened his eyes to see Peter tiptoeing through the door of the loft.

"Well, Peter was the last one to leave Derek's party. I mean, we all left, and Peter was still there. Anyway, and then for the rest of the month, Peter came in at least like three times a week to the restaurant, in the morning when we were setting up."

And when I was sleeping, Nihil thought, irresponsible asshole that I am.

"Yeah, I know," he said. Peter had told him he'd made friends with the kids at Monty's. He had also told him he'd spent some time getting lost in various Vancouver neighbourhoods, seeing if he'd like to live in one, and checking out the Safeways, to see which one he might like to transfer to if he decided to move to the coast.

"Anyway," Deanne continued. Her inability to quickly get to a point, any point, was acutely maddening to Nihil he had to cut her. "Derek and Peter would go out in the afternoon lots of times, as soon as lunch was happening. We don't know where they went, or anything. But they seemed to be talking serious shit, I mean, I don't know what, but it seemed serious, cuz sometimes we'd see them out the windows sort of get into an intense conversation as soon as they left the restaurant, and Derek would sometimes put his hand on Peter's shoulder and stuff."

"And?"

"Well, what we feel you should know," Deanne said, with an earnest self-confidence that made Nihil almost want to laugh, kindly, "is that Derek has AIDS."

An instant fever of condensation dampened Nihil's sides, the back of his neck, his forehead. His heart shot against the wall of his chest, as if trying to get out. As it fell back into place, the sling of fear quivered with reverberations, which he felt in his stomach and through the length of his bowels.

Since Nihil wasn't saying anything, was only staring hard at her, Deanne continued, as if feeling some of the vulnerability of the messenger who should not be shot.

"Derek told us, when he got sick at the end of March. I mean, he's had it for like three years. The virus. But he wasn't sick before. He got pneumonia and some other stuff in March, and he was in the hospital for a month. Anyway, I'm not *saying* anything. I just think you should know. Because of Peter. Not that anything happened. But it could have. Not that Derek would have like done anything and deliberately not told Peter. But we have no way of knowing."

With the last sentence, her voice recovered some of the social-worker tone she had taken at first. "Peter didn't seem too experienced, y'know, and so we thought we should tell you about Derek, just so, y'know, maybe you could tell Peter."

Nihil opened the back door of the club, which they had kept wedged open with a board, and deposited Deanne inside.

"Have you got a way home?" he asked.

"Yeah, the door guy, he's a friend, he drives me if I want."

"Perfect," Nihil said. He squeezed Deanne's hand once, tightly and quickly, then closed the door.

Four a.m.

Tina lay curled against Lawrence's chest. The sheet covering them conformed to the single shape of both bodies, like a shell. They slept.

Madalyn was wrapped in a ball on the top of her dreaded bed, finally calmed by Tina's reassurances that she would be over the next day, and by the last of the wine. Stuffed and stuck like dry packing paper, in her head, her muscles, and in all the empty places of her heart, sleep held her fast.

Anguish, like an animal, stalked through Nihil, who sat shivering under a blanket on his bristled couch. The soft relief of sleep would not dare approach, and his eyes grew dry from fatigue and alcohol. Fear's grip, like fingers reaching down over his forehead and hooking into his lids, would surely keep his eyes open forever.

# Chapter Seven

It had been three weeks. Of crying and drinking, drinking and crying.

"It's been three weeks," Madalyn said, crying and drinking, "to the day."

She said this to Tina, who sat at the other end of the couch. Over the expanse of whiteness between them, they had been duplicating, once again, the same conversation. This post-breakup therapy was becoming a circular thing. And it was losing its force, its power to comfort, with repetition. They had been over and over the breakup. How Madalyn hadn't seen it coming. Why Madalyn hadn't seen it coming. Why Madalyn shouldn't have been expected to see it coming. Why Madalyn couldn't have been expected to see it coming. How Madalyn still felt so in love.

Concentrating on not dropping ash onto any of the creamy cleanliness of Tina's living room kept Madalyn focused, provided a point around which to shape her sloppily flaking grief, the same way she was carving the ash of her cigarette into a point against the side of a big glass ashtray.

Over the past three weeks, Madalyn had done a lot of talking. Tina had done a lot of listening. And watching. She had watched her friend repeatedly impale herself on this love of hers. Now Tina felt she could stand it no longer. She was becoming irritated by the spectacle, by her friend's embarrassingly low self-esteem, her repeated self-flagellation. Madalyn's spinelessness made her angry.

Tina decided to offer something more compelling, more shocking, perhaps more constructive than the twin sets of sympathy she had been doling out to her friend's impoverished heart. She started off slowly, with something relatively mild but conclusive, something she had said before, with which Madalyn had disagreed.

"I'll tell you again what I think of him," she began. "The man's an ass, and he cannot recognize something good when it's staring him in the face."

Her tone was not kind. "Why can't you see that?" she snapped. "He *doesn't* think you're too good for him. He's *not* afraid of an unconventional life. He's just a taker. He takes from everyone, anyone, it doesn't matter. As long as he gets something out of it. Some thrill. Some excitement. He cannot recognize something good when he sees it, because he's under the impression that he is as good as it gets."

She watched Madalyn retreating, watched a look of hurt come over her face as she cuddled herself deeper into her corner of the couch and covered her eyes with her hand.

"Why can't you see that?" Tina repeated, running her scalpel again over the spot where Madalyn bled. Her friend's condition was pitiful, in need of an aggressive protocol for healing to begin.

"He's a selfish, arrogant, dangerous, charming creep. He can't recognize something good when he sees it. Can't you understand? He's incapable. He's a waste of time."

"You mean, he has no concept of value?" Madalyn asked, jolted by a sudden excitement. Here was a flash of insight to which she might cling! She leaned forward toward Tina, drawing deeply on her cigarette. She flicked her hand away from her face, a movement reminiscent of her old dramatic style. Ash fell onto the carpet.

"Yes!" Tina said, refilling their glasses with more champagne, their drug of choice for these sessions.

"No concept of value," Madalyn repeated.

"Right. So, if you'll excuse my language, fuck 'im." Tina raised her glass in a toast.

"I'd love to," Madalyn said, her longing flaring up again like an oxygenated fire, refracted for a moment through this ray of weak humour.

"Madalyn." Tina's voice curved upward in warning.

"Oh, alright, fuck 'im." Madalyn knocked her glass against Tina's with enough vigour to slop wine over their hands.

"The way to really fuck him is by fucking someone else," Tina said. She hated to use such language, really. But she was herself quite drunk, and these kinds of words seemed to work on Madalyn. So she got into it. The more she practiced with the F-word, the more her inner blush diminished.

"Fuck the hell out of him!" Tina exclaimed. "Find someone far better looking. Rich. More high profile than the goddamn sleazeball. I'll make sure he knows about it, trust me."

"Yes! Flaunt it in front of his face! I just have to find the perfect guy, the guy John wants to be, the guy he thinks he is but isn't, and just flaunt the fuck out of him!" Madalyn was gagging on giggles, the first jets of relief escaping from the punctured package of her pain.

"And fuck 'im if he can't take a joke," Tina said. *This*, she'd always wanted to say this. She'd learned the line from John. It was one of his favourites—his all-purpose remedy for any slight or failure in business or office politics. "Fuck 'em if they can't take a joke," he'd often say to Tina during their frequent tête-à-têtes in her office. The line served to refinish his corroded ego.

John had made that very statement to Barry Klammer on a Friday afternoon two weeks earlier, just before he had jumped on the three p.m. flight to Toronto to celebrate his birthday with Monica.

"I'm gonna pull out in stages over the next few weeks," Barry had said of the Arizona condo deal. "You didn't hear it from me," he had drilled into John, whom he had run into at the corner of Howe and Pender. He'd pulled John into a doorway, away from the lunch-hour crowds.

"You got that?" Barry said, his tobacco breath assailing John's nostrils. John looked closely at Barry. He caught the intensity in his voice and noticed how the red veins on Barry's nose and cheeks seemed to disappear into the flush of his face as he continued to speak under the cover of noise from the street.

"You did *not* hear it from me. But I'm telling you."

What he told John was the gist of what a mole of his at the Securities Commission had related to him the previous Sunday, over glasses of icy liquor on Barry's concrete slab of a patio, which stuck out like a tongue into the waters of Barry's personal stretch of ocean, which lapped at the front three hundred feet of the Klammer property.

The Commission was sending the Arizona Offering Memorandum over to Revenue Canada for scrutiny. Some overzealous compliance officer had questioned the legitimacy of the tax structure under which the units had been offered.

"If Revenue Canada feels like getting tight-assed enough, they'll freeze the thing," Barry said as he flipped the lid on a pack of Players and drew out a cigarette on which he began to chew. Disgusting habit, John thought to himself. "And I don't have to tell you that they're already watching the market," Barry continued. "I bought in a variety of vehicles. And like I said, I'm pulling out now, easing out real smooth. You're not invested too heavily, isn't that right? So for a small fish like you to sell, they won't notice. The market's great right now . . . yeah, good, you've been keeping tabs . . . so that's a good enough excuse. But do not wait."

"And I don't have to tell you that if this information gets out to too many of the investors, we'll all sink heavily into the shit. So I'm telling you, and I've told Jerome, but that's it. For some reason, he's hanging tight, for now. But he's watching the situation. I don't have to tell you what happens if the thing freezes up," Barry continued, then enlightened John anyway. "The banks down south will be after all of us for the payments, and if the units are off the market, we're all fucking stuck picking up the tab."

John's mind worked as Barry spoke. It worked over his fears for his own investment. It worked over the ethical dilemma, which, theoretically, he guessed he might be in, vis-à-vis, say, Lawrence, a colleague to whom he was close enough to warrant such a dilemma. His mind worked over these things—and it soon came up with some answers that felt pretty good.

It was a legitimate deal, available to anyone through their local broker. All legal. But the information to which he was being made privy was utterly illegal. However, if he himself got out, and if he kept this information to himself, he could save himself and, like Barry said, he wouldn't be responsible for upsetting the market, drawing attention to increasing divestment activity, which would be a sure thing if he told any of the other investors, like Lawrence. They were all in a straight deal. If it got held up by some inquiry, well, that was par for the course, part of the gamble. He'd seen it before. The fact that if the deal was frozen and people like Lawrence would be left holding the bag, would very likely lose all of their original investments to the banks, well, that's business for you.

"I didn't hear a thing," John said to Barry. "I decided to pull out because I determined it was probably the height of the market for the product, and I could realize twice as much as I put in." He recited this to Barry, who immediately recognized it as a practice speech for use in the future, if necessary.

Barry smiled and clapped John on the shoulder. "Atta boy."

"Fuck 'em if they can't take a joke," John said, his face flushing slightly. "Thank you. It's been very nice talking with you, Mr. Klammer," he added out of respect for the more senior slime.

The two men parted company. John felt good. Barry felt good. Each had made a new friend.

Lawrence was excited as he drove over the bridge to work. It was a Friday morning, and another long weekend was coming up—July first. Another long weekend with Tina. He glanced away from the car ahead of him for a moment, his gaze sweeping down over the side of the bridge to the glinting water, the white boats, the creamed forget-me-not sky that fell to the distant western horizon like a kitchen curtain grazing a windowsill, prettily muting the fresh-scrubbed sunlight that shone into Lawrence's morning.

As he drove onto the causeway, which cut through the park, he was thankful for some time alone to review and organize all he had to tell Tina that evening.

Last week he had received the latest reports on Arizona, which outlined both the pre-selling of the condominiums and sales of the partnership units. The units continued to do well, were pumping capital into the development like clockwork. And the condos themselves were being snapped up at a rather brisk pace. But Lawrence had noted a slight tapering on the product side of things and, given that he'd already doubled his investment, he had decided to pull out in a couple of weeks. He'd been smart to wait. If the product market was topping out, well, it wasn't particularly discernible, but he was the cautious type and had made a very decent percentage. Just about time to cash in.

Two hundred thousand dollars, give or take. In Tina's name. That's where he'd put it before he started up discussions with Susan, discussions that were going to come straight out of the blue, for her. Boy. He wondered how she would react. Anger? Tears? Or the cold silence she was so good at, and which was so effectively alienating. He prayed they'd be able to keep things civilized, for the sake of the kids. He *had* to make sure his children did more than just survive this divorce. He had convinced himself they would love Tina as much as he did.

He felt, as always, the pull she possessed. He felt it all the time. It was as if her skin were magnetized in a special way, coded just for him. It was how he knew it was the real thing. How else were you supposed to tell? He often imagined himself lying with her, his arm curled around her head, protectively, sheltering her, keeping her.

As he pulled into the underground parking lot, was swallowed by the hole in the paved-over downtown core, as he parked his car in his very own spot and rose twenty-five storeys into the air, as he left the Birk & Samuels receptionist all shaken up by the unexpected personal charm of his good-morning smile, as he settled himself into his box in the sky, surrounded for blocks by thousands of other such boxes, his well-planned fate was being quietly amended.

In another tower, on a lower floor, in a shabbier office, a Revenue Canada clerk was filling out the courier forms to dispatch the Order to the Commission—to freeze all trading, pending an investigation.

Madalyn lay on her stomach in the middle of the living room rug. She turned her face to one side and stared down a dustball, as fragile and dry as a tumbleweed waiting for a desert wind to pick it up and toss it away. It was Sunday evening, the worst time to be single and alone. She'd gone for a walk on the seawall that afternoon, what she thought might be a therapeutic foray into the land of the living. The world had passed her by like a kind of slick, surreal film. Her loneliness and angst had only been exacerbated by the deafening sunlight, which seemed to fill her ears and shoot into her body, where it decimated everything except the hard lump at her centre, which felt as heavy as lead. Her body around it felt dried up and weightless. The useless, happy activity of the people around her began to create a psychic claustrophobia, which soon became unbearable.

After an hour or so, she returned home to the relief of her cigarettes and wine. She pulled the curtains shut, wanting to ground herself in darkness, but light still managed to permeate the room. She began to drink.

She watched a movie about teenage love and dreams fulfilled. *Pretty in Pink*, it was called. The movie saddened her dangerously, the hope and promise of a beautiful sixteen-year-old, with her life ahead of her, who will rise from poverty, you could tell, by sheer force of talent, and will get whichever guy she wants—the wacky and sweet and loyal poor guy, or the brave and sensitive rich one.

The wine began to numb and soothe, something it did so well. She was nursing yet another glass, which was nursing her, coaxing out the tears. When they began, she felt which way each one ran down her face. She got up and went into the bathroom to look in the mirror, auditioning her tears. That one would make a perfect close-up shot, she thought, a big drop rolling down the middle of her cheek and actually falling off her face, not veering to the centre and thinning out as it rounded the curve of her nostril.

She went back to her wine. She laughed out loud when she found herself regretting that now she probably wouldn't be running into Mr. Stoller anymore. Maybe this means I'm getting over it, she thought. Then her whole face puckered and the tears ran together, creating a glossy finish all over her face; she smeared the tears into her makeup with a Kleenex. Don't call us.

On Monday morning, it rained. Madalyn was running late and missed the bus she liked to catch because it was usually only moderately full. Instead, she barely made the next one, packed with denizens of daytime downtown—showered, coiffed, resigned and grim, they would not "move to the back of the bus" but stubbornly hunched together near the front, in clumps of misery, hung onto the poles and waited for it to be over.

A fellow standee's umbrella dribbled onto Madalyn's ankle. Her patent leather was being nicked and marred beyond repair, she could feel it. She was wedged between a perspiring fat lady and a short, middle-aged man in a bowling-league jacket, whose baseball cap she was forced to read for the duration of her ride: "I snatch kisses and vice versa." Madalyn interpreted the resentful look in his eyes as an admission that no one had ever given him a chance to do either. She felt contempt. She noticed a hair growing out of a mole on the fat lady's face. She felt nauseous. She wanted to slap everyone. They *could* help it, being so stupid and unattractive.

When she finally got off the bus, the digital clock on the outside of the Air Canada building gladly repeated itself for her: 9:10, 9:10, 9:10. As she rushed to the intersection to cross the street, her light turned yellow. An older, boxy grey BMW, a car that looked just like John's, sailed through the light, turning it red.

Madalyn and Tina met for lunch that day. Tina had called; there was something she needed to discuss, quite urgently. Madalyn was cheered by the prospect of one of their Bloody Mary lunches at the Hyatt.

"I knew it," Tina whispered heavily, leaning toward Madalyn as she sat down across from her. "Lawrence wants to get a divorce."

"Oh my God," Madalyn said, setting down her glass, which was rimmed with seasoned salt. She licked her lips and pulled in her chair. "My God," she repeated, her voice bundled up into a squeal.

"It's not funny," Tina said.

"No, of course not."

Tina settled herself. Her blouse was so white it glowed like phosphorous in the weak, wet light coming through the windows. And her hair looked unnaturally shiny, appearing to Madalyn to be curlier than usual, although she knew it wasn't—the gleaming, marmalade coils seemed to bounce thickly with pent-up energy.

"Um, a Bloody Mary, please, for me also." Tina smiled warmly at the waitress. "Thank you."

Madalyn waited until the waitress was out of earshot. And she waited for Tina to begin talking again. Tina's news was still thudding through the middle of Madalyn's body, creating dull, painful vibrations, which made her want to curl up into a ball.

"It's too *real*," Tina said. Her eyes, so shiny and gaudily green, flashed with fierce delight. She clasped her hands and leaned across the table toward Madalyn, her head ducked down. "You know?"

"I know. It's one thing to think about it, and it's another when it actually happens, I guess." Madalyn paused. Flatly she asked, "Um, do you want to see the lunch menu?"

"No. Not right now. This could be a strictly liquid affair."

"Are you scared?"

"No, what do you mean? What's to be afraid of?" Madalyn was hurt by the tone of Tina's voice, felt as if she were being treated like a child. Who wouldn't be at least a little afraid of being involved in something of this magnitude? Something this adult?

"Um, well, I just meant what could happen if he goes through with it, you know, lawyers, court battles, gossip and scandal. There could be some major fallout. Like you said, it's pretty real."

"I just want things to slow down," Tina said.

How many times had Madalyn heard *this* before—some poor guy wanting to finalize things with Tina, to commit, and Tina, of course, never wanting to, and asking Madalyn's advice, as if she needed it, on how to let him down gently.

"So, um, are you asking for my advice?" Madalyn asked on cue, feeling something like a growing kinship with Lawrence, trying to stop her eyes from tearing up, thinking she was probably just being overly sensitive.

"Well, yes. What am I going to do? I'm not prepared for this dumping-of-the-wife scenario. I'm not prepared to inherit three kids every weekend. I never wanted *reality* in this relationship!" Tina laughed.

"Aren't you thrilled that he wants to be with you? Don't you find the prospect of a normal relationship attractive? Don't you wish you could call him whenever you want? Don't you miss him? Don't you want to be with him?" Quietly, her voice thin with resignation, Madalyn let it fly. As much as she dared.

"I *am* with him," Tina drawled in her mother's tumescent, fatally effective southern tones that never missed their mark. If voices were scented, Tina's and her mother's would have enveloped the listener with the drug-like perfume of an evening garden, thick with accumulated humidity and jam-packed with rich and poisonous blooms. I *am* with him, Madalyn heard. It was a statement of fact, there being, as usual, no one to convince.

"Two exhausting times a week," Tina continued. "What more could I want? And we talk every day. During the week, anyway, and most of the time on the weekends, he manages to get away and call me. Or I call him on his cell. I haven't been missing him. And to tell you the truth, I *love* the secrecy."

"You mean, normalcy could spell the death of love?"

Tina's drink arrived. She took several sips. "Precisely."

"I was kidding," Madalyn said, looking at her friend with a mixture of jealousy and fear. How did she manage it? Her lack of need?

"I enjoy having a love affair with the man. I don't necessarily want to *marry* him."

"Well, what did you say?"

"Not much. He was just so excited. He said he wanted to ask Susan for a divorce so that we could be together, that I was what he had been looking for so long, that I was what he needed and, y'know, on and on."

Tina's face had a look to it that Madalyn recognized—the same look she always had when discussing Lawrence, as if her enjoyment of him was a chocolate melting in her mouth, or some emotion felt only by the muscles of her face as they moved through a sequence of expressions and controlled pleasure. And it was obviously not a guilty sort of pleasure.

"It was so cute. Basically, I told him to wait. To think it over. I said we should give it a few more months, to see how he feels then."

"Or do you mean to see how you feel?"

"Well, is that so terrible? I have no particular desire to change the relationship at this point, or to be married at this point in my life. I enjoy the sex," Tina said with such matter-of-fact truthfulness that Madalyn slipped even further into Lawrence's camp.

"If it were me," Madalyn said, "say, in my former situation, can't you just see me jumping at the chance? Can't you just see me? Poor, desperate Madalyn. If some guy asks me, how could I help but say yes?" She felt the hurt Tina had inflicted deepening as she nurtured it with her own perverse expressions of self-pity. "Except that, well, I feel I haven't *done* anything with my life yet. Haven't got anything to show for myself. Y'know? Like I need to accomplish something before I get married."

"Marriage as a goal?" Tina asked.

"More like a prize."

"Oh."

It was frozen and there was no way out. By Monday evening, Lawrence's joyful excitement of the previous Friday had turned to fear. Tina wasn't sure! And he was stuck in the deal. He was out of pocket a hundred grand, including the mortgage, and bloody well could not get his hands on the hundred he'd made! His broker said there was no telling how long the inquiry would take, and who knew what was going to happen to the product market in that time? And jeez, Lawrence was thinking during dinner that night, every day that goes by, I'm losing, the partnership is paying, every single day. God, what a mess. Maybe in a few months, things will be back on track. And maybe Tina will be sure by then. Why isn't she sure now? *He* was sure, so completely.

She had really kicked the proverbial chair out from under him on the weekend. It had taken his breath away. But she'd explained herself so sweetly—that she didn't want him making any rash decisions, that if it was right, then he would feel the same way in three months. It had been hard to argue with her logic. But for the remainder of the weekend, subtle doubt had evaporated some of the elation he always felt when he was with her—a balloon gone ever so slightly soft, imperceptibly wrinkling. A germ of fear had begun to swim through his blood.

He already felt drained by the effort of maintaining the status quo in his home life. Three more months would be almost too much to bear. He quailed at the thought of the three-week family holiday coming up in August. He'd dreamt of being out of the house by then, of maybe taking the kids to California, or somewhere, for half that time, to help ease the transition for them.

Dinner was almost over, and Susan was repeating herself for the umpteenth time.

"I *said*, are you still going to be able to take next Friday afternoon? We were going to get away early. Are you still able to do it?" She pressed her husband, then paused, turning to acknowledge her son's quiet efforts to get her attention.

"Yes, Michael, you may be excused."

Michael got up from his place at the dining room table and went to stand beside his father.

"Dad? Dad?"

"Yes, Michael, what is it?"

"Is tonight okay to help me with that social studies project? Remember? The Constitution?"

"Right. Um, okay, you go up and get started. I'll be along soon." Lawrence tried to focus on his son, who had inherited his dark eyes in which, lately, Lawrence had often imagined he'd glimpsed a heartbreaking sort of fearful reproach.

Marisa, seven, and Megan, five, had their pale little heads together. They were sharing some secret. Lawrence looked over at his daughters, making a conscious effort to get his mind back into the family dinner scene. He hadn't made much of a conversational contribution that night, and now dinner was over.

"What are you two monkeys up to?" he asked.

"Nothing!" they said in unison, turning up their pink-cheeked faces to look at their adored father. The giggling resumed at a pitched volume.

"You two may be excused also," Susan said. "Dishes, Michael!" she called. "And you too," she said, getting up to close the door to the kitchen behind the girls, leaving herself alone with Lawrence, who had begun to leaf through his ever-present *Time*.

"Are you going to read through your coffee, as usual?" Susan asked.

"I don't have to," Lawrence answered, glancing up. He set the magazine aside, pulled himself up to the table and took a sip from his My Dad's the Greatest mug.

"The Swansons next door on the island are selling. Lorraine confided in me that they've run into some trouble. They're devastated about having to sell, and she said now is certainly not the time. Apparently the market for recreational property on the islands is really abysmal these days."

Lawrence did not trust himself to say anything, was acutely aware that his heart had begun to thump monstrously in his chest. He took another sip of coffee.

"Hmmm," he said from behind his mug.

"Well, it's really too bad, isn't it?" she prodded, looking intently at her husband. She fluffed her bangs with the tips of her fingers. Lawrence looked back at her, focusing on the bump on her longish, delicate nose, which was sunburnt and shiny.

"Mmm, yes, really too bad."

"They've been there since long before we bought. Gosh, I think they've had their place for over fifteen years. I hate to see them go. I feel so badly for them."

"Hmm," he said again, draining the last of his coffee. "Think I'll have a little more." He rose in the direction of the kitchen.

"I'll get it. I'd like to talk to you, without an audience."

Lawrence heard her in the kitchen, telling the kids they were doing a great job, but that she'd finish up. They could get some fresh air for a while, and she'd call Michael when his dad was free. She returned to the dining room with the pot of coffee.

"I hope last weekend will be the last one you'll have to miss on the island this summer," she said. "It's a lot of work for me, keeping tabs on the kids the whole time. And of course your mum and dad will want you to be there on the Labour Day weekend when they're here. I trust there are no problems with August."

"No. No. We're all set." Lawrence always took the last three weeks of August for the family summer holiday. For seven years now, they had spent most of this time at the house in the islands. Earlier that year, they had again discussed driving across the country with the kids, but Lawrence had persuaded Susan to hold off on the trip for another year.

"It's just that none of us have seen much of you for quite some time," Susan said. "Is this going to become a permanent condition?"

For the past six months, there had been a number of sarcastic remarks, which Lawrence had appeared to ignore, and long silences, during which he had struggled to feel comfortable, but no direct questions, which he had been dreading. He looked closely at Susan, trying not to be obvious in his scrutiny. Did she suspect, or what?

"It's been a particularly busy year. The Stackhouse people especially are shoveling work our way. I can hardly turn it down."

"Maybe you should, sometimes. You do have other things in your life. You have a family. Children. A wife. Remember?"

"Of course I remember," he said overzealously. "Why do you think I work the way I work? So we won't have to go the way of the Swansons." The sharpness of his voice brought a flush to her face. Guilt surged through him. He softened.

"Is there anything else you'd like to discuss?" he asked with great care, playing his voice with the lightest possible touch, leaning forward on his elbows, trying to alleviate the coldness between them with a look of concern.

"I wouldn't call this much of a discussion," she shot back, her arms crossed over her chest.

Whoa, Lawrence thought. No luck with the soft sell.

"Well, I would." He gave up. "I'd better get to Michael. Great supper." He smiled and rose from his chair. "Think I'll change first," he added, beginning to untuck his shirt from his suit pants. He turned away to leave the room.

"Well, I'm not finished!"

Her voice was shaking. The word "screech" popped into his mind, unbidden. He turned around. Still seated, she had a hand planted on either side of the table, as if she was about to stand and bring a meeting to order. Her nose looked even brighter. His guilt, and the absolute need to conceal it, wrapped themselves around each other in his gut.

"Can this wait until later this evening?" he asked evenly.

"No. It cannot. Sit down, Lawrence, please. I am quite desperate to get through to you."

Down he sat, lounging in his chair, one arm hooked over the back. He waited.

"It's about neglect," Susan said. Her voice still sounded strained, and he could also hear the beginnings of hoarseness, which meant, probably, that she had begun to cry, dryly.

"What a typical wifey thing to say! But it's true. I never see you, I feel like we have some sort of business arrangement, our sex life is so clichéd, it's almost funny. Saturday nights! And then you fall asleep! Never in the mornings anymore."

"And I get the feeling it's all you can do to sleep in the same bed with me, that you can't wait to get out. That's the worst of it, in a way, but I miss you, Lawrence, not there, but all the time! You're hardly ever home for dinner. You're out so late so often, supposedly on 'business,' but I really have to wonder."

She paused, searching his face, which he was keeping straight, clean, unresponsive.

"I certainly don't begrudge you," she continued, "your one night out a week, your squash night, but you're here for dinner on Friday evenings, and that's usually it. I mean, we are truly blessed if we get to see you any other weeknight. And on the weekends, I know you try to spend time with the kids, but what about me? We haven't been out together for months and months. I can't remember the last time . . . I mean just the two of us. I feel like I'm living out some magazine article. I really do. It is just so suburban . . . so typical," she finished, sounding tired.

She looks tired too, Lawrence thought, noticing the hollows under her eyes. They were almost blue. Against her sunburnt cheeks they made her look pretty, he realized. Pretty and fragile. The way she had looked when they used to make eye contact, late in the evenings, in the library at university. He had, back then, felt like taking her home, feeding her, putting her to bed, tucking her in.

"What do you want me to say?" he asked, scrambling for ideas. He should have rehearsed this kind of thing better, in his head. But then he had been hoping to skip this part. "My work is very distracting. Maybe that's it." Lame, he thought, my God, how dangerously lame.

"Daddy!" It was Megan, shrieking from the front door. Lawrence sprang out of his chair and went to her.

"Daddy, can we get ice cream from Dicki Dee?"

"Mum?" Lawrence turned to Susan.

"Alright. Yes. You had fruit for dessert, so it's okay."

"I wonder if I've got enough money. Do you think I do?" he asked, teasing his daughter by jingling the change in his pocket.

"Daddy!" Megan squealed, hanging onto his arm. "You have money, Daddy. I can hear it. *Daddy*," she admonished as he continued to tease.

When his daughter had left, slamming the door with the remarkable, thoughtless strength of small children, Lawrence turned back to Susan.

"I'll see what I can do," he said. "About being here more. We've got the holiday coming up, and I'll be on the island, so I won't be able to escape, right? I guess we have been having a bit of a rough patch. And I guess I haven't been paying attention. Give me some time, okay? Um . . . just give it a little time, okay?" He smiled at her. And he willed himself to look directly into her eyes and not be the first to look away.

She did not say anything further. She raised a hand and waved it backward as if to dismiss him. She did not look particularly angry, and this surprised Lawrence. He felt guilty about his relief.

"I'm going to go change, okay?"

She nodded her head, a gesture he interpreted as a signal that he'd bought himself some peace and some time. When he left the room, she retrieved a cigarette from the package she kept in a drawer in the buffet. She rarely smoked. But now it was the only thing she could think of to do. Something mindless and soothing and somehow depressing in its basic uselessness.

"Where have you been?" Madalyn asked Nihil over the phone. "I've been calling you for weeks."

"Had to go up to Prince George. A family matter. But I'm back. What's up with you?"

"What's down is more like it. Let's get together and drink."

Nihil suggested tequila on the Asphalt Patio. He said he'd spring for it if Madalyn would bring the limes. When he answered his door, the first thing she said was, "Your roots are showing!"

"Yeah, I know," he said, running a hand over the inch and a half of hair he now had. Dark roots were indeed evident. "Growing it out."

Nihil had spread towels over two rusted garden loungers. Between them, on the tar-papered roof, he had set the tequila, a cooler of beer, a shaker of salt, a plate and an X-Acto knife for the limes, and two glasses. They settled themselves on the chairs and each cracked open a beer.

Madalyn kicked off her sandals and stretched out her legs, past the towel on which she sat onto the plastic webbing of the lawn chair. She looked out over the rooftop, past the tangle of telephone wires, past the rotting railway track, to the harbour. She watched a seagull, plump and white, dive against the backdrop of a stalk of blackened pilings, turn on its wings, rise again and disappear into the hot, flat sun. She turned her head to look at Nihil.

"So," she said.

"So." Nihil looked down through his sunglasses at the beer can in his hands. She felt tears scratching at her eyes behind her own dark glasses. She had expected him to have picked up on what she had said over the phone—"What's down is more like it"—and to have put his usual charming and open-hearted self at her disposal. She had expected him to draw her out, to gently grill her, it wouldn't have taken much, until her sad little tale would begin to pour itself out. Now that she was with him, she felt, frankly, a little stunned by his closed-off manner. She needed him. Where was he?

"Are you alright?" she asked.

"My brother has AIDS."

"Oh my God!"

She sat up straight and drew her legs around to the side of the chair. His words had freeze-dried her thoughts, she had responded automatically, she did not have a clue what to say, what to do. She took off her glasses and reached over to touch his arm.

"Nihil, talk to me, my God, I am *so* sorry. Tell me what happened. I'm so sorry."

Like a machine, its gears grinding slowly through sawdust, he told her about Peter. About that night at Monty's, and the Tile Room, about Derek and Deanne. About assuming the worst. About assuming the worst about Derek. About the lonely, hot and horrifying bus ride up to Prince George the next day. About his mother being so surprised and delighted to see him, about his father's usual gruff and critical questions.

He told her about taking Peter out for some beers to a tavern on the edge of town. About how they had talked and what they had talked about. About how Peter, with his clear, young voice and his eyes, in which hope threatened to swallow up devastation, had blasted away so many of Nihil's assumptions and had left his cynical, pompous ideas about life smouldering on the floor.

"Pete didn't get it from Derek," he said. He sounded disgusted. "It happened in Prince George over a year ago. It was a one-time thing. The relationship. He said it just happened. He met this guy. He said the guy was real nice. *NICE!* They got to be friends. The guy was gay. Pete tried it out. End of story."

Nihil poured beer down his throat. Madalyn did not dare say a thing. Nihil sounded as if his voice was coasting on the edge of a razor.

"How could I have been so *fucking* in the dark?!" Nihil paused for another long guzzle. "Pete went and got tested. Because this guy had just been sort of passing through, and Pete got scared about what he had done. I mean, he had a girlfriend. So he went and got tested. And it turned out fucking positive."

Madalyn was still sitting up straight on the edge of the chair, staring at Nihil, who had yet to turn and face her.

"Um, his girlfriend . . ."

"She's fine. She's fine, thank God. And get this." Now he turned to face Madalyn. She watched his lips moving below his sunglasses. She could barely hear his words over the roar in her ears. The sun was too loud again. "She's still with him. She's standing by him. She's the only other person who knows, besides me. Peter's not sick. He's just positive."

Nihil's words had begun to flow, in viscous spasms, his guilt and pain falling away from his insides in chunks, as he confessed himself for the first time. "And Derek wasn't after him. Peter came down to Vancouver to check out the AIDS organizations. To see if there was more information, better doctors, more or better support systems down here, like if he thought he needed them sometime, or something. And Derek was fucking wonderful, he said. He said he found himself telling Derek, that night after the party when everyone else had left. He said he was so fucking happy, so fucking happy to have found someone else who was in the same boat, who knew the ropes. But why didn't he come to *me?* Why didn't he tell me? Why did he fucking have to *experiment?* Why did he fucking have to experiment with *that* guy? I am such a royal fuck-up, it's sickening."

He sat up abruptly and leaned down over the space between the two chairs. He unscrewed the top of the brand-new bottle of tequila and poured a large inch into a glass.

"Lime?" Madalyn asked in a whisper, beginning to slice one up, relieved to have this small activity to occupy her frozen fingers, thankful for this slightest, entirely inconsequential offering of service.

"What?" Nihil asked. "Ah, no thanks."

"I think I'll have some too," she mumbled, pouring tequila into the other glass. As she was leaning over, she slipped her sunglasses back onto her face.

"You're not a fuck-up, Nihil. I don't understand why you think you are." She said this quietly and with kindness, but she was angry. Where was this misplaced blame coming from? How could it possibly be Nihil's fault that this terrible thing had happened to his brother?

"Because I should have told him."

"Told him what?"

"About AIDS."

"That is truly ridiculous. It's obvious he wasn't that out of it. He went and got tested, didn't he? He may be young and seem innocent, but he obviously knew something about the issue. Why is it your fault?"

Nihil was silent. Madalyn took a sip of tequila, then bit into a wedge of lime. It did what it was meant to do—the tequila tasted wonderful. She tried it again.

"Because *I'm* the fuck-up in the family," Nihil whispered.

"You know," Madalyn ventured, about an hour later, finally feeling drunk enough. "A lot of people don't seem to ever get sick, with it, I mean. I mean, I've read about people who've had it for years and still aren't sick. A lot of people are into health regimes and spirituality, y'know, positive thinking, well, I mean, y'know, a New Age approach. It seems to be working for some people."

"Huh?" Nihil grunted.

They had made quite a dent in the tequila. Talk of Peter had stopped for a while, and they had actually laughed a bit, had joked about their elegant rooftop patio, about how hard it was to get good help these days. And they had been silent, growing sweaty in the sun, enjoying the beginnings of a good drunk. Pointed pain was dulled into a more homogenous ache, and the more they drank, this feeling too began to ease.

"You know," she said, "taking care of your immune system. No smoking or drinking, lots of vitamins, meditation, thinking your way to health, getting in touch with your higher power. I know I sound absolutely illiterate right now, but what do you think?"

She took a drag off her cigarette.

"My brother's going to die of fucking AIDS," Nihil said, his voice barbed with anger. "Why are you sitting there self-destructing with me if you believe that shit? You're saying you believe in that shit when you don't practice it?"

"Don't be so simplistic," she said quietly after a moment, suddenly finding herself crying. When enough tears had fallen that she had to wipe her face beneath her glasses, he noticed.

"And judgmental," she finished.

"I'm sorry." He tried to clip his irritation for her sake, but she heard it. "But *fuck*."

Her tears grew in volume, she sniffed loudly, she drank deeply.

"John left me, not that you care. I'm sure you always thought he was an asshole. And what I'm going through can hardly compare to what you're going through, so I guess I shouldn't even have brought it up."

She had taken her glasses off again and was sobbing heavily into one hand. Her other hand held her tall glass, which she appeared to cling to like some stubborn relay runner unwilling to pass along the baton.

"Well, I didn't know."

"I'm sorry, I know I'm wallowing in self pity crap . . . I know it doesn't compare . . . I'm sorry . . ." She uttered the words in quick soundbites that stayed at the back of her throat as she gulped in air.

Nihil took the glass from her hand. He opened another beer and wiped off the wet can with a towel. He relieved her of the tequila glass and put the can in her hand. He held it there, crouching by her side. Her hair had fallen over her hand, and as he gently drew the strands back over her shoulder, his chin began to pulsate below his smile. He kissed her cheek and his eyes swam in their own juices, finally.

Madalyn took three weeks' holiday in August. During the first ten days, she and Tina drove down the Oregon coast. It had been a draining holiday for Madalyn. Doing anything other than being alone with herself and sinking into the comfortable groove of her depression required a great deal of energy, felt like moving through deep water. But the trip had helped distract her, had offered some new activity in which to lose herself for short periods, just as Nihil's disclosure had galvanized her emotions for a short time. But as the shock wore off, her admonitions to herself that she was really so incredibly lucky, so blessed, became less frequent and less potent.

She returned home, with relief, to the familiar emotional terrain within her apartment. Here, the same sun that lit up the rock and sky and ocean of Oregon, illuminating foreign and lovely scenes in which she had felt her pain shrink and float more lightly inside her, this same sun shining into the rooms of the apartment and creating little boxes of stagnant light, seemed to exacerbate the heaviness inside, just as the dust in the air was brought into relief and made to seem larger than life.

She tried to hide from it. From the light. From being outside in it by herself in the noisy city. The sun seemed to sear her brain, scuttle her thoughts. And being alone in the crowds, always thinking she had caught a glimpse of John, was so disorienting, she feared she might stumble into traffic sometime.

So she stayed inside and watched a lot of television.

She became quite addicted to several soap operas. The only thing she looked forward to on awakening each morning was making a pot of coffee and finding out what happened. She kept the phone off the hook much of the time. She got into the habit of sleeping late and developed a dreadful insomnia, which kept her up until three or four in the morning, the late late show blinking and flickering before her like a hearth fire. Sometimes, during the day, just stepping out onto her balcony would start the tears, and she would begin to feel her mind becoming transparent in the sunlight. She would darken the living room, turn on the television and smoke like a fiend.

She gave her heart to Jesus a number of times, like she'd done all those years ago at summer camp with Tina. It never seemed to work.

One afternoon, which had been turning out just like all the others, after she had finally had a shower, she thought she might attempt a trip outside. She was running out of wine. But thinking of the bright and busy city lying in wait eighteen storeys below convinced her to put off the excursion for a few more hours, to wait until the evening. Although the sky did appear to be hazing over, any extra waning of the light would help.

She turned on the TV. Oprah was beating even deader the subject of child abuse. The guests sat lined up together on the stage, eager to offer up their privacy to invading millions. Madalyn muted the sound. Abusers and abused mouthed what must have been, respectively, remorse and shame, and the interspersed shots of Oprah's practiced concern all looked the same. Madalyn, omnipotent, restored Oprah's powers of speech and was told not to touch that dial, because coming up after the break was a convicted child molester live via satellite from prison.

Madalyn changed channels. On the *New Dating Game*, bachelor number one was saying that it's like if he knows a girl likes him, then, like, it's like he knows he's got her and he'll, like, immediately lose interest.

Madalyn changed channels. *Wild Kingdom* had its camera crammed into a clump of baby sea turtles. Just born, they were struggling out of sandy holes—nests—and Madalyn saw that they were pathetically handicapped by stubby flippers. But finally they managed to climb out and toddle away. Then, horror. Nature told an obscene joke, deadpan. As the tiny creatures made a brave run for the sea, they were picked off by swarming birds of prey. Few turtles, apparently, survive.

# Chapter Eight

"I am *so* glad to be back," he had said over the phone, and in his voice she heard the strain of the past three weeks.

As she prepared herself to see him that Thursday evening, she thought about what he had said and about how his voice had sounded: "I missed you so much." If that was all it was . . . well, good. She found herself wishing again that she could have imagined him having a terrible time spending three perfectly sunny weeks on a beautiful island with his children. This was a troublesome train of thought that could complicate things if she let it. She dwelt on it.

He had said he would arrive at seven o'clock. It was around six-fifty when she opened the wine, helping herself to a glass. She stood by the big picture window in the living room, waiting. When she saw his car approach, she moved away from the window, an instinctive habit. He would never know that each time she had waited, she had also watched.

His suntan came as a surprise. Of course he would have one, but for some reason it was a shock. She wished to touch his hand, browned and strong-looking, stronger than before. He took her in his arms in a deeply suntanned sort of way, and she burst into uncontrollable laughter.

"Is it something I said?" he asked, not having yet said a word. His joke sounded to her more like the kind of teasing that has the power to bruise than like the charged, verbal tantalizations with which he had caressed her ego for so many months, their sole purpose to delight her.

"I don't know what's come over me," she said, feeling the laughter she was struggling to control threaten to heave itself up through her throat, transmogrified into tears.

Casually, she invited him to have a glass of wine and tell her about his holiday. She retrieved the bottle from the fridge and tried to infuse her smile with comfort and efficiency as he let her pass by him in the hall—a wifely sort of smile.

"Don't I even get a kiss?" he asked as she sat down. She stood and put her arms around his neck and tried to avoid his eyes. But he held her away from him and said her name, and so she looked. She saw the viscious resolve in his eyes, saw that if he had spent the last three weeks recounting the cost, then he still found her to be worth it.

She knew also that if she let him rip himself out of his present life by the roots, the life that tamped him down much more than he realized, the resulting disaster would be her fault. She had no intention of taking on that kind of responsibility. I miss you so much.

Naturally, the intensity of her kiss was misinterpreted, and as he let her up for air, Lawrence felt as if he were standing on the edge of a cliff and, for the first time, standing there without any fear.

"You had a great time, didn't you?" she asked. She had seated herself once again and was busily pouring the wine. "You had a great time with the kids, you relaxed and you slept with Susan and it was okay. Right?" She handed him a glass.

Lawrence accepted the glass, then set it down, then picked it up, stared at it, and finally raised it to his lips. His hand shook. "It was a good time for the kids."

"You did, didn't you?" The softness and kindness of her voice made him want to retch.

"I . . . it keeps the peace, you know that. Why would you even bring it up? I wouldn't have gone on this holiday if you . . ."

"I know," she said, her voice like wax.

"Do you? Can you really say you know what it's like?" He stood and paced. "Listen, Tina." He paused, stalling for time, trying to figure out how to get this thing back on track. It wasn't going at all the way he had expected. Or maybe his hope, both fantastic and craven, had disguised itself too well as expectation. He sat down beside her and touched her hair, felt against his palm the spring of her curls instead of the finely planed curve of her cheek, soft as talc, which had fit his cupped hand every day in his mind's eye for the last three weeks.

"Let's just do it, okay? Let's just do it. I want to."

She placed the two words "I can't" in front of him quietly and deliberately, and he stared at them as if they were the malignant product of surgery, slipping and sliding horrifically in the bottom of a stainless steel bowl, presented to him as the physical evidence.

Through the open window, he heard music rippling out from a passing car, shreds of a summery song, ". . . up the ladder to the roof, where we can see heaven much better, let's go up the ladder to the roof . . ."

"Closer to heaven . . ." were the last of the words he heard as the car drove away.

He spent close to two hours at Tina's, and none of the things she said, about his children and Susan and his life, came close to answering his only question: "Why?" He answered it himself, sitting in his car a few blocks away in the parking lot in front of the planetarium. She doesn't love me. Oh dear God in heaven.

He did not feel it yet, but his rage was beginning to build. Susan would get the brunt of it over the coming weeks.

But she did say she loved me. So why?

She had said it would be better if he didn't call her, that she had made up her mind, that it would be easier this way. He had told her, a number of times, that he would call her in a few days, or in a week or so, or a few weeks, if she wanted, whatever time she needed to think things over. She had said no each time except the last, when, standing at her open door, she had said goodbye instead.

Although he was not, he had felt drunk as he stumbled down her stairs. Sitting behind the wheel of the Volvo, the seat burning from exposure to the Indian-summer sun, the air around him chokingly thick with heat, he found himself at a complete loss as to where to go and what to do. All he wanted, of course, was to race back up the stairs and set free the gargoyle of need that kicked and screamed inside him.

"An actual job," was what Nihil had said to her when he started working for Derek in September. Derek had offered to train him to manage Monty's. Nihil dyed his hair back to brown, changed his name back to Ron and threw his keyed-up energies into his new career. "Just temporary," he said to Madalyn.

He learned quickly and before long had established himself as co-host, with Derek, to the post-theatre hipsters whose fawning displays of pseudo-friendship Nihil managed neatly, keeping the crowds by the bar, waiting for tables, feeling calmed and happy with his personal attentions, applied sporadically enough to maintain both their appetites and their self-serving assessments that Ron was their man on the inside.

Madalyn spent many evenings that fall sitting at the bar at Monty's with a glass of wine and with Derek or Nihil, who introduced her to a number of the regulars. She became something of a fixture and developed a reputation as someone who could be counted on to stab the conversation with remarks of deeply cynical humour during the impromptu soirées that sprang up almost nightly after closing time.

When people asked what she did, she'd say, "I'm in transition, waiting on the gods for inspiration." This was a line she and Nihil had cooked up to describe both their states of existence, and Madalyn uttered it with such perfect pacing, her deep pauses between words made the listener wonder and wait, respectfully and in vain, for the spaces to be filled. She was rarely pressed for detail.

She became concerned about her work suffering because of the late nights, but had managed to hold it together. A routine had evolved. She would force herself up at eight and, after showering, would swallow almost an entire pot of coffee and smoke, hard, as she dried her hair and dressed. At a quarter to nine she would order a cab and was usually delivered to the office just in time. She would also return from work by taxi—the extra expense was well worth it, as she had no patience or energy for anything at all except the most essential efforts needed to make it through the days, which she spent, in her head, in constant anticipation of those autumn evenings at Monty's.

After work she would doze for several hours, then once again force herself vertical and ruthlessly expunge the drowsiness out of her head with splashes of cold water, gasping, talking to herself. After donning a pair of black jeans and an old black leather jacket Nihil had lent her, she walked the four blocks to Monty's, where she would sit at the bar and eat an appetizer for dinner.

Nihil had instructed whoever was tending bar to open a bottle of house wine for her, to serve it by the glass, but to charge her at cost only for the bottle. He'd concocted a vague but dramatic story about her for his staff, something about her getting back on her feet after some unspecified personal tragedy. No one appeared to think anything untoward about her drinking. In fact, she drank more slowly at Monty's than when she was alone. She found the welcome reception and the human contact both stimulating and relaxing. After two in the morning, Nihil would walk her home, and they would continue their ongoing discussions about what they were going to do with their lives.

"Summer was the shits, September to December—an hiatus—then in January, we make decisions and take action," he had said.

Lunch hours were Madalyn's biggest challenge. She could not bear the lunch room at work: the sickening smell of other people's food, the crowds of women—she could bring little emotional energy to their conversations about calories and complaints about their jobs. She often wandered the streets, trying to find new out-of-the-way places to eat.

One day in mid-October, she stepped into an empty elevator on her way down to scrounge a late lunch. Just as the door was closing, she saw Lawrence running toward it, and she jabbed at the Open button to let him in.

"Thanks," he said as the door closed. "How *are* you?" He stood close to her, was in fact in some of her personal space that she usually guarded, but she felt no discomfort.

"Oh, you know," she said, deliberately looking into his eyes, sharing with him what each knew about the other.

"Yeah," he said.

Several floors down, the elevator door opened. Two men and two women got on. They were exchanging chitchat, obviously from the same office. Madalyn and Lawrence stood together at the back, enjoying the wordless comfort of each other's presence. When they stepped out into the lobby, Lawrence guided Madalyn ahead of him out the door and onto the street, his hand resting lightly on her back.

He said, "I'm off up to Robson Street for lunch, a meeting, actually . . . um, you take care, alright?"

She wanted to stay with him, had an urge to take hold of the lapels of his overcoat and just stand next to him, absorbing his empathy, letting him feel hers.

"You too," she said. He reached out and touched her arm, gave it a gentle squeeze above the elbow. They looked at each other as he backed away. Then he smiled, erasing completely whatever lines of office hierarchy she might think separated them, and each knew the face of an ally.

Lawrence turned and walked away. Madalyn headed in the opposite direction, walking around the corner of the Birk & Samuels building and into yet another office tower, stepping onto an escalator and descending into the mall below. Her half-hearted search for lunch lasted about a minute. Finding herself in a sudden sweat, she strode up the escalator and found relief outside as she made her way down Burrard Street toward the hotel on the water. She walked along the deck outside, where the cruise ships docked. There were no ships that day, but there was a raw wind, which smelled like snow. She stood in the cold, waiting for numbness.

Lawrence, early for his meeting, took a corner table and ordered an uncharacteristic double scotch. He drank it in three gulps, and he too waited for numbness.

"Jere. I hear your pal Pickard over at Birk & Samuels has something going with your *Miss* Tyhurst," Phil said.

"Tina?" Jerome asked, startled. A stalk of celery swatted his lip as he rushed to put down his Bloody Mary.

"She's quite the fox, or haven't you noticed?" Phil and Barry laughed like girls.

"Tina?" Jerome repeated. "She's a virgin!" he insisted, using his encompassing term for girls who may sleep, but not around. "Where'd ya hear this crap?"

"It's getting around," Phil said.

"Who said what? I want facts." Jerome leaned back, loosening his tie, the reverse version of the more honest, feminine hunkering.

"Jeez . . . let's see." Phil began to recite. "Nance—you know my wife?—is like this with Mare, my accountant—they went to school together—so anyway, they were jawing over lunch the other day, and it turns out Mare knows Pickard's secretary, who told her." He leaned back too, satisfied that the story was complete.

"Told her *what?*" Jerome asked.

"Told her that 'all the signs were there,'" Phil said, wiggling his fingers next to his face in mock horror.

"That doesn't tell me a whole helluva lot," Jerome said. He was stamping his stick of celery against the bottom of his glass.

"The wife said she reviewed everything Mare had found out, and it was obvious to her that Pickard and Tina were getting it on, 'involved, definitely involved.'" Phil paused and turned toward Barry.

"It's probably all bullshit," Phil continued. "Bare, old buddy! This is the last time I'm picking up your seed stock, you know that. Extar's been listed, what, a month? When can I bail?"

With a man's infuriating inability to gossip properly, Phil left Jerome hanging, without Details, with a gaping curiosity—the worst condition of the Interested. Jerome took a bite of celery. It was bitter and stringy.

On a Friday afternoon at the end of November, at a quarter to six, Tina stood at the Stackhouse reception desk, signing for a package. The office was notorious, even by Vancouver standards, for closing up shop early on Fridays, and the courier was teasing Tina for working so late. But she'd been waiting for a set of documents from Birk & Samuels, which she wanted to take home with her on the weekend. There was a big closing on Monday afternoon, and she wanted to review the lot descriptions and organize her paperwork at leisure, spare herself a frantic Monday morning. As smooth as possible, that was how she wanted her life to be. Every part of her life.

She was anxious to take the documents home with her for another reason, could not wait to open the envelope and enjoy the mordant sensuality of feeling her heart drop when she read Lawrence's formal business letter addressed to Stackhouse Developments, Attention: Tina Tyhurst. She would have anticipated even more shuddering in her chest had she known that the letter had been signed, not, as usual, with Lawrence's fine vertical strokes, which looked like long grass, but with a rounded, childish hand, "Renata Clarke for," and typed underneath, "Lawrence Pickard," and underneath that, "Dictated But Not Read."

"You have a great weekend, eh?" the courier guy said, tugging at his fingerless leather gloves and giving Tina a big smile, which creased his face under its fashionable stubble. Tina promised him she would, and he turned and left, lanky swatches of dirty blond hair sashaying around his shoulders.

She was in her office, cramming the envelope into her briefcase.

"Tina."

She whirled around, startled. It was John.

"Oh, hi, you scared me."

"Sorry." He stood in the doorway, his trench coat hooked over a finger.

"I thought I was the only one left," she said as she shouldered her coat and snuck an arm into each wide, white sleeve.

"Nope. But I'm sure we're the last two diehards. You off home?"

"That was the plan. And you?"

"Yeah, I guess—I've got kind of a nothing evening coming up."

"Join the club." She brushed against him in the doorway on her way out.

"Feel like going for a drink?"

Tina said she had to get out of downtown—it was too depressing, the emptied-out core of the city on a rainy Friday night. They each drove in their own cars, to her place.

"I think I'd like to change," she said.

"In that case, we could even grab a bite somewhere in the neighbourhood," he suggested.


"There's some wine in the fridge—help yourself," she called from the bedroom as she peeled off her pantyhose. She tossed the wretched things onto the bed. When she came into the living room, in jeans and a sweater, a pale turquoise angora cardigan, John had the wine opened and sat with his stockinged feet on her coffee table.

"Should I turn on the fire?" she asked.

He laughed loudly. "Absolutely."

"So, um, what are you doing for Christmas?" she asked, sitting cross-legged in the boxy, creamy leather chair that matched the couch.

"Um, going back east, Monica's. Um, I guess I haven't told you we're engaged."

"Oh. Great. Minor detail. Madalyn will be thrilled. Just *thrilled*." She looked at him, watched him react to the sting in her voice.

"What can I say?" His voice was flat but slightly corrugated with a world-weary tenderness. She wondered if he meant it. They managed then to detour, for awhile, pouncing with relief upon trivial pieces of office gossip. The first glass of wine led, without any discussion of dinner, to the next. They continued to drink past those critical moments when decisions about food must be made. It was raining hard. The room was warm.

Relaxed, emboldened by the wine, Tina began to grill him about Monica.

"I'm not sure how much I should tell you," he commented to the bottom of his wineglass.

"Well, everyone's heard of the Baxter Group," Tina said. "It's no secret who her family is. Do you have a picture?"

John laughed again, slipped a snapshot out of his wallet and half stood to reach over and hand it to her.

"I'll come over there," she said, in one fluid motion uncoiling herself from her chair, gliding over the few feet of carpeting between them and rearranging herself beside him on the couch.

"Hmmm," she said, of the pink-cheeked, round-faced young woman in a beige crew-necked sweater. Her short blonde hair was flung up on one side of her head into the blue sky behind her. She was standing on a sailboat beside a tanned and grinning John, who had an arm draped over her shoulder.

"She looks athletic," Tina observed, and again John laughed, with an irritating obstreperousness.

"She's a strong and healthy young lady in every way."

"Jeez." Tina batted the photograph against his arm before examining it again.

"You won't find out what you want to know that way," he said.

She continued to look at the picture, took her time about it, then placed it on his leg. She looked up at him.

"Perhaps not," she said.

They were both silent. They continued to drink.

"Just forget it," Tina said, all of a sudden.

"What?"

"About Madalyn. I'm not a spy, but just forget it," she said, her voice rising onto the cusp of a whine.

"She's twenty-one. Did a year of university, hated it, works for her dad as a receptionist at one of his companies, sails and skis like a fiend, and very well."

Tina felt her eyes watering. But the serious look on John's face, what seemed to be a look of the gravest sincerity, helped soften the tension she was feeling.

"What are we talking here, booze-wise?" he asked, swishing the dregs of the wine around the bottom of the bottle.

"Let's see, I think all I have is, yeah, I'm sure I do, some champagne. Californian. And unchilled," she added apologetically. "I could put it in the freezer."

"Why don't we open it now, have it with ice."

Didn't need to worry about the niceties at all, she thought to herself as she opened the bottle in the kitchen.

While she was gone, John removed his tie, rolled back the cuffs of his shirt and began to rummage through her tape collection. From the kitchen she heard Harold Melvin and the Bluenotes begin to croon.

She tinkled the ice cubes against the insides of the glasses as she carried them into the room.

"You probably know way too much about *me*," John said, accepting a glass. "Or maybe we shouldn't get into that."

"I guess I know enough. At least one version."

They both stretched their feet onto the glass top of the coffee table and fell silent again.

"What are *you* doing for Christmas?" he asked.

"Texas."

"Mmm. Tell me about it."

She related the kind of time she could expect to have, riding with her many cousins, attending endless rounds of parties. "They're always trying to set me up with one guy or another."

She was guzzling her champagne, and she knew it. But the effect of it mixing with her blood was too good, producing an obliterative sensation of relaxation.

"We're sort of getting drunk, aren't we?" she asked.

"Yeah, getting there." More silence fell down around them, but it felt more comfortable than before.

At some length, he said, "I know about you, y'know."

"Meaning?" she asked, but she knew, of course. Pillow talk is generally uncensored.

"Mr. Pickard."

"That's over."

"How long?"

"Two months and two and a half weeks."

"But who's counting, right?" he teased her gently.

"*I* did it," she said, turning to look at him. Her throat felt full, she swallowed, and her tears clouded his face.

She drew her legs up in front of herself, and John reached over and placed a hand on her knees.

"Rough scene, eh?"

It was an irresistible kind of comfort—a masculine voice, pitched low, sounding as if it suffered with her, as if it had suffered itself. She nodded and looked over at him, wiping her face, one brush of each cheek with a single finger.

"It's okay," he said, his hand rocking her knees. "You cry beautifully."

She smiled, lowered her legs into a sitting position and reached out for her glass. John picked it up and handed it to her.

"Got it?" he asked, holding both her hands around the glass.

"Yes. I'm fine."

She took a sip. She swallowed. She set down the glass. She tucked up her legs again, turned toward him and curled up against his chest. She felt his arms around her immediately. Then she felt a sexual twinge, medium-sized but unmistakably an erotic unzipping of sorts as she huddled closer to him. No wonder Madalyn was so crazed, she thought, feeling his strength as the muscles of his arms tightened around her.

The Bluenotes had finally gotten to her favourite, "If You Don't Know Me By Now." Tina closed her eyes and let her head lose its balance—it swam with wine—and the notes of the song strained through her longing like sweet syrup. She continued to cry, with no discernible shaking or shuddering. When John began to straighten her legs, and when he drew them over his, she let him. He gently stroked her back. They sat there for the duration of the song, immersed in its sensuous ache.

She felt her crying subside, and pulled away and looked at him. Whatever the look on his face, whatever she felt going through her body right then, was much more than medium-sized. His hand ran slowly up her back, over her shoulders, and came to rest on the side of her face. They kissed.

What is mental motivation, or even emotion, when sexual energy appears to rule the world? Why fight it? She ran her hand down his shirt front toward his waist.

Oh yes, oh absolutely, who cares, who cares, yes!

She readjusted her body without undoing their lip lock and knelt, one leg on either side of him. She let him press the small of her back, pulling her against him, as close to him as he wanted, which was as close as possible.

"I've always wondered . . ." he mumbled.

"Try not to say too much," she whispered into his ear, before pressing all of her accumulated sexual energies onto his mouth again.

"Just one thing . . ." he said moments later, when the kiss had wound itself down a little. "I'm, ah, sort of getting to be in the family way, and . . . um . . ."

Tina stood up, took him by the hand and led him to the bedroom.

The next morning arrived, not without some private agonizing and hangovers, when each of them awoke in their own beds. And John did not come in to see Tina when he returned at noon to pick up his car. Both knew it was a one-time thing. Both knew it had been a product of the moment. And both would carry those few hours with them, those few hours of pure physical pleasure, of supremely singular sex, isolated in their memories, as something good.

Jingle bells, jingle bells, jingle all the way . . .

Mind empty except for the endless carol, rotating like music on a player piano, Madalyn typed in time. Only another forty-five minutes of boredom. Mind-numbing is such an apt description, she thought sarcastically of her job.

What relief to finally sink into a seat at the Garden Lounge and let Tina talk her into the cranberry juice and vodka. They each had two and, thus tranquilized for their first attempt at Christmas shopping, headed out into the mild, rainy evening. Madalyn knew she would regret her choice of coat once in the muggy stores and wished she had worn her trench. But it should be easy this year, she thought. She needed gifts only for Gordon, Evelyn and Tina. And fast. Last year she had spent many excited hours searching for witty, memorable stocking stuffers for John.

Just for the high of self-pity, she imagined him charming the daylights out of Monica's mother in some tasteful, firelit living room in Toronto. She pictured him, for some reason, in a shirt and tie and sweater, like the models in catalogues' menswear sections.

While making the rounds on Robson Street, the two women ran into an old friend from high school in a closet of a shop filled with such knickknacks as satin sacks of potpourri for fumigating drawers. Laurel Miller, now Williams, was crouched by a stroller, negotiating with a glossy-chinned child over taking its bottle and letting Mummy shop. Tina bent over the baby, and Madalyn felt suddenly hot in her winter coat, and claustrophobic.

Their classmate was as cheery as ever, although Madalyn noticed the figure that had pumped Laurel's cheerleading outfit into such taut symmetry had been retired into just enough fat to rule out competition, now unnecessary anyway. And the cheeks that had fluffed out her face as a teen now had a jelled, permanent look to them, which Madalyn found encouraging.

It had been a very good year, notwithstanding that blip in his personal portfolio, which he'd slipped out of just in time, so Jerome went all out that December—the Stackhouse Christmas party was held in the ballroom of the Four Seasons Hotel.

People brushed gently against each other in their good clothes, wools and silks. The light from the chandeliers high overhead and from lamps cupped against the walls by dulled brass sconces was soft and flattering, lifting faces. Voices created an uneven hum, rising and falling like the scratching lines of ink from a polygraph machine.

Madalyn paced the edges of the darkened ballroom. She passed by an ashtray and tapped her cigarette. She surveyed the couples and clusters. Her eyes rested on a man's back, and she noticed how it shaped his shirt. A familiar excitement opened her up inside, then she recognized a stranger, and a more familiar disappointment clutched her closed.

She had arrived fairly early and had not yet seen anyone she knew. Eventually she found herself in the midst of a group that, she thought to herself, Nihil should really be there to see. Dear God, does this town not produce *anything* other than lawyers, brokers and real estate agents?

Glancing away, she noticed Lawrence, about ten yards away, nodding his head and rocking on his heels, looking painfully bored with whatever the brown suit standing next to him was saying. What could you expect from someone who wears brown suits, Madalyn thought, anticipation and irritability mixing together inside her.

Lawrence looked up and she caught his eye. He raised his glass and she smiled. Her eyes swept the entrance yet again. Ah, there was Tina arriving with Jerome. Madalyn's distractedness was having no apparent deterrent effect upon the round little tax lawyer who was exercising a small-man-syndrome sort of cockiness on Madalyn, trying to pique her interest with a description of his recent trip to Italy and the really kinky time he'd had touring around on motorcycles with an eclectic group of rich Euros, including the alcoholic, sexually ambiguous son of a famous clothing designer.

Tina was walking out of the powder room on the far side of the ballroom when the commotion began, so she did not notice right away. She felt a hand on her back and turned around to receive a compliment from John.

"Quite stunning, my dear," he said of her dark green velvet suit with the deep vee in front. She put a hand to her neck and smiled, her lashes casting shadows on her face.

Madalyn and Lawrence were closer to the action and saw most of what happened. Yes, it was definitely some deranged street person, people were saying of the man who was pacing in circles over by the bar, muttering invectives against some unseen enemy. His short beige trench coat was saturated with grime. His long grey hair was pinned into a bun at the back of his head. He wore bright orange jogging shoes, the tips of which pointed upward in a slightly clownish fashion, above which a pair of flared brown polyester pants flapped at his bare ankles. His age was not discernible in his long-boned face. His equally fine fingers swept through the air and slapped at the hem of his coat.

"Goddammit to hell, I tell you, goddammit. Goddammit to hell. Dammit. Goddammit to hell," he said in a voice that, although loud, seemed turned in upon itself, a voice lacking the bitterness one might have expected from the vocabulary of his rhythmic recital.

Jerome approached the man and put a hand on his shoulder.

"How are you this evening?" he asked, his voice cranked up for his audience.

"This your place, goddammit to hell?" the man asked declaratively.

"Well, I, no, well, yes, I guess you could say it's my place," Jerome answered, his arm around the man's shoulders now. Jerome slowly steered him toward the door.

"*Your* place," the man said in an even-tempered conversational bellow. "*Your* place, goddammit to hell."

The crowd heard this same response to whatever Jerome was saying as he walked with the man out the door and down the wide mirrored hall.

As Tina approached, she saw Lawrence and Madalyn standing together, looking out the door after Jerome. She walked toward them.

"Poor guy," she heard Lawrence say. "I wonder what's gone on in *his* life."

"I wonder if Jerome's putting him up in the hotel for the night," John's voice said behind Tina as she reached Lawrence and Madalyn.

Isn't this a cozy little group, Madalyn thought, thankful for the quality of light in the room, which would hide her involuntary blush. She moved closer to Lawrence with an imperceptible shifting of her feet. She turned her head toward him and flipped her hair over her shoulder, to afford John a good side view of her long neck and her slim, white, shapely shoulder, visible under the thin, see-through fabric of her black blouse.

"That would be thoughtful," she said.

"I'm positive Jerome will give him a generous amount of money, at least," Tina said. "He's really a softy."

"The guy'll just spend it on booze." This from John.

I never quite realized what a true jerk he can be, Madalyn thought, feeling her gnarled heart instructing her body to press itself up against him, her treasonous body, a perversity-seeking missile.

"God, you're charitable," she said.

"You have to feel for the guy," Lawrence commented. "Out on the street, at this time of year, especially."

"It's a wonder he got past the doorman," Tina said.

Turning slightly closer to Lawrence, Madalyn said, "He probably came through the mall. Remember, Tina, how many people were asking for money when we were Christmas shopping there last week? I finally had to put a bunch of quarters in my coat pocket."

"Why would you do that? It's a racket," John said.

"I guess we won't be nominating *you* for patron saint of the great unwashed."

Lawrence chuckled at Madalyn's rejoinder.

"John's a fascist when it comes to politics," she continued.

"God, I really hate it when people throw that word around," John said. "Do you even know what it means?" The obvious irritation in his voice shook Madalyn, and she found herself speechless.

"I think Madalyn was kidding," Lawrence said with gallantry, looking at Tina. He allowed his eyes to rest lightly upon her face, consciously keeping himself from staring too deeply, even though the sponge of his gaze threatened to soak her up completely.

"You know what *I* hate?" Madalyn said. She spoke to Lawrence. "Has this ever happened to you? You're walking down the street and somebody walks by you, singing, and they deliberately sing louder as they walk by you, just to show they're uninhibited. I hate that! Just *be* inhibited. No one cares that you're so fucking evolved." She said "fucking" quietly, with obvious de-emphasis, with a slight apologetic grimace for Lawrence.

"Know what you mean," he said. "I cherish my inhibitions. They're good company."

The group fell silent. Lawrence, playing the host, sifted the tensions down by asking if he could procure refills for anyone.

"Me, please," Madalyn said, passing him her empty glass. "That was a vodka tonic. I'll have another." She met John's eyes and held them deliberately, as if to say, what of it?

"Back in a sec," Lawrence said. "John? Tina?"

"Beer's good for me," John said.

Champagne was Tina's choice. "Jerome's serving it," she said in response to Lawrence's raised eyebrows. "Why let it go to waste?"

A small conspiratorial laugh issued forth from John's smug smile. "Hey, there's my man Barry," he said all of a sudden, having just spotted Klammer heading in their direction with Jerome.

"Barry, my man!" he said, shaking Klammer's hand, hard.

"John, Tina—I don't believe I've met this beautiful creature," Barry said, extending a hand to Madalyn, then turned toward John. "That's quite a young lady you've got. Joanne and I really enjoyed meeting her. Monica, right? Was it last month? Baxter Group. Whoa! Way to go, guy. Now that you've got a ring on her finger, when're you gonna tie the knot?"

Lawrence returned, juggling four drinks.

"Ahm, well . . ." John stammered, turning to assist Lawrence. "Oh, here, let me get a couple of those."

Madalyn observed John, watched him being saved so neatly, and it seemed only natural.

John asked Jerome who his friend was, and Barry said, "Hey, don't laugh, that could be me, a couple of bad deals down the road!" The three men snickered like teenagers, and Madalyn thought they might break into high-fives at any moment. She wondered when Lawrence or Tina or herself, for that matter, would think up an excuse to leave the group. The three of them stood in the circle, smiling at whatever in-joke John and Barry and Jerome seemed to be sharing. These sorts of situations were hard calls—one didn't want to smile too largely, let alone laugh, lest those who were in the know looked askance at you, as if to say, "We know you don't get the joke, so what's so goddamned funny?"

Maybe I'm becoming paranoid, Madalyn thought. She was drinking at a fair clip, hoping to numb her jealousy and her anger toward John. Or was she trying to revive these things, drowning as they were in desire?

Above the rim of her glass she shifted her eyes over to John. His face was a study in light: his cheeks, shaved almost shiny, and his eyes, which shuttled between the people around him, scuttling over Madalyn's face like crabs over rock, resting for extra beats on Tina, on her eyes when he could catch them, and on the vee of her jacket, charging up when he looked at Lawrence, headlights on high beam, on purpose, in order to blind.

Lawrence was the first to excuse himself. After wishing everyone a Merry Christmas or a Happy Hanukkah, or whatever the case may be.

He turned to Madalyn "See you in the salt mines," he said smiling, then turned to make his way toward the door. Madalyn glanced at Tina, who was fast becoming the centre of attention. Barry was teasing her about her love life. Madalyn touched her friend on the arm.

"I'll see you later," she said, and then she too left the group, but not before making quick eye contact with John. He winked.

Madalyn walked away as quickly as she could, sidestepping guests, smiling her *excuse me*'s, intent upon reaching the powder room as soon as possible, where she could allow her disciplined face to crumple in the privacy of a stall.

"Hey, Madalyn," she heard. She turned to find herself face to face with the tax lawyer. He had his glasses off and was wiping them with a cocktail napkin. His eyes were already bloodshot, and perspiration moistened his round face.

"You remembered my name," she said.

"I'm Neil," he said. "I didn't expect you to remember mine," he added goodnaturedly. "So, those kids I was with, we were talking, and we've decided to head over to Dick's on Dicks a little later, as soon as we've had enough free Stackhouse food. I'd like you to join us." Madalyn noticed, with a small stab of anger and distaste and a little perverse attraction, the way Neil had turned an invitation into a command, so like John.

"All expenses paid and no strings attached," Neil said, all negotiative charm, "if you'll forgive me for being so crude. How about it?"

"Well . . ." She hesitated. She was at a real loss. One part of her wanted to flee to the comfortable isolation of home, where she could revel in the sickening mix of emotion her encounter with John had engendered. But she also supposed it might be good for her ego, not to mention all the free drinks, to go out with this man, whom she had no need to impress. That would have required much more energy than she could spare. Plus, John might see them leave together.

"Come on. You'll have a good time. I promise." Neil pushed his glasses onto his nose with a finger. He patted his silk tie, the colour of dried blood, which lay on his sloping belly.

"Well, okay, I guess, sure," she said, forcing a warm smile. The effort made her almost regret her decision.

"Have you eaten yet?" Neil asked.

"Yes," she lied.

"Well, then, let me get you another drink, and I'll start to round up the gang."

By ten thirty, Madalyn was horrendously drunk. She could not remember having felt that drunk for ages. The alcohol had given her energy, and she had danced and flirted, had made meaningful eye contact with every good-looking male who had entered her line of sight. And all the while, Neil had kept her supplied with drinks—they were now on a bottle of Dom—and had protected her from any unwanted attentions. There had been one particularly nefarious fellow, a greasy-looking stock promoter named Rick, with a waxy, caramel-coloured tan accentuated by mounds of chunky gold jewelry. He had recognized Madalyn from the office—he was one of the more ill-bred and morally questionable of the firm's securities clients.

Two-thirds of the way through the fourth battle, almost a whole pack of cigarettes since they had arrived, Madalyn told Neil she was going home. He insisted upon escorting her, not just *to* the taxi, but all the way *into* her home, Madalyn realized, and when they got as far as the lobby of the nightclub, she found herself forced to be rude.

"Neil. You're not taking me home. I appreciate that you want me to get there safely, but I'm fine."

A huge baby-faced doorman, whose small silver name tag labeled him "Garry," opened the door for them, and Madalyn tripped out onto the street in front of Neil. A taxi appeared almost immediately, hailed by a wave of Garry's tuxedo-clad arm. He opened the door for Madalyn with great élan.

Neil gave her a hasty but very wet kiss on the cheek, which she wiped onto the sleeve of her coat with some vigour as the cab pulled away. She sat back, hugely relieved to be going home, to be free of Rick, whose greasiness she could still feel like a nausea-inducing coating over her entire body, and of Neil, and of pretending to have a good time.

As soon as she got in the door, she sank into the couch, still in her long, heavy coat. She lit a cigarette, then lurched a few feet to the stereo, flipped on the AM band and cranked the volume. A love song sprang to life in the room, the kind played by one of those long-haired, Spandexed, louder-than-loud metallicky bands, whose members are nothing but skin and bones and lips, and who record their anthemic numbers with full symphonic backup. The lead tore the tortured ballad from his throat, with great musical knowingness, and Madalyn cried, wept, choked, sobbed. The pain felt limitless.

# Chapter Nine

Lawrence cracked the squash ball like an egg. Over and over, his frustration sought out the fragile in order to smash it. But this activity brought no relief. And he wanted no relief. Keeping his despair going was keeping him alive. His partner Nils had observed the changes in Lawrence's game over the last few months.

Since September, Lawrence had played without much zeal, had given Nils straightforward but fairly lackluster competition. But his skill had not waned. However, for the past month, since the end of January, Nils had watched Lawrence fling himself around the court like some caged, crazed animal, the intensity of his play overshooting his technique. He was missing more shots, but threw himself into the hits and misses alike with such overweening vigour that he often crashed against the walls, his racquet scraping and crunching. Nils knew the reason for this frenetic overkill: Lawrence had been told by Jerome, during idle conversation and to Lawrence's horror, that Tina was soon to be married.

"Some Texan," Lawrence had said to Nils.

Madalyn's bouquet shook as she walked down the aisle of Houston's Evangelista Baptist Church. She struggled to control her involuntary reactions to being on display. A lot of good those acting classes are doing, she thought, if I can't even do the bridesmaid routine.

The place was packed. More than four hundred guests watched her proceed slowly toward them, saw the trembling flowers and her straight-ahead stare, as if some fixed point at the front of the church was the only thing ensuring her balance. As she passed by, they saw the white roses tucked into the sleek, fat chignon of her upswept hair and the giant periwinkle blue bow, which looked both saucy and absurdly theatrical in such a colour at the back of her white dress.

Madalyn was the last of four bridesmaids down the aisle before the bride, who, on the arm of a serious, not entirely convinced Don Tyhurst, drew as many gasps as she had intended in her froth of whitest organza. This is such a trip, Madalyn thought, imagining what Nihil would say if he were there. God, I feel so bloody *pretty*, she thought, mentally noting her reflexive apology for taking God's name in vain while in church. Then Don Tyhurst handed his daughter over to a tall, sungroomed

Texan, and for the duration of the ceremony Madalyn fought back tears of the sweetest, most luxurious and ancient longing. Just keep it together 'til you get to Mexico, she told herself.

Tina had re-met her new husband during her Christmas trip to Houston. He was the one who had kept appearing by her side at the dance over a year and a half ago. Darcy "D.W." Whipple, forty-eight, was a man of few words, the possessor of thousands of inherited cattle and acreage and no children. He had been ripe and ready for a second wife when he scooped up Tina at her cousins' Boxing Day barbeque, and that had been that.

Darcy had travelled to Vancouver in January to meet "Tina's people." Expecting, for some unreasonable reason, a loud and rough-edged cowboy wearing one of those string ties, Madalyn had been jealously surprised by his social polish, the way "Deedubya" cherished and protected his adored fiancée, who, in her highest heels, came only two-thirds of the way up his dulled silk tie, next to which her head often rested.

So just three months after "that fateful barbeque," as Madalyn repeatedly teased her best friend, Tina had a new last name. Whipple. And how apt a name it was, Madalyn thought, standing on the church lawn after the ceremony, next to Tina, who looked a little lost in her couturier's orgy of a dress. Her husband had a big, sexy, suntanned hand on her waist. Madalyn stared at that hand, stared at Darcy's face, the agates of his eyes, winged by tantalizingly mature-looking crow's-feet, at his smile, which left generous amounts of open space around the compressed slats of his white teeth. She stared at the broadness of his shoulders and thought of the decades of sexual experience he must have under his flat cummerbund. And she felt her feminine powers threatened by Tina.

Madalyn made a conscious effort to look alive and to try to catch Darcy's eye, feeling the instinctive competitiveness engendered by looking upon a claimed man who was not hers, a man who therefore might not dab upon her ego the validating balm of his lust. But for the first time in many months, she felt energized and excited. She imagined that this, perhaps, was what Tina might have felt about Lawrence before the affair had begun.

Madalyn acknowledged to herself the conditioning of civilized society, the obvious fact that Darcy was in love with his bride, and her own loyalty to Tina, which, she realized with only a little surprise and with a kind of perverse wisdom, was not a thing to be assumed. And although these thoughts put a damper on the pangs of sexual rebirth she was feeling, she determined to stick with it. Surely she would be able to find realistic opportunities and to abandon herself to them the first chance she got.

Back at Tina's aunt and uncle's home, before the reception, which was to be held at the exclusive Cattlemen's Club, Madalyn managed to sneak a smoke, grab a glass of champagne and pop a breath mint before the interminable wedding pictures were taken out in the garden. Pretty maids all in a row, the bridal attendants were lined up on one side of the happy couple, in order of height. This put Madalyn, the tallest, next to the smaller Tina. The bridesmaids wore white ballet-length dresses with their periwinkle sashes and held long, trailing bouquets of white roses, as did Tina, only hers was even longer.

Four tuxedoed groomsmen likewise cascaded down in height next to Darcy. The photographer urged them all closer, issued endless instructions about foot and head placement, and when all thought they might break with the strain, he admonished them in a cheerful voice to "look natural!" and started snapping away.

"Daddy?"

"Yes, sweetie?" Lawrence looked up from *Time* to see his youngest daughter.

"I have to show you what I made for Mummy's birthday." Five-year-old Megan came and stood against his legs, stretched out on the upholstered footstool, beige stippled with beige, matching the chair. She held out a piece of construction paper.

"It's a princess!" she announced. Lawrence could indeed see—the crown of gold sparkle rested on a yellow Crayola swath of hair, which fell to the top of a pink cotton-batting skirt.

"It's a beautiful princess, sweetheart. Mummy will love it! And what is she doing? Is she opening the door of her castle?" he asked, referring to the fuchsia stick appearing from beneath the hair and attached to what looked like a knob on a block of brown paint.

"That's what I made it. I tried to draw the prince, but he, um, he, um, got all messy. So I made him into the castle."

Lawrence looked at his daughter's face, the wispy blonde hair, which would probably grow into Susan's light brown, and the hereditary puffs under her eyes, also from Susan, with the pale blue hollows underneath. Megan had been smiling her biggest smile, which showed most of her upper gum, and which she would try to train down closer to her teeth in her teens. The smile had deflated slightly, and a dry patch of lip was left stuck to her gum.

"C'mere, Mite," Lawrence said softly, lifting her onto his lap.

"It has to go in the box," Megan said, opening a sweater box in her lap, "or else the sparkle will all come off."

Lawrence put the boxed princess on the couch beside them and gave his daughter a hug.

"What are you getting for Mummy?"

"Well, we'll have to see." Lawrence held her wrist, which lay on his chest as she played with the button of his shirt pocket. So tiny, I could fit my little finger around it, he thought, noticing the blue veins, tiny, still, but not as tiny, surely, as the one on the top of her head that the doctors had found. Lawrence had been amazed they had been able to find it, let alone insert the intravenous, which had kept her alive during the first three incubated weeks of her life.

"Pickard, Girl," the sign had read, but she was a prenamed baby. Susan and he had spent every possible hour urging her on with "Megan Veronique" as they stroked her back, no bigger than one of their hands, through the armholes of the incubator, as if using both names would more strongly affirm to the Powers That Be that she had been identified, with love, and would not be given back. Megan Veronique Pickard was how they introduced her with we-knew-it-all-along relief when they finally got to take her home. "Just needed a little more time before she was done," the pediatrician had said in response to their concerns about her present and future health. "Just treat her like any other kid on the block." Which, of course, they never would.

The day after the wedding, Madalyn was on a plane to Mexico City. From there she would catch a connecting flight to Cancun, where Nihil would meet her.

Her first night in Mexico found her admiring the sunset through a glass of amber-coloured beer. The sun looked like half a penny as it was ever so slowly sucked down into the flat, black horizon. She moved her glass through the air in front of her face.

The air was a thing unto itself down here. It had dropped onto her as she stepped onto the tarmac in Cancun, like a warm, moist towel. Now that she had adjusted, she loved the fact that in the evening the air was the same temperature as her body, and she felt no sensation as she moved through it.

She and Nihil had boarded an overloaded *barco* in Cancun for the hour-long ride to Isla Mujueres, during which the carefree Mexican captain and his cohorts laughed at the anxious *touristas*, who struggled to maintain a semblance of adventurous holiday joie de vivre as the forty-foot boat, layers of paint peeling off its decrepit wooden decking, chugged with slow and steady determination through the wild waters. The tail end of last week's storm, one of the other passengers told Nihil.

He had found a small, cheap hotel, a squat white building on a village side street, five minutes from the beach. He'd been staying there for the past week. "It's clean and quiet," he'd told Madalyn, "and the cockroaches are your better class of roaches, really."

Now the two of them sat on the beachside edge of an outdoor restaurant in front of one of the more posh hotels. Torches lined the swimming pool next to them.

"You look like a different person!" Madalyn said. "I can't get over it."

His suntan seemed to add weight to Nihil's frame and to fill out his face. He wore a billowing white shirt and khaki shorts, which fell to his knees. He told her he had already scouted out most of the village, which covered much of the small island, and said he felt pretty much at home. He had spent the past week on the beach "plastered to the sand," snorkeling in the ocean, a painfully beautiful turquoise, wandering the main streets of the town and practising his fractured Spanish on a few of the indulgent, somewhat somnambulant local tavernkeepers.

Madalyn related some of the more amusing and traumatic details of Tina's wedding, including how she had risked her friend's wrath by making herself scarce during the bouquet toss, "a barbaric ritual."

"Which serves," Nihil teased, "both to identify the unmarried females to the community at large and to allow the unclaimed maidens to scratch and claw for the symbolic prize—unbridled competition unmasked and at its best."

Madalyn groaned.

"So she's taken the plunge into holy matrimony. Well, here's to her." He raised his bottle of beer. Madalyn looked at him with exaggerated suspicion.

"I mean it," he said. "If she's happy, more power to her."

So they drank a toast to Mrs. Darcy Whipple "of Houston, Vancouver, Palm Beach and Bal Harbour," Nihil added.

"That's not far from the truth. Darcy has *mucho dinero*."

"Speaking of dinero," Nihil said, leaning forward on his elbows, his eyes full of new ambition, "I've found a way to actually make some. It's peanuts, really, but I'm on an actual payroll, second assistant director! Fuck! Gavin gave me the job, I don't know why. And I'm overflowing with ideas for my own first film. Gavin was the independent film director who was teaching a university course that Nihil had begun in January. Gavin had hired Nihil to work on the production of a film being shot locally. He had picked Nihil out of the class, having been familiar with the work of Nihil's previous incarnation, and the two had become more like peers than student and teacher.

"A new medium is exactly what I needed," Nihil said. "I want to do something in black and white, a quote unquote small art film—I want to take a complex relationship, or several, and follow the actors around with a hand-held, record their faces, the whole thing will be, largely, talking heads, and I'm thinking of how to play with this—say, delaying the sound of their voices as they're speaking. The viewer would see the facial expression, and a few seconds later would hear what they've said . . . could be some interesting juxtapositions . . . want to be in it? How are the acting classes going? Are you fabulous?"

"No, I'm not *fabulous*. My energy is somewhat *blocked*," Madalyn said with florid theatricality. "Although I'm by no means the worst in the class. We've been doing camera work, and while the camera likes my face, it seems I have camera-friendly bones.

The instructor says I need to learn to access my emotions and let them play themselves out more on my face. Really! *Please.* But it's just not happening. If I could manage to take a deep breath for once in my life, maybe some of my inaccessible emotion would be able to show itself. I don't know. I guess the classes give me some sort of a focus, like you said, but I don't feel committed to them. I mean, I am *not* blessed with overwhelming talent. Trust me."

"But you have to work with so-called talent. Just work with it for a while. I also told you I thought acting might be therapeutic. Are you finding that?"

"No." Madalyn dropped her head onto her arms, which were resting on the table. "Like I said, I'm so fucking *blocked*."

"Darling, how devastating for you."

She raised her head. "No, really, I can't seem to make a connection between the mess inside and the expression of a specific emotion in class, which should draw its energy from somewhere *in* that mess. I can't make the connection! Maybe it's not the right medium, I mean, it's me, myself, as the medium . . . I think I do need one, though, but please don't try to talk to me about painting again." She heaved a rough sigh and looked hard at Nihil, a pointed look in her smiling eyes. He raised his hands as if to say, You won't hear a word from me.

"It's just so dead and stale for me," Madalyn continued. "I can't bring myself to go near it. So much has happened since I last painted, it's been years—I have this huge mental or emotional block about going back to it. Because it's *going back!* And I don't want to go back. I just can't face a canvas, it does nothing for me, it terrifies me. And I don't have any ideas, for Christ's sake! That's death to an artist." She stretched her legs out to the side of the table and crossed them, placed one hand on her chest and the back of her other hand on her forehead, tilting her head back, punctuating and acting out her pseudo despair. They both laughed.

"And who says I'm an *artist*, anyway?" she said, reverting to her real self. "I may have *done some painting* when I was younger, but am I an artiste? You tell me, because I don't know. But I need to do something, because the longer I don't do anything, the more uptight and neurotic I become. If I could become any more uptight and neurotic than I already am."

"Let me say again, without you biting my head off, please, that fiddling with your medium, whether it's paint or words or clay or your body and emotion, just fiddling around often brings out ideas. I think it really helps to fiddle with stuff. And the other thing I would suggest is to make some more changes in your life. I mean like big changes, radical."

"*Babe,*" "Well," Madalyn continued chuckling, "it has helped to start working nights, at least that change has made me feel like I'm out of the nine-to-five scenario, which I *loathe.* I get to wear jeans to work, it's quiet, I hardly run across any lawyers, which is such an incredible blessing. And even if it is the same firm I'm with and even though word processing is so thoroughly fucking mindless, at least it is a change. I love having my days free . . . I ruminate. That's my calling, my avocation, I think, I'm a ruminator."

"That's cool," Nihil said seriously.

"I think this holiday will help. I hope." Madalyn stretched her arms above her head, then draped them about herself, one extended onto the table, her hand resting lightly around her glass, the other up behind her head, where she played with her hair, lifting and sprinkling swatches of it onto her pale shoulders.

"Well, you look good, if that's any consolation. Better to be miserable and beautiful than just miserable."

"Oh, thank you." She smiled, grazing his eyes with hers. He watched as she lit a cigarette, an act of comfort-level maintenance.

They took a walk along the beach. With their sandals dangling from their fingers, they waded in the residue of the warm surf as each broken wave crawled over the flat sand with creative irregularity. Nihil's presence close beside her, made more familiar by the foreign shore, was a comfort. In the light of the moon and the torches in front of the hotels, she noticed Nihil's forearm where his hand disappeared into his pocket. She felt like reaching in for his hand and holding it, or slipping her arm through his. But, she reasoned, this might send out the wrong signal, the results of which she didn't want to cope with. He was too much of a friend. He knew her too well as a plain old person. So she did nothing.

They came upon what seemed to be a party, people spilling out from the poolside patio of a large pink hotel. They had heard the sounds as they approached; the music, talk and laughter carried without buffer through the still air. They stopped to look. Nihil began to walk up the beach toward the crowd and, with his hand on her back, she went with him. Two men ran past them toward the ocean, drinks held high in their hands. When they reached the water, they turned and ran back—an impromptu running race, it appeared, perhaps a variation on the egg and spoon. Madalyn recollected a cartoon she had seen on a set of cocktail napkins in a gift boutique on Robson Street: a man saying to a woman, "I used to jog, but the ice kept falling out of my glass."

One of the runners approached them and, very politely and largely soberly, invited them to join the party.

"It's being given by Enrique for some of his North American friends," the man said.

"Enrique?" Nihil questioned.

"Just Enrique, *I* don't even know his last name—I'm not sure anyone does. Owns probably two-thirds of the island. He's got real estate and ex-wives scattered all over Mexico, Costa Rica,

Florida. A great guy. I'm not even sure he's still here. But come on up."

Nihil and Madalyn edged through the crowd, approached one of the poolside bars and asked for margaritas. They were given an enormous jugfull, along with two salted glasses. Enrique was certainly generous, if nothing else. They carried the jug onto the beach and settled themselves on the sand, far enough from the noise so they could hear the water lapping, but close enough so the music from the band made them feel part of the party.

"Here's to Enrique," Nihil said, his glass raised in the first of many toasts to their unseen host. The first jug was fairly quickly followed by a second. The night became black, the copper sun completely enveloped. As they started in on the second jug, they romped on the shore, giggling and dancing, their glasses set on the sand. The lights from the hotel and from the torch-lit party played in large, soft, magnified licks on the sand around them.

Madalyn lay down on her back, her legs in the edge of the tepid water. Nihil stretched out next to her on his side, supporting his head with a hand.

"From here to eternity," he said, as the tag ends of the breaking waves flowed up and down their legs.

Madalyn's arms rested on the sand above her head.

"Mmm, right."

Nihil reached an arm over her and braced above her on his elbows.

"Grand passion," he said, kissing her mouth lightly and softly.

It felt good, she felt good, she felt drunk and relaxed, and she felt something sputter to life in her groin, which she pressed into Nihil as she put her hands in his hair and pulled his head back down until he was kissing her again.

Her mind was as black as the sky, and for some moments she let herself feel, only. But as their kisses grew more intense, and as she started to run her hands over his shoulders and back and felt his tight, slim body and so much of his bones, her sexual excitement subsided. Nihil's body felt strange, unfamiliar, out of whack with the images of John, which now filled the eye of her heart. She remembered being in the same position with him, hanging onto his arms with her fingers, like a bird on a perch, underneath him as she now lay underneath Nihil. These images squeezed at the hard lump in her chest, threatening to soften it enough to wring out tears.

She let her arms fall onto the sand and turned her face to one side. Nihil rolled away from her. He kissed her cheek.

"Let's finish those margs," he said, getting up and striding to where they had left the glasses and jug propped in the sand.

They both sat cross-legged, the jug between them.

"Please don't brain-cramp over what just happened," Nihil said. "Really. I'm your friend, you can relax."

He smiled at her and raised his glass.

"Thanks," she whispered, raising her own glass.

Drinks finished, they returned the empty jug to the bar. Walking past the band, Madalyn grabbed Nihil and they took a few spins together, holding each other up for the most part, and smiling at the brown faces of the musicians, who smiled back and played on—some Spanish love song—the words repeated over and over in controlled cadences, which swooped carefully up to and only slightly past the edge of polished professionalism.

During the five-minute walk to "our hotel, such as it is," as Madalyn called it, she enjoyed her inebriation. She felt a bubbling sense of well-being, the enjoyment of being on a safe adventure. She enjoyed feeling the loosened grip of her internal control, the absence of her ever-present tension. She enjoyed not knowing what would happen next, like when they got back to their one room with the two beds.

She played with possible outcomes, each one a dramatic scene that revolved around herself, each born out of the vortex of her own need. Cozily she tossed scenarios around in her mind, each one as light as a beachball, and each one, whichever one would land, she imagined landing smoothly and heavily and richly around her, for her own enjoyment, gratifying in its intensity, its drama, its motherlode of ego-enhancing emotion.

When they arrived at their room, Nihil tossed himself onto his bed, reached over to the floor beside him and unscrewed the top of a large bottle of water. He was half sitting up against the wall behind the bed.

"You should have some," he said, taking a swig, "or those margs will be with us in the morning in a big way."

"Good idea," she said, half-heartedly pouring a little water from her own bottle into a glass. She took a small sip, not wanting to dilute the alcohol in her blood too much. She came and sat on the end of his bed.

"So," she said.

"So, why don't you join me, put your feet up." He moved over to one side of the sagging single bed. Madalyn crawled up to the space and sat beside him.

"Cheers," she said, tapping her glass against Nihil's bottle.

"Cheers."

Madalyn took a package of cigarettes out of the pocket of her shorts.

"Smoke?" she asked. Nihil would join her occasionally, although officially he was a non-smoker.

"No, thanks. Those Marlboros are brutal."

"I don't actually really want this," she said, lighting up. Restlessly, she bounced her legs up and down on the bed. She looked over at Nihil, who had his head resting against the wall and his eyes shut.

"You're not going to sleep on me, are you?" she asked.

"No," he said, his eyes still closed. "I mean, if you want to talk, just slap me around. I am pretty bagged, though."

Without another word, she put her glass on the floor, dropped her cigarette into it and lay down next to him, her head on his shoulder.

"Mmm," he said.

She began to cry. She could feel the tears moistening his shirt. She wondered when he'd notice, as she was crying silently, at least making a deliberate attempt.

"Don't cry." He pulled an arm up behind her head and cradled her shoulder.

So he had noticed. She felt free to add the sound effects.

"That bastard," he said.

"I don't want to want him," she croaked and snuffled, "but I can't help it. Everyone just thinks he's an asshole, but obviously we had *something*." She remembered but didn't mention the long looks into each other's eyes when they were making love. She'd been convinced those looks had deep and profound meaning, although she could never tell, really, what was going on behind his eyes, which had not looked, to her, to be quite the wide-open windows of adoration and surrender she was sure hers had been. He *had* looked sincere, though, most of the time, she recalled, and she had reasoned that he just always kept his emotions in check, more than she did. She had guessed it was sort of a guy thing. She had found it irresistible.

She had found it irresistible because she had imagined a scared little boy inside of him who, if she could just love him enough, would eventually come out through his eyes, and she would finally feel completely gratified by his love, which would imbue every cell of her body, every perpetually starved nerve ending of all of her skin, every cranny of her needy heart, and would light up the dark place inside, wherein huddled her terrified soul. Her gazes, though, she knew, had also been a little orchestrated, in the sense that she remembered making a rigorous and conscious effort to try and communicate her adoration with her eyes. John had occasionally commented on the intensity of her look during those times.

"But I like it," he would tease.

"You never got a chance for closure," Nihil was saying. His voice above her head was soft and deep and felt like soothing relaxation music plugged directly into her ear. "I mean, he just tore himself away from you, and so of course you're grieving. I mean, it's never easy, but you never got the chance to wind things down with him, to wean yourself from him, so to speak."

"Sounds like an addiction," she said lightly, a little amusement in her voice.

"Well, love often is. Not that that's a bad thing. Necessarily. I guess the trick is not to expect another person to try to fill up whatever is empty inside you."

"I know, I know." She felt that big, empty space reverberate with loneliness and with great, fat, dry gusts of familiar kinds of pain, which she did not understand and had not ever been able to assuage. She cried and cried into Nihil's neck.

# Chapter Ten

Lawrence and Susan spent the last week of May at their house in the Gulf Islands before it went on the market at the beginning of June. Lawrence had dreaded having to tell Susan about the second mortgage he'd taken out on the property and how he had lost it for them. Her reaction, however, had surprised him: she had wanted to know what had *really* been bothering him for the past six months. They had a battle one night, back in March, the culmination of months of tension and alienation. The shouts and cries of this seminal argument had reverberated throughout the house and still echoed in their minds, dulled for the most part by time, but still stinging, occasionally and unexpectedly. Afterward, they had succumbed to each other, exhausted and contrite.

Since then, since they had both agreed to make an effort at renewing their commitment to the marriage, things had been smoother, though no less delicate. During the argument, Lawrence had come so close to spilling the beans about Tina.

Susan made her decision. She let go of her suspicions when she knew she had won. She would let Lawrence have whoever "she" might be, in memory, as long as Susan could have him in fact. After a bitter war of attrition, her sole accomplishment, as she secretly defined her marriage, was hers to keep. The marriage would last and although sometimes precarious, was never again fatally so.

After the two had made love that night, and after Susan had fallen into the deep sleep of the emotionally spent, she never knew that Lawrence had stayed up for hours—staring into the darkness from the front steps of the house. Still suffering the burden of grieving in secret, he cried away many, but by no means all of the tears he still had left to cry for Mrs. Darcy Whipple of Houston.

By May, Madalyn had developed and grown into a more ordered, although rather lonely and monotonous state of daily existence. Working nights, and not doing much of anything during the days, she slowly allowed her residual sadness to work its way out of her twisted and bunched-up heart. She and Nihil were still drinking buddies, but in this area she was not quite so relentless as she had been in the fall. And after Mexico, their relationship had pushed itself up over the edge that Nihil, at least, had been teetering on, and now sat firmly upon the shelf of friendship. Platonic, he said to himself, sounds so noble.

One matted-down Saturday morning, with the weekend stretching out emptily before her, as usual, although slightly less fearsomely lately, Tina called from Houston, where it was severely sunny. Madalyn flapped to the phone in her mules, drawing the curtains on the way, to let in the thin grey light, which could hardly call itself day. April's showers had become May's, without much letup.

"Hello?"

"Hi, Mad, it's me!"

"Is this *the* Mrs. Darcy Whipple?"

"Madalyn!" Tina groaned, laughing.

"I'm so glad you called," Madalyn said. "I mean, I really need this call. I can't stand you being down there," she lamented. "I mean, you know I'm happy for you, but I feel stranded. Work is soooo boring these days and my social life is non-existent and, oh my God, I'm positively wallowing in self-pity, aren't I?" Madalyn felt she should infuse some affection, dab it on gently. "How are *you* doing, really?" she asked.

She was fine, Tina said. Still, her new life continued to be a little nerve-wracking, the social life down there was so large-scale and practically all-consuming.

"If I get sick and tired of being a professional wife," Tina said, "I can always go back into real estate." Not that she needed the money. "Lord above, you should see the real estate babes down here. Stiff blonde hair, power suits, Mercedes and the scariest fingernails you've ever seen. The money they make is atrociously excessive."

Tina paused. "So . . ." she ventured, the word dipping in its approach to the topic, "is there still gossip going around about me and Lawrence?"

"Oh, I didn't tell you!" Madalyn responded with gleeful vengeance. "Renata's left the firm! She is now, oh, get this, the *personnel director* at Greyell Webster. Can you believe it? It's the perfect job for someone like her. She'll be privy to the dirty lowdown on everyone there. 'Oh, you need a few days off for medical reasons? What for? An abortion? You can tell me.' She'll have a ton of shit in which to bury her fucking, fucking self-righteous nose."

"I will never forgive that bitch for what she did to you. I hope it's the reason Lawrence fired her. Though I doubt it. Men are so oblivious to gossip. I mean, he is such a sweet man, but it's highly likely he was largely oblivious. Anyway, I'm still so fucking angry. I mean, I heard rumours before there was even a reason. It had to have been Renata. Christ, what a priggish witch!" Madalyn's voice was liberally coated with disgust, fortified with anger.

"Anyway, since she left, things have died down pretty much at B & S, at least I think so, because pretty well everyone knows we were friends, so they don't say anything about it to me."

"So, no new dirt?" Tina asked, digging.

"Well . . . just a sec." Madalyn lit a cigarette, wondering how much she should indulge her own weakness for passing on gossip, since Tina *was* asking.

"It's really sort of filtered down to the second-hand level, y'know—I think people at B & S like to criticize Lawrence, the senior partner. Someone way up in the hierarchy, has *sinned* . . . but you are achieving sort of mythic qualities in people's minds. People who don't even know you."

"Really?" Tina sounded intrigued. "Like what?"

"Well, I've heard 'gorgeous,' 'dumped him,' um . . . I just sort of get the impression people think of you as some kind of totally in-control femme fatale. Which of course you are!"

Madalyn was deciding against sharing the opinions of that new secretary who wore the leather skirts, knew nothing and had really taken over the lunchroom lately.

"So that's it? Don't leave out anything 'cause you think it will upset me. I'm interested in how badly that provincial, uptight little town has screwed things up, no offence to you about Vancouver."

"Well, okay." Madalyn switched gears again. "But I wouldn't take this seriously, because it was a real *chick* who said it," she advised, referring to the leather-skirted newcomer. "This person said you had to move to the States to get over it."

There was an inch of silence, long enough for the wheels to turn. Once.

"Spare me," Tina said.


The next week, Madalyn worked days for her former boss, Ross White; he had asked her to cover his secretary's holiday time. At about two o'clock on Tuesday afternoon, Ross called her into his office.

"These Stackhouse contracts are perfect. Thank you. They should go over now—I'd like you to hand them personally to that obnoxious Smilie. Hounded me all week. Christ, give a guy an MBA and a telephone . . . bad as lawyers." He winked at her as he handed over the stack of agreements with one hand and whipped up his ringing phone with the other.

"Sure. Put him through . . . John! Fear not! My secretary is on her way over with them." Ross stuck his finger into his mouth and pretended to gag, rolling his eyes at Madalyn. "Fine, yes. Your guys should sign up first, right . . ."

Madalyn put the contracts into an envelope, grabbed her purse and ran to the ladies' room, where she redid her face and thanked God she had not overslept that morning and that her hair was okay and oh, thank you that I have on *this* suit.

Over a year, and only a few glimpses. Surprisingly little contact, really, given the small and incestuous nature of the city's legal and business community. One day in a downtown restaurant at lunch. And of course last year's Stackhouse Christmas party.

When John's secretary ushered Madalyn into his office, he lurched to his feet, and with nervous solicitude escorted her into a chair. He sat back down behind his desk, leaning forward on his elbows.

"Here are the Mitsu agreements," she said.

He threw them onto a corner of the desk, a mere excuse. His eyes were still glued.

"You look fantastic."

And so did he. He's so ridiculously masculine, she thought, noticing how trapped he looked in his noosed shirt.

They chatted for over half an hour, comparing notes on once-common friends. He asked about her love life, politely but with his old mocking tease, which made superficial to her slow but steadily learning heart any authenticity of emotion. She silently praised herself for the tone of her voice, which sounded richly healed, and for her contented restraint when describing several men she had been dating. She felt she was lying quite convincingly. John did not mention Monica, only joked that he had to behave himself now. Madalyn knew he was to be married in less than a month.

He walked her to the elevator, and just before the doors closed, still looking into his eyes, she caught the prize of his choked goodbye—a longing in his voice that she recognized immediately, because she had, on absolute purpose, kept it out of hers.

Victory was hers. Oh God, thank you. Thank you, thank you, thank you God.

The evening of Saturday, June sixteenth, John's wedding day, found Madalyn dressed to the nines in black, hoisting glass after glass of champagne at a private party at Monty's. It was Derek's birthday bash, and the restaurant was closed to all except his inner circle, in which Madalyn was now firmly ensconced.

It was the tequila that did it, really. The way she swallowed her second shooter with such smooth-faced professionalism really made an impression on Gavin, who, Madalyn discovered to her pleasure, was a terribly attractive green-eyed blond with an excess of cerebral charm. She was very comfortable with him and very drunk when the taxi pulled away from Monty's just before two in the morning. They found themselves quite naturally in an embrace, and after all the flirting they had done, eagerly and naturally kissed each other all the way to her place.

It was exhilarating, after almost a year of not being touched. She loved the way he held her hands above her head and ran his fingers down her sides, the way his fingertips rounded the curve of her breasts. It was thrilling, the pure sensation of him thrusting strongly into her, bringing her back to sexual life as his hips moved automatically, helplessly and hard above her and against her. It was gratifying, the compliments they lavished upon each other. It was cozy, the way they sat up in bed afterward, in agreement as to what a nice guy Nihil was. And it was unencumbered and not sad for Madalyn when he left her at her door with a hug and a smile, without asking for her number, as if they would naturally meet again, friends, in the overlapping circulations of their lives.

"Dieter Schnitker, 81, uncle of the wife of Baxter Group Chairman, Hart Baxter, was arrested this week in Amsterdam on war crime charges. Schnitker, a captain with the German occupation forces in Austria in 1939, is being charged with the deportation to the death camps of as many as a thousand Jews . . ."

Madalyn had read the news story earlier that week. In subsequent articles, she read of the publicity in Toronto. The business and political press were having a field day analyzing the possible impact on the Baxter Group, speculating about Monica's mother, Kirsten Schnitker Baxter. Had she known? And if so, what was the extent of her knowledge, and, if she had known, what was the nature and extent of Hart Baxter's culpability? And how was the Jewish money reacting? Madalyn's heart went out to John. She did not even know where he was living, although a month earlier, she had called directory assistance in Vancouver, out of curiosity, but there was no listing for a John or Monica Smilie.

She found out, on a Sunday near the end of August, when she ran into Geoff and Mia at Granville Island. Madalyn brought it up. What did they think about this Baxter Group Nazi war criminal thing?

"It's not a very auspicious beginning for John as a new Baxter Group VP," Geoff said. "Did you know he and Monica have moved back east? No? They moved a month ago. Were only here for about five weeks after the honeymoon. Belize. Anyway, John Boy's in the thick of it now. Not an auspicious beginning at all."

Mia examined Madalyn's face with much sensitivity, touched her on the arm and, with a knowing look, said that at least she wasn't involved.

Madalyn finished her shopping in an emotional glaze. She had to force herself to concentrate, hard, during the drive over the bridge. On arriving home, she poured herself a large glass of wine and tucked herself into a corner of the couch for a good brood, sucking in the smoke of one cigarette after another. These things felt necessary to soften the brittle clog in her heart, to alleviate the scatter of confusion.

She could not quite make herself feel the glow of retributive justice. It would be obscene, she thought, to interpret one of the most evil demons of history as rising from its shallow grave of scant decades to cast a shadow upon the face of John Smilie, just for her gratification. Still. In lieu of the anger she could not yet feel, she let her usual sadness flow wetly down her face.

After a time, something reminded her that he would be able to rise, laughing, above even this. Even this thought produced no righteous anger. She did, however, dimly realize that sadness for herself was what she was really feeling. Knowing this, she supposed—although she found the idea difficult to conceive—that the time was near for the stream of sadness to slow. This infancy of hope, however, left her unconvinced that she would not love John forever and ever.

Stabbing with her vacuum at the carpeting beneath her bookcase one evening the following week, Madalyn discovered the package of brushes and paints John had given her over a year ago. She opened the package, found a large soft brush and grazed it over and over against her cheek. She emptied the brushes and tubes into her lap and fingered them. She had an impression—weird, she thought—that these objects were innocent. It struck her that they had come into her possession through John Smilie, merely as the courier. Pristine and magical, they had been delivered to her and kept safe by the gods through the heart-sickening morass of the past year.

Lawrence took his daughters to the Children's Festival that August, an annual event held on the large grassy fields between the planetarium and the boat-spotted waters of Burrard Inlet. After having their faces painted as butterflies, and to their great delight, Lawrence bought each girl an ice cream cone and a balloon, and they strolled toward the water. At least Lawrence attempted to stroll as he watched the dartings and scuttlings of Megan and Melissa with much more conscientious effort than usual. Given the locale, Lawrence could, if he snuck a look behind him to the south, which he did several times, obtain a fairly clear view of Tina's former residence, the baked white stucco and broad glass planes of her condo, through the branches of the maple and walnut trees in full leaf in the park across the street.

Lawrence heard a sudden cry from Megan and saw immediately the cause of her alarm: her pink balloon—"my favrit colour"—had slipped from her small, sticky hand and was shooting upward with wondrous speed toward the summer sky of perfect blue, that particular blue that covers us neither like a lid nor even a veil, but like the tease of a promise that it really does exist, although we can tell, if we really look, that it is completely without substance. Into this existentially irritating sky Megan's balloon soared, and Lawrence was amazed at how far away it seemed to be, much higher than the planes heading in and out of the city's airport, but there it was, the dot of pink that Megan mourned.

Tears were dried with the edges of a chocolate-soaked napkin. Back to the balloon man immediately they strode. Megan got a bigger one this time, and this one purple, her "new favrit," she declared with deep satisfaction as Lawrence tied its string firmly around his daughter's tiny wrist. Sister Melissa pondered the wisdom of releasing her own balloon, accidentally on purpose, so that she too might obtain a larger one. Her eight years of maturity won out, however, and she grasped her string firmly, showing Lawrence. Pride shone in the eyes of both.

It was a rainy Sunday afternoon in August. Her father called while she was setting up to paint. She told him she was getting back into it, and that her friend Ron was ready and willing to help her promote her work to some of the local gallery owners, if and when she got a group of paintings together. She guessed she must be feeling better.

"Atta girl," Grant said. "Sounds like you're away to the races."

Literally. Once you were out of the nest and onto the beach, that was it, run for your life. Madalyn wondered if the turtles who got to grow up were possessed of some special instinct, a kind of turtle radar that kept them from being plucked into the sky. Or perhaps they were just lucky, or destined, or blessed—one of the choices Grant had examined, sincere in his search.

Whichever—movement was everything. Madalyn twirled a brush in a worm of red paint. Possibilities suggested themselves from the palette, and combinations began to colour the bone-white future in her mind. She dug around in her disused imagination. A few forgotten ideas that had once excited her came to the surface, and she considered them, like shards of broken artifacts being dusted for clues. Her brush made flicks through the lightless afternoon. The canvas, a neutral ground that did not know a well-planned stroke from a slip of the hand, absorbed them all.

Edwards Brothers Malloy
Oxnard, CA  USA
December 2, 2014